Orion
Escape
Velocity

I. JAMES FORREST

◆ FriesenPress

Suite 300 - 990 Fort St
Victoria, BC, V8V 3K2
Canada

www.friesenpress.com

Copyright © 2017 by I. James Forrest
First Edition — 2017

All rights reserved.

This is a work of fiction. Names, characters, places and incidents are the product of the author's imagination and are used fictitiously. Any resemblance to actual persons, events is entirely coincidental. To the best of my knowledge, Orion and aliens do not exist. That said; drop me a text if I'm wrong.
www.iJamesForrest.com

No part of this publication may be reproduced in any form, or by any means, electronic or mechanical, including photocopying, recording, or any information browsing, storage, or retrieval system, without permission in writing from FriesenPress.

ISBN
978-1-5255-0004-6 (Hardcover)
978-1-5255-0005-3 (Paperback)
978-1-5255-0006-0 (eBook)

1. FICTION, SCIENCE FICTION

Distributed to the trade by The Ingram Book Company

To mom and dad, who nurtured my imagination and encouraged me to put my dreams down on paper. Thank you.

To my friend Carson and his zeal for all things Sci-Fi. Good bye buddy. You will live on in the Orion universe.

PROLOGUE: Mountain plateau, Tibet - 990 C.E.

The fields were slick with blood from both sides of the warring factions and still they fought on, surrounded by the cries of the thousands injured and maimed. Monks, disciplined in spiritual meditation and swordsmanship, were dressed in red robes to hide the blood from their many wounds. They fought alongside peasant farmers, who were armed with only bamboo pitchforks. Together they tried to fend off the heavily armored attacking army, with tenacity and courage. Their only advantage in this losing battle was that they held the high ground, yet they were still outnumbered and outmatched by the professionals. In the distant lowlands, far from the plateau and many days march away, their emperor was not aware of the ongoing slaughter of his mountain people. The royal troops would not be dispatched. The runner with the monk's message died trying to leave the mountain. The enemy would soon conquer this sacred plateau and sweep down into the lowlands, taking the conflict to the rest of China and to the Ying Dynasty ruler himself.

* * *

The pilot could see smoke rising from the plateau, and as he got closer, he could see crops burning. The creature could smell the stench of death, which was raw and biting.

* * *

A thunderous roar came from the heavens—a sound so unearthly that it stopped the battle. The men looked to the sky. A gargantuan object blocked what little sun shone through the smoke-filled air. The combat-weary men ran, as a dragon from their ancient mythology crashed into the battlefield. Smoke belched from the side of the beast and vegetation hung loose from its body, furthering the illusion of dragon wings and instilling fear in the hearts of the onlookers as they fled in terror. Those weighed down with armor could not move fast enough to escape and died instantly, crushed as they joined the fallen under the great beast.

The great lumbering beast, weighed down by gravity and atmospheric pressure, lay exhausted from flight. Poisoned, its body needed the essential elements of copper, zinc, and calcium to purge a foreign substance from its system. Amid the smoke and ash, the pilot dispatched a stingray-like drone—a much smaller version of the great beast itself—to bore into the mountain, seeking out the veins of these minerals. With a second drone, the pilot exited the vessel then and floated above the debris of war—above the dead—before heading toward a small patch of wild alpine flowers untouched by the carnage.

At the edge of the meadow, a monk knelt, bandaging a wounded comrade. He was offering words of comfort as the life slipped away from his friend. The pilot floated near the monk, who raised his sword in defense before seeing the stranger and freezing in fear of his life. The tall stranger, with green hair and large glowing emerald eyes, stopped. Ignoring the feeble show of strength, he knelt down beside the care-giving monk, who was now wracked with fear. The stranger removed a thin silver necklace from around his neck, and gently touched the injured man with its black crystal pendant. The wound mended before their eyes. Minutes later, the injured man sat up coughing and spat out the blood that had collected in his mouth. Both men looked on in awe at this stranger who had fallen from the heavens with a giant dragon, had vanquished their enemy, and now healed their wounded. This must be a holy man sent from the gods.

The stranger gathered a handful of the flowers, crushed the blue petals in his fingers, and tasted the juices. Satisfied with the results, he touched his arm band and the stingray drone hovered over the field, gathering the flowers before retreating to the vessel. The stranger stayed behind to continue offering aid to the injured. No words were spoken between the two species, but trust had been earned. The monks, schooled in medicine, knew the power of the flowers' antitoxin properties, and sent word to the women and children who were hiding in a nearby valley, telling them to return with baskets of the little blue petals.

The people of the plateau, with the assistance of the drones and the stranger, created a paste from the flowers and ground minerals. The drones carried some of this mixture inside the creature, and the remainder was spread on the damaged and burnt skin of the 'dragon'. The stranger had befriended the people, sharing food and drink with them while the creature lay motionless, silently healing.

One moonless night, months after he fell from the sky, the stranger ate with the people around a large evening fire. He listened to them as they spoke with reverence, offering him various items and repeating their words slowly for his benefit. He had not spoken to the people, communicating only with gestures to indicate his acceptance of the food and drink given.

As the dinner fire turned to embers, and after dinner drinks of rice wine had been shared by the men, he smiled, cleared his throat, and stood facing his friendly hosts.

"I am a traveler from the heavens. My home planet revolves around the middle star in that three-star configuration." He spoke their language perfectly, as he pointed to the Orion constellation.

A hush fell over the gathering.

"Is that where the 'god of dragons' lives?" an elderly monk asked, bowing his head.

"I am not a god, only a mortal with advanced technology and knowledge that you could not understand."

"If you are not a god, how can you heal the wounded and now speak our tongue?" a younger monk inquired.

"How did your dragon get sick?" someone else asked from the back of the group.

The stranger answered calmly. "My ship is not a dragon, but rather a creature with incredible power, capable of traveling to the stars at unbelievable speeds."

"But how?"

"As I said, my people have learned to harness the powers of the stars, to advance our knowledge. Just like your people have learned to melt various ores and forge that raw metal into swords and other useful tools."

"Why are you here then?"

"I came to this planet years ago with two travel companions, to extract a rare ore for my home-world. My friends were killed and I barely managed to escape, but not before my creature sustained injuries. It was poisoned by the very ore we were mining." The traveler calmly told his tale.

"We were forced to leave the lush jungle mountains far to the east, beyond the great ocean." He waved in the direction he came. "We fled from the local people, our friends the Mayans, when they attacked us. I do not blame them. Our mining operation had contaminated their water supply, and the air ignited in flames due to an invisible, odorless vapor that was accidentally released. The village was destroyed and my travel companions, our wives, and our children all died." He paused and looked away from the growing numbers before him, wiping a tear from his eye. An elderly village woman handed him a cup of hot tea, touching his hand in the process, a gesture that conveyed sorrow, compassion, and hope.

The stranger continued. "The creature dove into the deep waters of the ocean to extinguish the flames and cool its skin. It swam through massive kelp beds, wiping off the sticky substance but more was needed to purge the poison. Weak and in need of minerals and vegetation, it surfaced and continued searching for the elements it needed to heal. The poison, fire, and flight had fatigued it to the point that death was near, and so it collapsed, dropping from the sky and falling to this plateau." He paused to gather his thoughts and sip the warm liquid before continuing.

"Neither I nor the creature have ever encountered this oily fluid, but driven with willpower and an inner strength, it is getting better, thanks to you, the good people of the mountain. I will forever be grateful for your compassion and generosity." He wiped a final tear away, finished his drink, and handed the cup back to the woman. Then he returned to his sleeping hut.

The people fed the creature a continuous supply of plants and minerals, but something was still lacking in its diet. Buried beneath its bulk, it found a protein source it craved. Methodically, it absorbed the fluids of the dead it laid upon. First the rotting flesh, then muscles, cartilage, and bones. It consumed the calcium in the marrow, and finally it found what it was seeking: amino acids, the building blocks of life. The creature was not familiar with this sensation, but the conditions were right; its base programming had mutated from the radiation this planet's new crystals gave off within its belly, and the overpowering urge of all living creatures took over.

It was creating an offspring.

***

Weeks turned to months as the village children painted pictures on their big sleeping dragon—pictures depicting the battle, its arrival, and the healing of the Tibetan mountain people. The creature lay motionless on the plateau, rebuilding damaged tissue, and unaware that deep within its core, cells were dividing, incubating life.

After six months of inactivity, the creature groaned and stirred, with its strength now returned and its system purged of the poison. Together, as symbiotic host and handler, the creature and its pilot decided that the time was right to depart and return to their home-world many light years away—a journey that would take years. While the pilot met with the people to thank them for their hospitality, the creature performed an internal diagnostic in preparation for leaving. Near one of its sub-light-drive engines was a mound of discarded ore slag from its earlier mining operation, and among the raw and finished crystals was an unidentified biological mass. This area needed to be kept clear for the engines to function properly. Performing a cleansing action, the creature jettisoned the unwanted matter before continuing its internal scans.

The creature—a bio-engineering achievement—was part being and part machine, and together with the pilot (in a synaptic link), it slowly rose above the plateau into the clouds. It continued its assent, increasing in speed and quickly reaching escape velocity, shaking off the confines of gravity. In the space between the earth and moon, the pilot activated the sub-light-drive engines. The twin engines were augmentations built into the creature for interstellar space travel, and was fueled by crystals. The trip to this solar system had exhausted the energy from the original crystals, and so their mining operation had needed to be successful or else there would be no return trip. Fortunately the meteor containing the crystalline ore, which had crashed into the earth before mammals walked upright, had yielded more than enough crystals to power the ship and still return with a substantial cargo needed back on his home-world.

The pilot had sent numerous communications to his two travel companions in the hopes they had survived the fire. With no reply, he had to presume them dead. As such, he applied power to the crystal energy chamber. The radiation from the crystal structure, when applied with the correct amount of pressure—exerted by the creature—sent a lightning bolt of power through the energy conduits to the drives, and seconds later the vessel would be traveling at near the speed of light. The creature-engineered elements were calibrated to the original power output of the crystals from their home planet. Unfortunately, this blue-green planet had richer oxygen/nitrogen levels than their own, causing greater than expected power output from each crystal. This was not discovered until the lightning bolt of power burned through the energy conduits and into the creature's nervous system. This massive jolt of electricity fried nerve endings and inner walls, as it traveled to the creature's brain.

Giant powerful muscles convulsed uncontrollably as bands of high-voltage electricity crisscrossed throughout the creature's innards. The bands of energy sizzled and crackled, leaving dead flesh in its wake before intersecting with the large nerve trunk that ran the length of the creature, terminating at its center of consciousness. The bolt of energy exploded along each synaptic pathway, overloading a brain larger than the planet's greatest whale. In milliseconds, the creature and its pilot were electrocuted, killed instantly. Without consciousness or power, the dead creature tumbled through space before impacting the orbiting moon.

***

The next morning, the Tibetan children were disappointed to see the sleeping dragon gone, leaving behind it a mound of slimy debris. Later that same morning, a heavy rain washed much of the oily slime away, revealing an egg. A black egg the size of a man stood upright in a nest of crushed ore and crystals—a shelled, embryonic progeny of a strange species.

Over the next few days, monks transcribed the story of the dragon, in pictures, onto the black shell. A few months later, a shrine was built around it where the devoted could pray and worship in the presence of the dragon's egg.

CHAPTER 1

NORTH BAY AIR FORCE STATION, ONTARIO, CANADA. PRESENT DAY

The little moose calf ventured out of the woods to graze on the new grass shoots, glancing back every so often to make sure the safety of its mother was within running distance. The large moose cow nibbled on the fresh spring buds, keeping a watchful eye on her first offspring.

A sound put her on alert. The early dawn glinted off the ripples of the nearby stream. Suddenly they both looked at the large gray building upstream of the creek. The water flowed faster. Something was happening.

They had no idea that they were looking at a leftover remnant from the Cold War. The North Bay Air Station had one of the longest runways on the continent, built for refueling returning bombers in the event their service was required. It was also the hub of the early-warning radar defense system that protected both the Canadians and Americans. Deep in the granite rock of the Canadian Shield, a labyrinth of underground tunnels connected the base to missile silos—a second part of the defense strategy. In later years, with the missiles removed and the threat minimized, the station became an integral part of NASA's radar telemetry tracking, and was deemed an emergency landing site for the Space Shuttle.

Today with the aid of the government and the private sector, it was now Canada's space port for satellite launches to sub-polar orbits, to monitor the polar ice caps and ozone levels in the upper atmosphere. With the influx of foreign satellite business and contracts with NASA, the North Bay Station could now launch heavy-lift rockets to the moon and beyond. It also had passenger capabilities, following other countries into the lucrative space tourism market.

"This is Flight Control for *Odin – Inuk 1* launch. Give me go/no go for launch."

"Booster?"

"Booster good to go."

"Retro?"

"Retro go."

"Guidance?"

"Guidance, we are a go."

"Telemetry?" "Telemetry a go."

"Network?"

"Network go."

"Recovery?"

"Recovery a go."

"CAPCON?"

"CAPCON, we are go for launch!"

T-Minus 0:05, 0:04, 0:03, 0:02, 0:01.

"Ignition Comit."

"Lift off of *Odin – Inuk 1!*" Flight Control shouted into his microphone, with the sound of applause in the background. *"Bonne chance, mes amis,"* he whispered to himself. "Good Luck guys."

"*Inuk1* has cleared the tower. Houston, you have control."

"Copy that North Bay; we'll carry the ball from here. Good jobs guys. Houston CAPCON out."

"Well there you have it folks, a beautiful pre-dawn launch from Canada's premier space port," the seasoned announcer remarked to his TV audience, in the early hours, from a remote location kilometers away from the actual launch site. "This Canadian unmanned flight, *Odin – Inuk 1*, will land on the moon, with essential supplies and equipment for the manned flight scheduled in three days from Vandenberg Air Base, California." The reporter then repeated himself in French, as was customary for the national network when reporting on major news stories that concerned the country. "This joint moon mission demonstrates the collaboration and friendship between our two great nations. The National Aeronautics and Space Administration, NASA, with its powerhouse of knowledge and resources, plus the Canadian Space Agency, CSA, with a large technical skilled aerospace population and a strong will to succeed, jointly constructed the two *Odin* launch vehicles for this mission. Although both ships have the capability to carry humans to the moon, only the US launch vehicle *Endurance* will actually be manned." The backdrop switched to the Odin space craft *Endurance,* sitting on the pad in California, illuminated by floodlights.

"Using the same launch-vehicle design, another mining mission to the moon is scheduled for later this year, with three additional flights expected for Mars early next." The backdrop changed to an animated close-up of the red planet and a ship bearing the red maple leaf landing on its surface.

The moose calf and cow were startled as they looked up at the pillar of fire that lit the early morning sky. Seconds later, a sonic boom resonated off the dense pine woods, frightening them and forcing a hasty retreat into the trees that surrounded the human habitat.

CHAPTER 2
LUNAR SURFACE. THREE DAYS LATER

The seismic alarm triggered the communication sub-system, turning it on and interrupting the six-wheeled machine's sleep mode as it recharged its batteries. Three minutes later, after bouncing off various lunar and terrestrial satellites, the signal was forwarded to an ornate blue-glass ten-story building in the Xichang Satellite Launch Center, Mission Control for China's National Space Administration (CNSA). On the communication floor, the alert was heard by subordinate supervisor Sun-Ching Liu, who immediately put down her English copy of a popular romance novel and focused on the monitor. She activated the high-definition and infrared cameras and notified her superior, Eric Yoo, currently sleeping in a bunk in the back room.

The night crew, or 'B' team as they were derogatorily called, had it easy, especially during the rover's twelve-hour recharge cycles. Their sole duty was to monitor the internal temperature and power status of this critical charging cycle. The geographic position of the lunar south-pole allowed for nearly 90 percent sun coverage, but unfortunately, it was at different angles throughout an earth day, which required the solar panels to adjust as it traveled. A design error on the angle of the solar panels range of motion hindered charging, and had already weakened batteries. Borrowing a page from NASA's *Mars Rover* playbook, the Chinese specialists would drive their rover up a slight incline to maximize the solar charge.

This had been the normal procedure for the last three weeks, as *Yutu 2*, the Little Jade Rabbit, drove to the South Pole with the intent of planting the Chinese flag weeks ahead of the Americans. That had changed four days ago with the unexpected announcement that NASA and the CSA (Canadian Space Agency), were accelerating the launch schedule of *Inuk 1*, the supply ship for the upcoming manned moon mission. The American mission was to descend into the Shackleton Crater and extract oxygen and water from the newly discovered ice.

With these condensed timelines, the Little Jade Rabbit's rest cycles were cut in half, with partial charges. It would remain parked on a slope for six hours, and after that limited charge, it would travel at a minimum speed so that the solar panels could still generate more power than it consumed. This was the challenge for the B team, who watched patiently as the charging indicator rose slowly. The graph showed that the rover now had a little over fourteen hours of driving time, which the day crew would use up as they took over the controls.

The day crew, or 'A' team, were from the best schools China had to offer, and they each had completed a year abroad in either Germany, the UK, France, Canada, or the USA. The eight-person team, comprised of six males and two females, were responsible for plotting the course of the rover, *Yutu 2*, to its destination. The mission was to prove to the Chinese people and the world that China had a strong and viable space industry, even after many failed attempts. This rover had already trekked twenty kilometers on the *Aitken Basin* in just under three weeks. It was a political move, proving that the once powerful USA, who had beaten the Soviets in the space race, was now going to lose to the Chinese in this new moon race.

"What's up, Suzie?" Eric asked his colleague, yawning and using her English name.

"Our Little Jade Rabbit just woke up. I think we are close to the American's landing site."

"They are four hours ahead of schedule. That was fast. Can we put the cameras on it and watch the landing?"

"Power is still coming online, so I can't get a clear picture with high definition, but the infrared shows the craft's thrusters coming in for a landing eight kilometers east of our position, and it's a big ship." The short black-haired professional responded in perfect English, with only a hint of a Chinese accent.

"Let's see it on the large screen!" Eric snapped.

Keys were entered and commands given before the wall illuminated with a burst of light into the darkened room. A fifteen by ten-foot image, in green light, displayed the faint ghostly flare of a long landing plume, indicative of rockets initializing prior to touch down. The brightness and heat of the rocket obscured the actual vessel.

"Bring up the map," he demanded.

Within seconds the screen was split in two, showing a zoom-in on the rover's coordinates and the new space craft landing only fifty meters from *Shackleton Crater's* towering perimeter rampart, a one-hundred-meter wall surrounding the actual crater.

Crater ramparts were formed when super-heated molten rock ejects from the depression that a comet or meteor creates. The ejected lava-like material hardens instantly in the sub-zero vacuum of the moon, forming near vertical walls. Depending on the impact velocity, angle, and density of the meteor composition and debris field, the wall height and thickness could vary widely.

"Do we have enough power to get over there and take some pictures?"

"Maybe, but it's off our planned route. We are heading south to the Pole, not east to the crater."

"I know; don't argue with me. I'm in charge! How long will it take to get to the crater?"

"Power is at 70 percent now, and if we travel at a medium speed, I estimate we can get there in two hours and still have power at 55 percent. But may I remind you that our instructions were to travel at minimum speed, so it will be at 100 percent charge before the day shift takes over? They want to take her into the shadows of the South Pole, where she will not receive the needed sunlight. If it gets stuck there without power, it's our careers on the line," the younger technician remarked.

"Don't talk to me like that. Of course, I know; I also don't want to be on the 'B' team forever. The 'A' team gets all the glory. We can get close enough to take pictures of the cargo ship and still have time to turn around before we are relieved in the morning. Besides if we post those pictures on social media, we would be famous, furthering our careers."

"We are scientists! Stop talking like that! It is not our jobs to make such decisions. Let me call the senior supervisor; he will know what to do."

"No! It is Thursday and he is with his mistress tonight; besides it will take him two hours to get here and by then I could have cameras on them. By morning I will be more important than the 'A' team. Now stop talking and make it happen."

The small rover backed down the hill from its sunny roost and turned to the new improvised route, heading east towards the crater to investigate. The topography had changed from light lunar dust to sharp volcanic glass, with rocks the size of a boxer's glove and boulders the size of subcompacts. The Chinese were new to moon exploration, with little experience, however what they did possess were superior skills in duplicating the equipment from nations that were experienced pioneers of moon travel. They'd had a choice between Russian or American designs for their new rover. They chose the Russian style and then modified it with less expensive materials and lighter grades of metal, to lower the cost and weight. Had they used the Soviet-style tires and added the extra thirty kilograms, a mere sixty-six pounds, the moon regolith would not have chewed up the light aluminum wheels. In all fairness to the design shortfalls, if the original route had been continued to the Pole, then a two-kilometer swath of the jagged rocks could have been avoided.

Instead, the Little Jade Rabbit struggled on, grinding down its wheels. Its autonomous on-board computer and sensors kept it on its new course as it scrambled around the last rocky outcrop, with power reserves dangerously low at forty percent. It raised its dual camera-lens head and focused on the towering Odin space ship, with NASA painted in large blue letters from top to bottom. Next to the writing were both the American and Canadian flags, vibrantly stenciled in the appropriate colors. The camera lens panned and zoomed in as an astronaut in a Surface Exploration Vehicle (SEV) maneuvered a thirty-foot inflatable habitat, setting it next to its equal-sized sister. A second astronaut was directing the move with hand signals.

The presence of the SEV was not unusual, but the presence of the habitats indicated a base camp for an extended stay. The existence of astronauts on an unmanned supply ship was most unusual and suspicious. As they watched the activity on the big screen, both Eric and Suzie asked the same question out loud: "What the hell is going on?"

The Little Jade Rabbit remained hidden behind a large boulder, thirty meters away from the ship, with one of its camera lenses peeking over the top.

Most moon-crater ramparts, over time, get partially or fully destroyed by secondary impacts. The far side of the moon showed evidence of multiple craters on top of each other, but the near side facing Earth has fewer. The South Pole region has the fewest craters and most ramparts are intact. Shackleton Crater, for the most part, is perfectly circular with an intact wall around the rim, except for the Cameron Cut, named after the Lunar Geologist, Doctor Tracy Cameron, who discovered the two-meter slice. Using satellite images and ground-based telescopes, she found a perfect slice that cut through the hundred-meter-high, twelve-meter-thick wall. The cause of this formation was still under discussion in the many scientific communities around the world. Seismic activity had been ruled out, because of the smooth surface of the slice. The prevailing belief is that an incoming shallow trajectory meteor exploded from internal gas expansion, prior to impact, creating a sharp edge that sliced the volcanic rim. The kinetic energy was low enough that it did not breach the opposite wall, and most likely, fell into the four-kilometer deep crater. One online group believed a supersized space diamond made the slash, and another group believed a flying saucers' edge did the job. Regardless of the cause, to access the crater and the ice at the bottom, it was the easiest entry point and the reason why the Americans were establishing a base camp outside the wall and beside the cut.

Eric and Suzie watched the activity of the astronauts on the large screen, possibly the only two people outside of the US who knew what was going on up there. They still had four hours before the 'A' team took over.

"Eric, we have enough pictures; let's turn around and get back to our original course."

"Yes, I agree, let's leave before we are spotted. If they didn't want the world to know about this unscheduled manned mission, they certainly won't want our Little Jade Rabbit and China to have pictures. Quickly plot a course out of here."

With new co-ordinates entered and uploaded, they waited for the three-minute delay before seeing any movement.

"It's not working Eric. Can you double check what I typed?"

Five minutes later, the senior 'B' team member finished his review.

"I don't see why it's not accepting our new course. I keep getting error code 'ERROR 900', which I am not familiar with. Can you look it up?"

After a thorough search of the error-code database, they uncovered nothing. On a hunch, she typed in 'ERROR 900 definition'.

'PROCEDURE 1 ACTIVE- MANUAL ENTRY LOCKED' scrolled across the screen.

"What is Procedure 1?" the junior technician asked.

"No idea, it was not part of any briefing I was in. Let's try a partial re-boot; maybe that will work."

After many attempts to send the re-boot commands, the Little Jade Rabbit ignored them all and remained stationary. The 'B' team technicians could do nothing but watch on the big screen; then suddenly the camera zoomed in on the big slice into the crater. They watched in amazement as a monitor came to life and pages of encrypted code started to scroll on the screen. A few minutes later, the following message flashed on the display: 'PROCEDURE 1 UPLOADING'

After the signal delay, the little rover came to life and started rolling towards the famous Cameron Cut, straight down the middle of the American's base. As it sped closer to its goal, one of the astronauts unexpectedly exited the cut, quickly bouncing over to the SEV, where his companion was out in front with the solar panels. They were unaware of the little six-wheeled vehicle passing behind him.

The astronaut had moved quickly for a reason. He had planted timed charges on the sides of the cut, to expand the opening for the SEV to travel through. The rover had just cleared the opening and started driving along the narrow ledge of the rim when the explosion went off. Eric and Suzie watched through the rover's eyes as it tumbled into the darkness.

'PROCEDURE 1 COMPLETE'

"Oh crap, we are in so much trouble!" Suzie cried, as she held her hand to her mouth. Eric could see his career vanishing and a prison cell materialize.

'PROCEDURE 2 INITIALIZED'

No further communications from the Little Jade Rabbit were displayed, as it was blown off the ledge, its status unknown.

❧ CHAPTER 3 ❦
THE NEXT DAY

The buxom, coco-skinned brunette cried out to her mother, sitting beside her in their Louisiana bungalow, as pictures of the crew were flashed in high definition. "Look Mama! They're showing my Tyrone again on TV!" The 25-year-old Coast Guard Lieutenant Tamara Gill and her mother were just two of the billions of people around the world watching the launch of the first manned moon mission of the 21st century.

"Honey, I'm so proud of Tyrone," the older women said softly. "I am honored to have him as my future son-in-law. I just pray that all that space travel doesn't prevent him from giving me grand-babies."

"Oh Mama, don't be so concerned about your future grand-babies. We have lots of time, okay?" Tamara laughed as she embraced her mother.

"I'm just saying, honey, that it could be dangerous up there."

"Hush! We don't talk about that. Only positive thoughts and prayers. No more talk about the dangers of space." "Good morning," interrupted a voice from the TV. "We're live at Launch Complex 6, Vandenberg Air Force Base, in beautiful sunny California. I'm Nancy Neilson-North and this is Jeffrey Potts. If you are just tuning in, you will see that the clock has stopped at T-minus ten minutes. Jeff, do we know why the countdown was halted?" The professional, blonde television announcer turned to her co-anchor, who was busy taking notes as he received information from Mission Control through his earpiece.

The gray-haired, seasoned reporter nodded then and looked up into the camera. "We have just been told that there was an intermittent sensor signal in the lunar-landing module that has now been reset and is operational. These new Odin-class space vessels are state of the art, with multiple backup redundancies, so there is no cause for alarm. NASA is confident that the countdown will resume shortly."

He looked towards Nancy, offering her the lead once more. She smiled professionally at him and then looked back to her audience.

"Although Vandenberg launches are usually of a military nature, for the defense department, the reason this launch is from Vandenberg and not Kennedy Space Center has to do with unseasonal weather patterns over Florida, and not because this is a military operation, as has been rumored. These facilities have been quiet for years."

"That's right Nancy," Jeffrey said. "There have been hints that there is a military agenda to this epic moon mission, similar to last Tuesday's launch of supplies from Canada's North Bay Space Port. These rumors of a joint Canada /US *military* mission are unfounded. The army is only there to provide their expertise with the equipment and logistics needed to get into the crater and down to the ice. The military certainly are not up there to protect the astronauts from the Chinese rover *Yutu 2*, the Little Jade Rabbit, which is also in the area. This idea, put forth by some of the less reputable news agencies, might be compelling, but is purely fiction nonetheless. In any case, as has been widely reported, the Beijing Mission Control unfortunately lost communication with their rover when it went off course near Shackleton Crater, named after the British explorer, Sir Ernest Shackleton, and his many expeditions to the Antarctic. His adventures also inspired the naming of the Odin space craft *Endurance*." Jeffrey shuffled papers for a moment before continuing.

"It has been half a decade since America was a space-capable nation, with the final flight of the *Shuttle Atlantis* in 2011, and of course, the last time humans walked on the moon was in 1972 with *Apollo 17*. This new space craft is not the Apollo-era craft but rather a perfect blend of space station, shuttle, and *Apollo*. This vessel has a crew capacity of ten, but on this its premier mission it will only carry six. The new Odin-class vessel is basically *Apollo* on steroids." He couldn't help getting excited as he described the new US space vehicle and moon mission.

In the lower right-hand corner was a digital countdown clock that had restarted, and was now showing eight minutes remaining.

On the left side of the screen was a live shot of the large space craft on the launch pad.

"This Odin vessel, *Endurance*, is bigger and faster, with more comforts and amenities than the shuttle or even the International Space Station. Mission Commander Tyrone Booker and Pilot Shirley Worthy, plus four mission specialists, will be the first of a new generation of explorers to land on the moon, beating the Russians, who are still months away from a similar launch.

"The mission specialists, using an array of instruments, will determine if the ice discovered by the Lunar Reconnaissance Orbiter, LRO, a year ago, is water or methane based. This American/Canadian crew will make that discovery live on our network in a few days.

"Water-ice is a key element for providing oxygen and water to sustain a colony." As the station alternated between coverage streams, more simulated pictures were displayed of the landing and of the crew taking samples of the blue ice.

The small picture in the corner switched places with the commentators, now filling the screen as Nancy and Jeffrey talked over the one-minute countdown.

"The Space Launch System, SLS, with the Odin vessel attached, is 360 feet tall and 27 feet in diameter, and lift-off weight is 143 tons. It is the most powerful launch system ever built—a mixture of *Saturn 5*, *Apollo's* legacy, plus shuttle-rocket engines and twin boosters with upgraded fuel-efficient technology giving it 9.2 million pounds of thrust, more than 34 times the total thrust of a 747 jet."

An extreme close-up camera captured the orange pillar of flame and the white-hot waves generated by the engines' ignition. Tons of cooling water poured out on the launch pad to disperse the heat. Microphones a mile away picked up the thunderous roar of the lift-off. Even with the broadcast volume set low, the sound coming out of most televisions rumbled and rattled windows.

"What a beautiful launch!" Nancy exclaimed. "Let the world know that at 10:02 a.m., the United States of America is back in space, no longer dependent on the Russians for a ride."

"Yes, that was a picture-perfect launch, into the clear blue California sky." Jeffrey sounded pleased and confident, although relief was registering as well. "This joint mission with Canada demonstrates a commitment our two countries have made to further space exploration. I just received word from Mission Control that telemetry is right on the numbers. That means our boys will be landing at *Shackleton Crater* in just over 50 hours."

"Don't you mean our boys and girls?" Nancy asked. "Let's not forget Shirley Worthy and Natalie Van der Hoose will be making the trip as well. They, in fact, will be the first females to walk on the moon. Do we know which one will walk first and if any momentous words will be spoken?"

"I apologize for that oversight," Jeffrey said, sounding sincere. "Yes, they will be the first females. We sometimes forget that NASA is an equal-opportunity organization and has been sending females into space for some time now, on the shuttles, the ISS, and now the moon. My money is on Worthy to be the first moon-walker, beating out both Van der Hoose and Commander Booker. Worthy is the oldest member of the team, and the matriarch (as it were) of the group." A series of photos of her appeared on the screen. "She is the pilot and second in command, which means she handles the actual moon landing and takeoff, and will be responsible for the final splashdown maneuvers when they return. She is also the flight medic, which means she can handle just about any medical emergency thrown at them. She is also the last trained shuttle pilot still active at NASA."

Nancy took advantage in a slight pause to ask a question. "With today's technology, where we can remotely control rovers on Mars and routinely fly drones on combat missions from halfway around the world, does *Endurance* actually *need* a person to pilot and land?"

Jeffrey nodded an acknowledgment of her logic. "Good point. In fact, the first *Odin* ship, *Inuk 1*, did not have a crew, and it was remotely landed on the weekend, but it's not leaving the surface nor reconnecting with its service module for a return trip. It's similar to why we have pilots on airlines. Auto-pilot will do most of the work, from takeoff, to navigation, and even most of the landing sequence. But it's always the human pilot that finishes the job, and Worthy's job is far more complicated than flying a plane."

Nancy asked an impromptu question. "Jeff, can you tell us more about this transport ship *Inuk?* That sounds like an Inuit word."

"Well Nancy, it is. The northern indigenous people of Canada, the Inuit, use the term '*Inuk*' to mean 'being human'. They have built large stone forms in the shape of a human all across the Arctic. These rock structures are a way to say, 'a human was here'."

"A true symbolic gesture for this moon mission," Nancy remarked.

"Commander Tyrone Booker will make sure everything runs smoothly," Jeffrey said, segueing back to the script. "Although the commander has spent time in the space station, he will be the first Canadian to walk on the moon. Maybe Worthy, an American, and Booker, a Canadian, will step on the surface together, but he may need to talk to his fiancée first." This prompted a chuckle from his colleague, as it was meant to. Smiling, he continued. "Commander Booker is engaged to a young woman from New Orleans, a lieutenant in the Coast Guard. Although Booker is Canadian by birth, he has made America his home and has been part of NASA's family for some years now. He was the youngest person to ever command the space station, and now, at 34, he will be the youngest to command a lunar mission."

"Well I'm sure the commander will be up to the challenge," Nancy said. "This will also be the first mission of Natalie Van der Hoose. At 29, she is the flight engineer and the only other Canadian on the team. Interesting side fact, she was part of the team that designed the Odin landing struts at MIT."

Jeffrey nodded. "That's right. And speaking of engineering facts, the Odin craft itself will actually land on the moon and not a lunar lander, as was the case in the *Apollo* missions." An animated presentation commandeered the screen, with Jeffrey's voice describing what the audience was seeing. "When Worthy puts them in lunar orbit, she will separate the command/crew module—that's their living quarters—from the service module—that's the rocket engines and fuel—which will remain in orbit for their return trip. Beneath the command module is the lunar landing module, which houses the decent and assent rockets and fuel, as well as the fold-out landing struts you talked about earlier, Nancy, which stay up there on the moon. Attached to that module is the payload module, which will be released on final approach. It has its own decent rockets and will make a soft landing. It contains the vehicle they will use to move equipment and crew down into the crater."

"So they just stack various modules together depending on the mission needs?" Nancy asked.

"Absolutely, and if this was a Mars mission, they would have included a secondary crew module with more supplies for the three-month journey. That said, the Odin command module is still big enough to provide comfort for the six crew members for their ten-day mission. They also have the use of *Inuk,* which landed in the same area. It has additional supplies as well as another vehicle for the crew."

Nancy picked up the narrative where he left off. "The three other members of the *Endurance* crew we haven't talked about are Major Adam Carson, Lieutenant Carlo Santos, and Lieutenant Ben Nuzzi. They are Army Engineers and not NASA personnel. Their responsibility will be to set up the necessary equipment to lower crew members into the crater and to the ice. Major Carson will oversee all lunar surface EVAs, Worthy is in charge of all on-board, in-flight activities, and Commander Booker has overall mission responsibility. We don't have much background on these three men, other than their rank and that they are listed as mission specialists."

"What we do know, Nancy, is that this is a collaborative NASA, CSA, and American Military mission, focusing on the ice at the South Pole."

"Jeff, this mission certainly has captured the interest and hearts of the American people, as well as rekindled the spirit of a space race. We are going to take a commercial break now, and will be back in just a moment with more live coverage of the historic flight of the Odin space craft *Endurance.*"

CHAPTER 4
STORNOWAY, SCOTLAND

The wheels touched down with a barely perceptible bounce, stirring him from his slumber. The cheers and clapping from the passengers—a common ritual to show gratitude towards the pilot and crew for a safe flight—brought Simon Richardson fully awake. He stretched and waited for people to vacate and clear the aisle while he drank from a bottle of water, compliments of British Airways.

A young cheery flight attendant, wearing a crisp blue uniform, assisted an elderly couple from India retrieve their bags from the overhead compartment. She paused briefly, catching his eye and smiling at him with a hint of sadness and consolation in her face. Earlier in the flight, she had struck up a conversation with the good-looking muscular blond guy in seat 38A. He had a Californian surfer tan and a well-built chest, hidden but not disguised by a tight black t-shirt. She was pleasantly surprised to hear a Canadian accent but saddened to learn that he was heading to Scotland to visit the estate of his late mother—saddened because she would not get the opportunity to ask him to escort her to one of the many clubs in Glasgow (or something more) during her two-day layover.

A mother and her young son, both with corn-country American accents, thanked him for his company and conversation during the long Atlantic flight. The young boy, suffering from pulmonary fibrosis—a rare lung disease that limits the absorption of oxygen into the lung tissue—thanked him for his "magic crystal" pendant, which Simon had allowed him to wear for the ten-hour flight.

"I can breathe better now. Thanks mister!" he jubilantly remarked, as he handed the homemade jewelry back to his new friend with the sparkling emerald-green eyes.

The mother had hard features, evidence of her long work hours, but she forced a smile for the benefit of her 7-year-old and his belief that the crystal had magically healed him. Only Simon knew the truth: that the black crystal had come from an ancient meteor mined in Central

America by beings of another world. These crystals, one of which he now wore as a pendant around his neck, possessed healing powers as one of its many traits. He had befriended one of the aliens' offspring, a human hybrid, who went by the name of Orion. This 900-year-old had been living under the ocean in one of their original space crafts, cut off from civilization and companionship except for his surveillance drones and a dolphin friend named Sheera.

Simon was traveling light with the largest carry-on allowed, and had enough clothes and personal effects for four days. With a little effort, he figured he could stretch it into six, if he decided to stay longer. He didn't know what to expect. The mysterious letter from his late mother, addressed to him and his twin sister, just said that they should come together to the country estate in Scotland. The document detail was sketchy as to why they had been separated at birth and later adopted by two different men, whom they each called 'dad'. It also revealed nothing about their actual biological father.

Simon had in fact only met Lieutenant Samantha Harding, or Sam (as she reminded everyone to call her), eight weeks prior to the reading of the letter. They had become friends—extraordinarily close friends—before he learned that she was his twin sister. In that short time, they had been so many things to each other, filled so many roles, that he felt her absence more strongly that he would have thought possible. But that was six months ago, when he'd last seen her on his boat, *Dragon Spirit* ... before the war called the lieutenant back to Afghanistan. This trip to Scotland was strictly a fact-finding mission—RECON, as his best friend and twin would say. He would meet with his/their late mother's attorney and hopefully get some answers about this previously unknown estate and their estranged mother.

After contacting the Scottish law firm that was handling the will, he gave them his flight plans and itinerary; then he sent an email to Sam's long-time girlfriend, Tamara Gill, who preferred to be called either 'T' or 'Lieutenant T'. The full-bodied Jamaican was still in the Caribbean, working with the DEA, and had recently sent him an email on his and Sam's birthday, congratulating them both for aging another year and also informing them of her engagement. Neither he nor Sam had ever met her new heart-throb, Tyrone Booker, but the texts that were exchanged between his sister and friend described (in racy detail) the six-foot-three, muscle-bound hunk with the gorgeous short black hair. He laughed to himself thinking about how the girls were carrying on. He thought of Tamara like a younger sister, but had concerns about her marrying a guy some seven years her senior, even if they *were* both Canadians. It also did not feel right that, after only a three-month romance, Tyrone had proposed to her on the same beach in Mexico where they'd first met. It seemed too soon, but who was he to talk? He had fallen in love with Sam very quickly and had needed to fall *out* of love just as quickly when he found out that his soul mate and lover was also his sister. His heart was still healing from the shock and the journey. This trip was his way of escaping his feelings.

Simon knew that talking to Tamara about his concerns regarding the engagement would not help anything. So he'd thanked her for the greeting, and conveyed semi-sincere well-wishes on behalf of his sister. That was the extent of the communication he'd had with Tamara, which was more than he'd had with Sam. Both gals were actively involved in missions, either with the navy as a chopper pilot or drug interdiction with the Coast Guard. The only person Simon stayed in touch with was Orion, and his dolphin friend, Sheera. Scuba diving down to see his friend gave him an excuse to take the big trawler out. Sleep deprived, he walked through the airport. Glancing at his watch, he realized that he was still on Nassau, Bahamas time. Glasgow was five hours ahead, and he couldn't remember the last time he'd had a solid sleep. Forty-eight hours ago, maybe. He remembered catching a predawn flight out of Nassau to Miami, with a two-hour layover, and then on to Toronto, where he'd met briefly with his father, Grover T. Richardson—who, he reminded himself for the hundredth time, was technically his step-father. Grover T. was the president of Richardson Geological Survey Company, the head office of which was in Toronto, Canada. Simon was a genius, completing two PhDs in less time than it took an average student to complete one. His last doctorate was engineering, from MIT, which he had breezed through just five years earlier. He had not been ready to assume the new vice-president's position his father offered though. Instead, he'd been anxious to get as far away from academia and the inevitable business world as possible.

He'd wanted to follow his dreams and explore the world around him, like any other college kid.

Grover T. allowed his highly intelligent, yet socially inept only child to take some time off and discover the man within. The boy was actually more of a research scientist than a spreadsheet guy anyway, a trait he'd inherited from his estranged and now deceased mother.

Aided by Mac, an old navy buddy living in the Bahamas, his father created a new research department, with Duffy's Dive Shop as its office. Together with Sam, they refurbished an old decommissioned spy boat: a seventy-foot trawler called *Dragon Spirit*. Their last adventure had led to the culmination of his lifelong research project: the identification and source location of the black energy crystals. With the help of Tamara and Orion, the twins traveled to the old meteor site and Orion's birthplace in Guatemala. In an old Mayan village, they found that all the evidence of the alien mining operation had been removed.

The smell of fresh coffee tickled his senses, and like an old blood hound, Simon tracked the scent to its source. He had discovered that Scotland, particularly Glasgow International, was populated by all nationalities with a variety of dialects. A petite Middle-Eastern woman with a light Scottish-Indian accent inquired as to how he wanted his brew. He wondered what part of the country his old friend and business partner, Iaan Mac Duff (or Mac, as everyone called him) was from. His accent, comical at times, was an extremely heavy brogue. Simon paused in thought, as he sipped his strong black brew, enjoying the revitalization of caffeine. He reflected on what circumstances could have led their two step-fathers to have a common association with Mac, and how the old Scotsman had brought Sam and him together. Further internal speculation led him to ask himself how Mac had known his mother. These were questions that should have been asked months before, and would be asked the next time they met. Glancing at his watch again, he noted that he still had an hour before his next departure, to Stornoway, on the Isle of Lewis in the Outer Hebrides island chain, which was a two-hour flight in a small twenty-passenger jet.

He sat down in a waiting area near the departure gate and caught a glimpse of the moon launch, displayed on one of the many television screens in the area. He turned his head to ignore it, preferring to watch people instead. A redheaded teenager was texting someone, probably a boyfriend, based on the smile on her face as she read his messages or perhaps viewed the pictures he had sent. Simon continued to sip his coffee, listening to the people moving about.

He was tired, but his mind was at peace, so he decided to try to test his mental skills, something that Sam had attempted to teach him numerous times. Closing his eyes, he relaxed and opened his thoughts to all that was around him. Sam could have easily read the minds of these travelers—an extraordinary side effect of an exploding crystal they had been exposed to during his research on an island near New Orleans. The other side effect was a telepathic bond between Simon and his twin, and again, she excelled at this new gift.

A stout woman with an overbearing attitude, wearing a BAW uniform, took up station behind the counter at Gate 20. The PA system distracted his thoughts as she barked out that the flight to Stornoway was now boarding.

The flight to the island was non-eventful and Simon managed to get a little shut eye. Half the seats contained cargo, and the rest were occupied by returning locals. They were a tough bunch, these islanders, living at the edge of the North Sea. Scotland itself was beautiful in its sheer rugged harshness. The country's national flower, a thistle, reflected this. Ancient armies and civilizations all had laid claim to this old land through bloodshed. Today the people are who they are because of their past, and now were the culmination of their diverse ancestors—the names of which conjure up myths and legends: Vikings, Druids, Saxons, and Gauls. Staring out the plane's window, Simon could see them in his mind's eye ... the many battles between the people who had occupied these lands.

His dream world was vanquished when the plane landed, this time without the pomp and pageantry associated with larger jets. Walking down the stairs to the tarmac, he was thankful that he wore a windbreaker, and pulled it up around his neck. The wind had picked up, blowing a cold rain from the north and further emphasizing the brutality of the land. Although he hailed from Canada, and should have been accustomed to this weather, he had lived in the tropical heat of the Bahamas for the past five years. He quickly entered the small terminal of Stornoway, and without the need for the Customs or Immigration inspections that were completed both in Toronto and again in Glasgow, he exited the other side of the building and approached the waiting cabs.

The law office that was handling his late mother's estate had promised to have a car and driver for him, and true to their word, he was greeted by a large, powerful black man with a hand-written sign that read 'Simon Richardson'.

"Good day sir, welcome to Scotland and to the beautiful Isle of Lewis. My name is Gregory Haroonton, the third," the man stated with a friendly Scottish accent with a hint of Caribbean patois, then gripped the young man's hand in salutation.

Simon was struck with the thought that this individual, if you ignored his rough exterior, sounded and acted like a gentleman's gentleman. It was as if he had grown up in the Elizabethan era as someone's manservant. After his bear-like grip released Simon, Gregory grabbed the luggage and loaded it into the boot of the car. The front left door was opened and Simon slid in. As a driver, Simon always found that right-hand-drive cars disrupted his perception, but this powerful and versatile Land Rover, with its luxurious leather interior was an acceptable distraction.

There was a familiarity about Gregory, a man he only just met. It was the same odd feeling he got when he'd first met Samantha, and later Tamara.

"How were your flights, sir?"

"Wonderful Gregory, I only had to take my shoes off once, and I was not selected for a strip search." Simon laughed and joked as he recanted his itinerary.

They drove along a coastal road with many twists and turns, with the turbulent waters thundering against the shore nearby. It was difficult to tell if the water on the windshield was from the waves or the rain.

He decided that the flights were long and too numerous and that sleep was more than welcome.

"What is the mood of the household now, without my mother?" Simon asked.

"About the same, but more somber of course," Gregory said. "The housekeeper has transitioned in well and has helped keep order, not that any was needed."

"Housekeeper? Is that necessary?"

"Not for me to say, sir. She was appointed by your mother's attorney."

"I see. I suppose someone needs to be in charge. What do you do there?"

"Me? Oh lord, just about anything and everything that no one else does." He let out a deep belly laugh, before continuing. "You know … odd jobs around the place that is forever in need of repair."

When they arrived at his mother's ancestral home, it was dark, but what light there was indicated a grand mansion. Gregory made Simon a locally grown tea, which he said would help him overcome jet lag. While he sat drinking the tea from a bone-china cup, in an ornate and richly decorated sitting room, he wondered who his mother really was.

CHAPTER 5

Van der Hoose opened her eyes, which had been tightly shut since they left the launch pad. Now that the second-stage rocket was jettisoned, the roar and vibrations stopped. The tightness in her chest from the G-force was gone. They were in zero gravity, weightless. She breathed deeply, still in her protective flight suit and helmet. NASA still used the heavier bulkier suits for launch, because they offered the best protection in the event of an emergency. Now that they were weightless, the suits could be removed and stored away until the return trip.

Although the roar was gone from the launch engines, the blood pounding in her ears was the only sound she could hear. Someone tapped her hand, still-clenched in a fist. The realization that she had made it finally hit home.

"Nat, your turn; you can take your suit off." Worthy was talking to her, as she helped the younger woman remove her helmet.

The hiss of pressure releasing and the smell of nervous sweat assaulted her senses. Looking around, she realized that she was the only one on the flight deck still with a suit on. The big commander was in a one-piece, blue-cotton flight suit, staring out a port window and floating horizontal to the floor. The pilot spoke again, holding the flight engineer's face as she gently tapped her cheek. "Nat, honey, come back to us. You're okay."

Suddenly the younger women took a deep breath, a reflex action from her adrenaline high. The ringing in her ears and pounding of her heart subsided, and she smiled at the salt-and-pepper-haired women still holding her face. The woman smiled back with gentle brown eyes and a motherly kindness.

"There you go, you made it. What did you think of the launch?"

"Oh my god, what a rush! The most intense sensations I have ever felt, but it scared the crap out of me!"

"How you feeling?" Shirley asked, as she lifted the bulky suit up over her crew-mate's head, an act made effortless in weightlessness.

"Better, but I have a headache. What happened to me?" she asked, rubbing her temples.

Shirley placed a small wrapped object into Natalie's hand.

"What is it?"

"Chocolate, it helps balance electrolytes after a stressful situation," Shirley replied seeing the questioning look on Natalie's face. "It's old school, and if you still have a headache in fifteen minutes, we will try something stronger."

"Hey, where are the army boys?" Van der Hoose asked, as she chewed the delicious sweet treat.

"They're down on the crew deck. The commander asked them to leave the flight deck to give you some privacy, in case you had an accident in your suit. Don't be embarrassed; it happens with first timers. No matter how much you train on the simulators, it's never the same as the real thing, is it?" her friend whispered.

The younger woman wiggled her feet out of the attached boots and floated up and out of the lower torso pants. She was thankful that there were no accidents to report.

Free of the confinement, she floated over to the port window the commander was looking through.

"This is a beautiful view," the big muscular commander said, as he caught the 140-pound woman floating towards him and shared the view of the receding big blue marble. "Worth the price of admittance."

"Why don't you two check on the rest of the team and get a bite to eat." the pilot suggested.

The commander exited the flight deck, while the flight engineer waited for him to clear the circular floor portal.

"Hey Nat, how's the head now?" the pilot asked.

"Much better, thanks."

"Good. Oh, and Nat, don't forget your suit. Stow it please."

The rest of the flight, for the most part, was smooth and uneventful. The new space ship, with all of its amenities, was everything it was promoted to be. The spaciousness of the crew quarters, with its many viewing windows, allowed the astronauts solitude to reflect on the majesty of the cosmos, when they were not on duty monitoring the ship's systems. The major and his team kept to themselves, as they privately reviewed the mission objectives.

At the mission's forty-eight-hour mark, the view of the moon was larger than the shrinking earth. Worthy made a minor course correction and confirmed the telemetry adjustment with Mission Control. They were still two hours from lunar-insertion orbit and *Endurance* was performing flawlessly.

Major Carson, in a slow Texan drawl, asked Commander Booker if he could speak to the crew, which was answered in the affirmative.

"Well hasn't this been a picture-perfect ride?" Carson asked rhetorically. "Worthy, you really are an extraordinary pilot. Thank you, ma'am. For those of us who have no space experience, I reckon this is better than a slice of peach cobbler pie." He paused, smiling at the crew with his disarming southern charm before continuing.

"I've asked the commander if I could speak to y'all, because I have more details about the mission. I'm sure y'all have questions, like why all the hushy-hush and stuff. Let me say a few words about that." The squared-jaw army major, in his late 40s, casually handed Booker an envelope with the Presidential Seal.

Ty carefully broke the wax seal and read the single page to himself, and then studied the attached photograph as the rest of the crew watched. He then slumped down in his chair and waved for the major to continue as he re-read the document.

"What I'm about to tell y'all is classified; can't be repeated. As of now, y'all are temporarily under US Military command, and not NASA. What that means is y'all will be taking orders from me. Booker is still in charge for the media and the public. Worthy is in command of *Endurance* and ship operations, but listen up. Once we set boots on the ground, y'all are taking orders from me and the commander in chief." Major Carson paused, to let his words register with the crew, before continuing.

"We will not be alone up there. Four days ago, *Inuk 1* landed at the crater's rim, and she carried a crew of two. They've been setting up a pair of big ole inflatable habitats, as well as equipment and supplies. So it's important that you land this ship on the coordinates given. We can't have you drifting. I reckon they opened up that crater cut by now, to give us more elbow room with those big ole rovers we will be driving." The major looked each of them in the eye to confirm that they understood the importance of his message before he spoke again.

"The reason this has been keep out of the press is because water-ice has been confirmed. Russia, Japan, India, and now China all want access to this supply. There may be other water sources, but I reckon this is the purdiest location, because the outer rim gets about 90 percent daylight, which y'all know means free solar energy. That's why Van der Hoose is here. She's the solar expert. It's also the perfect position to defend, because the outer rim's too steep to climb by hand or with a rover. That's why we took control of the cut. The Russkies are more than a month away from a manned mission and have not confirmed their landing site. When we leave, they could easily take over our base.

"Now legally, so I've been told, no one owns the moon, so no country can lay land claims. That said, we can claim the resources, so long as we show an active operation. The Moon Treaty is set up similar to the Antarctic Treaty, which is why we are being assisted by a few large corporations, Bigelow Aerospace for the habitats, Space X for rides, and Boeing for the infrastructure. A few mining corporations will be signing on shortly." He paused to receive appreciative nods from his team mates before continuing.

"So far all we have is a normal space race, just like with *Apollo* and the Russians back in the sixties, but there is one more little ole wrinkle that y'all need to know. When I said earlier that we wouldn't be alone, I was referrin' to more than just our sister ship, *Inuk 1*. Earlier this year, the LRO, or Lunar Reconnaissance Orbiter, satellite photographed something lying inside the crater. We did multiple passes at varying altitudes and with different sun angles. Commander, if you would pass around the picture in the envelope please."

The commander did as asked, handing the grainy image to Worthy, with Van der Hoose looking over her shoulder. Worthy's eyes widened and then her face hardened and her expression showed concern, as her eyebrows knitted. Natalie put her hand to her mouth in shock, but not before a gasp was released. She offered the picture to the two lieutenants, who declined, presumably being aware of the large black image from an earlier briefing.

The three NASA crew members had many questions for Major Carson, who did his best to answer.

"Do we know what it is?"

"Not really, but we have ruled out a meteor fragment."

"Why couldn't it be the remains of the meteor that created the crater?" Worthy interjected.

"NASA doesn't believe so, 'cause it's too angular. Meteorites are meteors after impact. Normally they're burned up in the atmosphere or vaporized on impact. We don't know a hell of a lot about lunar meteorites, but they reckon it vaporizes on impact if it's made of light or loose material. Now if it's made of heavy metals, like iron, then ya end up with a smooth, round rock ball. This crater was formed by a loose-packed, dirty snowball of ice and rocks, millions of years ago. That's the reason for the ice at the bottom. The *item* at the bottom, we reckon, is the result of a second impact, and one that relatively recent compared to the original. 'Cause of its irregular shape, the assumption is that it was not formed naturally."

"So are you saying it's alien?" Booker asked.

"Hold on there, sir. No one is calling it alien, but that *is* the working assumption til y'all get down there to investigate further. We have been calling it 'the item' and will till we know more."

"Do we know where it came from?"

"Not a clue."

"Do we know how long it's been here?"

"Nah, but we reckon less than 5,000 years and more than 500, when people started using telescopes and studying the moon."

"Do we know if it crashed or landed?"

"NASA and the NSA reckoned it crashed, 'cause of the debris field around it."

"Do we know how big it is?"

ORION - Escape Velocity

"Yeah, we reckoned a guess; part of the item is buried in the wall and part in the ice bottom. We are figurin' it's about one-kilometer long by a quarter-kilometer wide."

"Wow, that's big. Who else knows about it?" Worthy asked.

"The six of us, and my two guys already on site, CAPCON, the capsule communicator in Houston, POTUS obviously, 'cause of the letter, a few admirals, some high-ranking officials of the NSA, CIA, FBI, and Homeland, the guys that took that picture, your prime minister, and the Canadian Space Agency (CSA). I reckon about a hundred all told."

"What other countries know?" Commander Booker asked, following up on the same line of questioning his friend had started.

"That is still being assessed. What I can confirm is that India and Japan both have had close flybys and not detected the item."

"How do we know that?" Worthy jumped in.

"Classified, but let's just say that we sold them our communication equipment for their satellites and rovers; at a bargain price, so I've heard."

"That just leaves the Russians and Chinese who may know something," Booker added.

"Maybe, but like I said, it's an ongoing assessment. China's rover, the Little Jade Rabbit, was less than a kilometer from our site before it broke down and vanished from radar. And the Russians haven't been hanging their hat on this side of the moon for some time now."

"If the other countries find out and send a ship up here, are we in danger?" the brunette engineer asked nervously.

"Ah young lady, y'all were in a heap of danger when this big ole firecracker was strapped to your butt. Y'all are going to the moon; it don't get any more crazy dangerous than that, unless you want to go poking around inside a big ole alien thing." The major grinned and laughed as he continued. "Don't sweat the Russian or the Chinese; they are at least a month away, but I reckon closer to a year. So if there are no more—"

"Yeah I have one more question," Booker said. "How long have we known about this thing?"

"I only just found out about it when I was briefed forty days ago."

"That's not what I asked. How long has the US Intelligence Network or NASA known about it?" the commander asked sternly.

"I only knows what I've been told," the southerner drawled, averting his eyes downward for a moment.

Booker considered this for a long moment. "With the number of fly over's taken, without making it look too obvious, plus the planning of this mission behind NASA's back, it must have been known about for over a year. Does that sound about right, Worthy?"

"Sounds about right, Commander, and Major, for an army engineer who just got read into the program, you sure are knowledgeable about craters. The four of you have had little experience with zero gravity; your men and Nat have shown signs of motion sickness—it's an inner-ear thing that you get used to after a few days. The commander here has spent a year on the ISS and I ... well let's just say that I have clocked a few more space hours than he has. Our bodies know how to compensate. What I don't get, Major, is *you*," the veteran pilot challenged. "You act like a seasoned space traveler, with no sickness from weightlessness. My money says you've worked up in space on some Dark Ops mission with one of the shuttles ... maybe even piloted one, and the way you stand up to the commander, I would say that your rank is a little higher than 'major', if you even have a rank."

Major Carson met her eyes squarely. "I reckon I don't know how to respond to your accusations, but y'all better get them under control. What I have shared with y'all is what I've been told, and I believe it to be the god's gospel truth." He revealed his white teeth through a forced smile, with the soft disarming charm vanishing from his tone.

"Booker, you've known me for some time, right?" Worthy asked her commander and friend. He nodded.

"Would you say I'm a pretty good judge of character?" Again her friend acknowledged this with a nod.

"Has my 'bull-shit detector' ever failed me?" she asked, without taking her eyes off Major Carson.

"No Shirl, it has not."

"Because here's the thing Carson, if that *is* your name, that object didn't come from outer space. It wasn't inbound. It was outbound." She paused, taking in the shocked and blank stares from the rest of the crew before continuing.

"It was heading away from Earth. Look at its crash trajectory. A direct line from Earth, and when we get a little closer, I'll be able to tell you what latitude it left from."

"But Shirl, it has to be alien," Nat said, calmly putting her hand on her friend's arm. "It must have come from outer space."

"Oh hon, the *item* is alien, and it *did* come from out there; I'm just saying that the last planet it left from was Earth, and I think our new leader here, who probably works for some government agency with three letters, knows that and is holding out on us.

"What are you not telling us? I swear to God, if you don't come clean, I will throw you out the airlock myself."

"All right, all right … dial it down, woman. Okay … our probe reckons it's organic."

"WHAT?" she shouted. "It's alive?"

"Well, we're not sure if it's living. The scans only reckon it's organic, nothing more. Two months ago, NASA and the NSA launched a special, experimental lunar reconnaissance satellite to shoot a probe into the crater, to confirm water-ice presence. A second secret probe was purposely dropped on the object. The probes were reworked torpedoes with some cutting-edge technology loaded in 'em. We got some interesting infrared photos of the thing as the probe came down. It was designed to penetrate and analyze the first few inches, and we got lucky with a direct hit on a flat part, before it bounced off and stuck in the ice. When the probes internal chemical analyses were complete, they fired a small projectile containing the data results out of the crater and into low lunar orbit, where it was downloaded by the LRO satellite."

"And you weren't going to tell us that?" Booker asked, obviously struggling with his temper. "The fact that it's organic, and maybe even alive, isn't important? You are jeopardizing the safety of my crew and this mission; putting us in harm's way. Who the hell gives you that right?"

"I reckon that would be. the President," the major replied brashly, with a sneer across his face.

"You bugger! The damn thing *is* the alien! How dare you do this to us!?" the senior woman on board lunged at the major, but was easily restrained by the two lieutenants.

The major held up his hands in a calming gesture. "I assure you that this isn't a suicide mission; NASA and CSA were quite clear on that when I was read in on the facts. Y'all aren't going to the item, and in fact, y'all aren't even going into the crater. My team will make first contact and assess whether we make an incursion into it."

"Seriously?" the heavily built commander asked, not believing his ears. "HELL NO! We fly all the way up here, spitting distance from what has to be the greatest and most important discovery mankind has ever made, and you want us to sit on the bench? No flippin' bloody way! We are going with you to that crater—*to the item!*" Booker received strenuous agreement from his NASA crew-mates.

"Well now," the major drawled, slowly considering. "Y'all are real important to the mission, and I did promise that y'all wouldn't get hurt." He studied them silently for a long moment before coming to a decision. "Y'all can go, but it's voluntary, and if there is any sign of danger, y'all haul ass and get out of there, is that clear?"

He watched the crew's excited exchange and actually found himself regretting that he had to interrupt. "I'm sorry Pilot, ma'am, but you're going to have to stay with *Endurance* and *Inuk 1*... because you're the only one who can get us off this rock."

Shirley considered fighting this assertion, vehemently, but couldn't realistically argue the logic. "Bugger. What about the guy that landed the other Odin ship?"

"That would be a good ole boy in Houston who did all the work, and with the slight signal delay, almost smashed it into the side of the rim. Besides they'll be hitching a ride with us for the return trip, and you're the only one up here with the smarts to hook-up with the big engines in orbit. Sorry ma'am."

"Hell ... well if you guys go down there, and it wakes up and eats someone, I might as well be the one to tell Houston." She chuckled, easing the earlier tension, still disappointed but relieved she had gotten to the truth.

Major Carson smiled inwardly to himself, pleased that their meeting had gone better than expected.

* * *

Worthy entered lunar orbit after three successful two-minute burns and entered the circular parking orbit on the South Pole latitudinal line. After two complete rotations, with only one minor mid-orbital burn correction, she separated from the service module, leaving the big rocket engine in a safe orbit and in the care of Houston. She then began the landing sequence with a descent-orbit burn, when they reached the 2-km mark, the payload module containing the SEV was released to be guided down to the surface remotely by the flight engineer. Landing trajectory took them over the 21-km-wide crater.

All crew members ran to a viewing port to look down into its depths and try to catch a glimpse of the "item". Worthy had the best viewing port. From the read-out, the pilot knew that the bottom was more than 4 km away; the crew would never be able to pick out the black object in the darkness of the hole, but with her landing radar pinging away at the surface, she could make it out. The item was resting on a terrace shelf a third of the way down, with its nose wedged into the substrate. Using that as one position and the tail end as another, it would be easy to plot a trajectory back to Earth as soon as she finalized the landing sequence.

As they flew over the crater and the towering rampart wall, two glowing white-domed tubes, bathed in bright sunlight, came into view. On one were the letters USA, on the other, LUNAR BASE 1. Low on the horizon, in a jet-black starless sky, was a full Earth-rising. The twenty minutes a day that the South Pole would be in twilight would reveal a heaven of stars, similar to observations from Earth.

"Houston, *Endurance* on final approach," Commander Booker said calmly into his headset, as they crested the peak of the rim. "We are looking at one of the prettiest pictures a human could ever imagine.

Now we know how the *Apollo* teams felt, watching our home planet this way."

Major Carson was controlling the video feed with the aid of Lieutenant Santos, while Lieutenant Nuzzi monitored audio. Their orders were not to reveal the habitats on the live network feed, but rather capture the images for a secure feed after landing.

Worthy expertly controlled the big space craft, using the maneuvering thrusters for lateral direction and attitude orientation. The ship did not glide like the shuttle; it fell like a flat rock in water, but still with a measure of control. Using the descent thrusters, she worked with the one-sixth gravities' pull, making a slow sweep over her landing co-ordinates. At twenty feet, she turned the craft towards the crater and spotted the famous Cameron Cut, opening into the crater, and the recent excavation by some well-placed explosives. Beside this, and fifty feet from the wall, was the other Odin ship, *Inuk 1*. Worthy observed all this as the sensors signaled that she was a meter from ground contact, which followed a second later.

The six landing struts bore the weight of the vessel, flexing slightly as the joints locked into place. The final sequence was to shut down the power to the descent rockets and to breathe a sigh of relief.

"Good landing, girl!" Commander Booker patted her on the back. "You have the honors, Shirl." He handed her the portable microphone.

The pilot paused and took a deep breath, remembering her prepared speech. "Houston, Shackleton Base here. We're back. I am pleased to inform the world that humans have once again taken up residence on the moon."

❧ CHAPTER 6 ☙

Simon woke early the next morning after a restful, dreamless sleep—the kind of sleep he hadn't had since he was a boy. Feeling revitalized, he donned a pair of sweats and sneakers and headed out for a morning run, looking forward to checking out the grounds. Descending the stairs, he was warmly greeted by a young woman dressed in a conservative maid's uniform: black skirt, white apron, and blouse.

"Good morning sir, is there anything I can get for you?" the young lady asked respectfully.

"No, I'm good, thanks," he replied, as he continued down to the first landing, then decided he did need information. "Maybe you can help though. Are there any interesting paths I could use for my run?"

"Oh certainly sir, at the foot of the stairs, turn right and head down the hallway to the kitchen, and exit out that door. Out the back, past the rose garden on the left, there's a horse trail that will take you to the stables and then on through to the paddocks. If you continue on, you will come across the ruins of the old castle. Don't run through it, because it could be dangerous; go around it. Beyond that is a beautiful view of the North Sea. Be careful, because the cliff is slippery with the morning dew. It is lovely though."

"I will, thank you; you have been most helpful."

"Enjoy your jog, sir."

He followed the directions and was thankful that she'd also told him where the kitchen was. He would need a coffee when he was finished.

The first room on his left caught his attention, with the morning sun shining through a pair of stained-glass doors. In it, there was another young lady, wearing the same uniform, dusting the furniture. Looking into the room, he realized it was a great hall—the kind of room in which banquets would be held for a few hundred people. It was ornate and opulent in its splendor. He could see royalty hosting an event in this room. He realized that the whole house likely shared this palatial decor. Another room, this time on his right, looked like a reading room, furnished with fine old leather chairs against a backdrop of built-in oak bookcases. The molding detail was from an era when craftsmen took pride in their work. He continued past other doors, which were closed. As a guest, he decided they were best left unopened.

The aroma of bread baking announced that the kitchen was near.

As he pushed open the heavy ornate door, he was greeted by a middle-aged woman he assumed was the cook, based on her traditional chef uniform and hat.

"Good morning, sir. I was told you drink coffee; I will start a pot right away."

"No, it's okay; I'm heading out for a run. I should be back in three quarters of an hour … and please call me Simon."

"I will have it ready on your return, and you may call me Annie."

"You're up early. Guess you beat the traffic coming in?" the young man asked, enjoying all the sensational smells.

"No traffic at all. This is private grounds and covers the better part of the peninsula. Besides, my husband, Jeremy, and I have a little cottage out back, so I walk to work. If you are jogging near the stables, would you be so kind as to ask him to fetch me another bag of flour."

"Yeah no probs. How many people worked for my mum anyway?"

"Well, there is Jeremy and me, of course … my daughter Adriana and her cousin Michelle are the two maids. Zak, Michelle's older brother, works with Jeremy as a stable hand. So, I guess that's five who worked for the missus."

"What about Gregory? I thought he's the chauffeur, handyman, and groundskeeper?"

"Oh no love, he lives here. He wasn't employed by the lady of the house, but he does do all those things you mentioned."

"Talking with him yesterday on the drive in, he mentioned that the housekeeper is in charge of the estate now. I have a meeting with her around lunchtime. Is she not an employee?"

"Oh yes, that's right. She was appointed by the missus a few weeks before she…" Her voice trailed off as she avoided referencing his mother's death, quickly blinking away emotion before continuing with her description of the new housekeeper. "A lovely woman, kind and fair, a little older than me I suppose." She cleared her throat. "Now away you go. I have work to do. I don't want to be caught lollygagging. Away with you now! GO."

Simon left without any further questions. He had the distinct feeling that he was being thrown out and that she had not been completely forthright in her responses.

He jogged at a leisurely pace, enjoying the fall colors throughout the numerous gardens. The side of the limestone building was covered in ivy, from the foundation up to the fourth-floor roof line. He was not an expert on architecture but guessed that the building was probably a few hundred years old and in excellent condition. He jogged on, noticing that the path had changed from flagstone with mossy joints to crushed red brick. A wide path wove through maple and pine trees surrounded by wild flowers. In the wooded section, the trail floor was soft bark mulch, and made running easier. After fifteen minutes, he saw his first confirmation that he was running on a horse trail, which he avoided, and that the animals were near.

The stable was made of the same old field stone as the main house, and was large enough to board at least a dozen of the four-legged beasts.

"Hey Jeremy! You around?" he called.

"Oy! In here!" a Scottish-accented voice roared back.

As Simon approached the door, a broad-shouldered man with a receding hairline exited. He had the typical muscular build of a man who had worked outside with his hands for many years. His face showed his age to be about sixty.

"Hi, I'm Simon." He extended his hand in greeting. "My mother owned this place."

"I know who you are, son. No need for formal introductions," the working man wheezed back, sounding much like the horses in his charge. "We were told you and your sister would decide the fate of the Ferguson land." "No, it's just me. My sister couldn't get the time off. I spoke to your wife, Annie. She asked if you could get her another sack of flour."

Jeremy mumbled a curse under his breath before asking a question: "Well son, what do ye think of the old place?"

"I got in late last night, and this is my first real look at the grounds. Haven't seen too much of the house either. I plan to jog out to the cliff, and then head back for a shower and breakfast. How long have you worked here?"

"Most of my life. I grew up here. Your mother hired me on after I finished high school, and I have been looking after the stables ever since."

"Hmm," Simon said, nodding. "Yeah, she was a kind and generous person." Feeling he had Jeremy's trust, he pushed further for answers. "So what's your take on the housekeeper? She everything they say?"

"No idea who you're talking about, son."

"You know, the lady who runs the house now that my mum has passed?"

"Don't know that; I keep to myself out here and out of other people's business. Suggest you do the same," he grunted, as he turned and went back inside.

Simon scratched his head and continued his run. *What the hell? Is everyone here evasive? How can that guy have been hired by Mum right out of high school? He's at least twenty years older than her, and why is everyone avoiding the subject of the housekeeper?*

The path continued through an apple grove that extended up a hill, and when he reached the top, he could see the ruins of the castle below and the dark waters of the North Sea beyond. The walls were mostly down, ranging from ground level to ten-feet high. The outer stones were black from weather and the inner were still white. Many of these had been removed, probably to erect the buildings around the estate. At the ocean side of the ruins was a tower, or at least the thirty-foot remains of one. Two of the four sides stood erect, ready to defend an enemy from the sea.

Pushing himself the last few hundred yards to the cliff, he stopped, panting for air as he stretched out on the grassy edge. Crawling closer, he peered out over the rock precipice to look at the surf below. Off to the side on a rock shelf, he saw movement. Two men emerged from a rough opening in the wall. One was a large black man, who looked like Gregory, the man who'd picked him up at the airport. The other, who was doing all the talking, was older and had reddish hair and a beard. The waves eliminated any chance of their voices reaching him, but he knew by the mannerisms that this was his old friend Iaan Mac Duff, the owner of the dive shop he worked out of in the Bahamas. Mac was his friend and mentor. Simon wondered what Mac was doing there, at his mother's estate. *Did Mac know my mum? And if he did ... why didn't he say anything to me or Sam?*

He was about to yell out to get their attention when they touched their belt buckles and leaped into the water, fully clothed. As strange as the action was, what was even stranger was that their belts had started to glow, before the light fully surrounded them. This was something he was all too familiar with. Orion had shown him and Sam the same alien belts, which protected their wearers from the elements. Sam had taken to calling them EVA (Extra Vehicular Activity) belts.

Simon lay on the cool grass, trying to think of a logical answer, but none came to mind. Direct confrontation was in order.

CHAPTER 7

Cheers and clapping resonated through the capsule from the cabin speakers. The *Endurance* team applauded, slapping each other on the back and each taking turns congratulating Worthy. No one noticed the sensor for the fourth landing strut's middle joint flash from green to red and then to green again. It took only a millisecond and could have been a sign of an electrical failure or that the strut joint was not fully locked.

The camera cart was remotely activated and rolled out from its storage garage under the landing platform, capturing a forward view of the lunar surroundings before pivoting 180 degrees to zoom in on the exit hatch from which the team would exit.

The excited crew quickly but carefully donned their space suits, the next generation style from the ISS or shuttle, and four generations from *Apollo*'s. These suits were lighter, with better flexibility in the joints and quicker and easier to get on. The suits were modular, with parts that could be interchangeable, with different size legs, arms, and upper and lower torso sections, comfortably fitting any body type and size. The pieces clipped together at the hip, shoulder, elbow, and knee joints with connectors for the internal heating and cooling coils that kept the wearer's body temperature normal during the hundred-degree temperature swings.

The back and front packs were integrated into the upper torso and provided air, power, and communication.

The SEV was a pressurized cabin mounted on a tractor chassis, and unlike the Apollo's non-pressurized lunar rover, it could carry a crew of twelve for thirty-six hours without spacesuit constraints. This SEV also carried a crane assembly and a six-passenger elevator cage, which would be lowered down into the crater, to the mysterious item. The *Inuk 1's* SEV was outfitted with bulldozer and backhoe attachments, which had already been put to work making holes for explosives and removing the resulting debris.

Booker and Worthy entered the ship's elevator to reach the lower deck and airlock, where they would don their suits.

"You ready for the camera, Shirl?" her large friend asked light-heartedly.

"As ready as I'll ever be. Do you think I need to fix my hair and makeup?" she teased.

"Nah, why mess with perfection," he joked, as he double-checked her helmet seal.

"Hon, at my age this is as good as it gets," she mused, performing the same procedure on him.

The pair entered the two-person airlock, and once secured, the air was pumped out into a pressure tank. This system differed from the *Apollo*-style system, which vented the air outside. With this new system, the air could be reused over and over to re-pressurize the air lock on their return, or for the next set of crew members to exit the craft.

The two crew members walked slowly down the ramp to the surface, arm in arm—symbolic of the group effort that had facilitated this historic event. With Houston and the world watching and listening, Commander Tyrone Booker calmly spoke into his headset.

"We follow in the shadows of brave men, and now we step into humanity's next greatest venture."

Worthy continued. "For all you *Apollo*-hoax believers out there, we are using a different sound stage." They raised their joined hands.

Van der Hoose, and Lieutenant Santos exited next, with their arms over their heads and waving like celebrities, followed closely by Major Carson and Lieutenant Nuzzi.

"Hey, to all my fellow MIT grads, top this," Van der Hoose called out excitedly into her open microphone.

"The earth looks quite small from up here," Nuzzi spoke in a serious monotone.

Lieutenant Santos raised both hands like a boxing-ring champion. "Wow! Sure beats my last tour."

Major Carson stepped onto the surface last, put his arms around the two closest crew members, and said solemnly, "We hope to do Neil, Buzz, and all the others proud." He saluted the camera.

They all held their places as the camera cart took a series of photos, guided by a technician at the Houston Command Center. When the last of the public pictures and videos were taken, the live TV feed was cut and switched to encrypted feed, for NASA eyes only. The robotic camera cart's flashing green light changed to red, and slowly pivoted around to capture the second Odin craft, *Inuk 1*, and its two crew members who were bouncing over to greet the new visitors.

From this point on, Houston would maintain an additional six-minute delay on top of the normal three-minute moon broadcast delay. A team of eight video technicians scanned and scrubbed the feed of anything that was not *Endurance* related. This included shadows and footprints where they shouldn't be, as well as the two additional crew members. The second Odin craft, *Inuk 1*, would be shown later, but not the lunar base. It went without saying that evidence of the item would also never be made public.

"Crew of *Endurance*, I would like y'all to meet the fellas from the *Inuk*," the major drawled into the short-range communication channel.

Major Carson introduced Master Sergeant Donny Butcher and Corporal Jon Pierce to the NASA personnel.

"These guys and I recently worked together on a special project in the Gulf. They are two of the best field engineers the army has. They have a reputation for fixing mechanical problems in remote and dangerous locations, and I reckon it doesn't get any more remote or dangerous than the moon. The boys upstairs and I figgered we could send up a couple of crackerjack engineers, on the QT, to set up camp so that my boys from *Endurance* could hit the ground running. All right, Butcher, you fixing to make history?" He slapped the sarge on the shoulder.

"Let's do it. Good to see you guys; it's been real quiet up here with just Pierce."

"Let me introduce y'all to *Endurance*." The major made introductions on the command frequency so all could hear. "Commander Tyrone Booker, he's the PR face and voice of the mission. Shirley Worthy, our pilot and driver for the trip home. Natalie Van der Hoose, flight engineer. These two bubbas to my right are Lieutenant Carlo

Santos and Lieutenant Ben Nuzzi. I brought them on the mission for their expertise."

The crew's communication default was the command channel, allowing all of them to talk and/or listen on the scrambled frequencies. They each had the option of taking a conversation off-line, from command to one of the private frequencies, but if there was an emergency, command would break in. It was as close to normal conversation as technology could provide in a soundless environment.

Worthy wondered what the major meant by the lieutenants' "expertise".

"Okay Butcher, Pierce, where y'all with the base construction?" Carson asked, getting down to business.

"Both habitats are set up and pressurized; we have been sleeping in HAB1." Butcher pointed to the nearest big white inflatable dwelling, tucked near the wall beside the crater's cut.

"Is it big enough for all of us?" Worthy inquired, light-heartedly.

"I believe it should be," Carson said. "There are four sleeping quarters in each habitat, with four bunks and two bathrooms with those specially designed low-G space showers and toilets. I know y'all are accustomed to the ones on the *Endurance*, these work the same, with more comfort and luxury. For obvious security reasons, we couldn't train y'all on this design version, but y'all are bright folks. I hope you don't need any special instructions," the major remarked, focusing on the two females of the group.

Van der Hoose turned towards Worthy and rolled her eyes at his remark, mouthing the word 'pig'. Worthy responded with a smirk, and mouthed the word 'ass', which generated a chuckle out of the younger woman over the command frequency.

The major walked up to the crater wall and moved into the cut. "How did the excavation go?"

"We had a challenge at first, drilling into the crater wall using the SEV drilling tool, but we managed and got it done in just over two hours." Sergeant Butcher spoke informally to the group as they walked into to the cut. "We used the C4 charges, and let me tell you, it was quite a sight, seeing the blast without a shock wave or sounds. We picked up an extra two meters on each side. We now have a fairly clean cut, six meters wide, that extends up ten meters. That's plenty of room to drive the SEVs through." A few feet into the opening, his helmet lights winked on, as did the rest of the crew's when they became immersed in darkness.

"Damn good work boys ... damn good! I reckon smoother than the simulations," Carson praised, as he ran his gloved hand over the newly excavated wall, careful not to rip it on any potential rock shards, before continuing his address to the *Inuk 1's* crew.

"How's the air extractor working, Pierce?"

The young army engineer was excited to be part of the conversation and show off his expertise with the new experimental extractor, which squeezed any existing oxygen from the newly pulverized rocks from the wall.

Corporal Jon Pierce was 23, tall and lean, and had brown hair that was almost black and cut into a spiked crew-cut—"number one on the side, three on the top", as he would say to his barber. He was quick-witted and held a deep respect for those in authority, both traits he had inherited from his mother. He had a muscular physique that was a result of army training and amateur hockey, although it was hidden in his bulky space suit. He was a Canadian on loan to the US Army Corp of Engineers.

"It's a slow process, sir. The extractor has only generated half a cubic meter of oxygen in twenty-four hours. We need more power for the microwave to work."

"Butcher, why are the solar panels not producing enough power?"

"Don't know, sir. We set up the six banks just like in training. Pierce is right; they don't kick out enough juice. The power drain from the extractor is more than what the panels can provide. I think someone in Houston screwed up on capacity specs," the gruff sergeant explained.

"Listen up y'all! Without that air extractor working at capacity, I reckon we might as well scrub this mission and go home." This brought a groan from the rest of the astronauts.

"Van der Hoose, you're an engineer. Work with Pierce and Worthy, and get that damn thing up to speed. Otherwise we aren't going to be able to do what we came here to do. The rest of y'all are with me. If we have to cut this mission short, I want a close-up of the item. Now move out," the mission commander barked.

"Butcher, one more thing, did you spot the Chinese rover when you flew over?"

"No sir, I thought we picked up a faint transponder signal after we landed, but it disappeared."

"Well maybe Worthy and Van der Hoose can do a walkabout to see if it's hung up on some rocks. Don't want anyone to say we didn't offer a helping hand to our Chinese friends," the major remarked sarcastically.

"What's the status of communication in the crater?" he continued.

"I installed signal repeaters on both sides of the cut, and another about ten kilometers on the wider south-ledge side. We will need one more to cover the remaining fifteen kilometers and the crater interior. I had to come back to recharge, but we can install that last one at the same time we set up the crane."

"I reckon that will work. I would have preferred communication up and running before we ventured in, though. Okay, we do a COM check every hour. Let's haul ass and git 'er done."

CHAPTER 8

Kai Yung sat with his back to the door of his opulent Hong Kong office, in the tower that adorned his company's name: Yung Global Enterprise. He looked like a caricature drawing come to life. He was short and round, with a thin strip of brown hair growing on his jaw line and continuing up and over his clean-shaven head. His face was accentuated with thick burgundy-framed glasses that sat low on his wide nose. Yung grew up in the days when Britain influenced and controlled Hong Kong, when wages had been fifty times greater than in the rest of China. His entrepreneurial father had started the company back in the early fifties, with a few lucrative manufacturing contracts from the West. At first he made plastic toys, and then added small appliances to the list of products made in Hong Kong, under the original umbrella of Yung Enterprise.

In preparation of the transfer of sovereignty back to China, on July 1, 1997, and with the fears of major changes to the industrial machine that was under British rule, Yung Senior sent his son to the UK to get educated, so he could succeed in this new industrial revolution. In the spring of 2005, 40-year-old Kai Yung returned home, armed with western-styled management ideals and major American and European corporation contacts. The parent company had done well, making it a multi-million-dollar business, which the son quickly grew to a multi-billion-dollar conglomerate, and renamed Yung Global Enterprise, reflecting his worldwide reach.

Today he sat in his office, fashioned to resemble a stylized Buddhist temple with all the trappings, to emphasize his prosperity yet still show his clients that he was humbly rooted in the culture of China's past—a past his grandfather taught him about and that he had now learned to exploit.

He studied the frozen image on his Apple-clone computer, sipping an Earl Grey tea, which he preferred to the nation's traditional green tea. He replayed the video again in slow motion, and watched as the red and yellow smudged hanzi script materialized. Copying the screen image, he pasted the ancient Chinese letters into a program that would clean up the little pictures and translate them.

His people had already performed the same task, but he didn't become a powerful business man without occasionally checking on the competence of subordinates. These translations came back: dragon, sky, great battle, monks, and mountain. These words matched those etched on the surface of the object that had the honor of occupying the center of his office, protected within a glass case.

Switching programs, he pulled up the video surveillance of the enclosure in the subterranean depths of the building, and marveled at how much the creature had grown since emerging from its egg. His grandfather had discovered the egg in a mountain shrine, and had it stolen after an earthquake devastated that region of Tibet. The senior Yung had the egg examined. The composition was unknown but the ancient hanzi script written on it had been translated, revealing a great battle in the mountains of Tibet, where a dragon of enormous proportions had descended from the heavens, severely injured. It spoke of a being that resembled a man but was not a man, who had healed the wounded with only a touch. The egg was all that remained after the dragon creature left.

Studying the same satellite images as the American scientist, Doctor Tracy Cameron, his people were able to determine that the now famous Cameron Cut had been caused by this egg creature's mother, who most likely still lay at the bottom of that crater. With his contacts in the Chinese Space Agency, he was able to secure the contract to build the Little Jade Rabbit and secretly modify its programming. He replayed the video again at regular speed, as the little rover drove through the moon base towards the big cut, and watched its recording of the writings, transferred from the big dragon's body. He knew why the US had astronauts up there, prior to the official manned launch; he already had his people there too—people who were his eyes and ears, with the skills to do what was necessary. The egg creature's mother was going to be his!

Taking another sip of tea, he flipped back to his live feed from the moon, and watched the green monochrome images being transmitted back from the Little Jade Rabbit. He was pleased that he had talked the space agency into adding infra-red optics to the cameras, and even happier when they'd agreed to pay the extra. He'd already had to absorb the cost of the second transmitter and the small thrusters hidden by the wheels. He'd been careful to hide the compact hydrogen fuel cell, which he acquired from a questionable Japanese businessman. The extra weight, unfortunately, had been discovered by an overachiever on the government's payroll, who recommended changing out the heavier-gauge steel wheels for lighter aluminum. Such were his business dealings: substitute or use inferior materials, but get the contract at all cost.

With the Americans up there now, the race was on. Not for water or bragging rights, but for so much more.

CHAPTER 9

Major Carson, with his hand-picked team of Lieutenants Santos and Nuzzi, Master Sergeant Butcher, and Commander Booker, boarded the SEV from *Endurance,* equipped with cable, elevator cage, and a crane assembly strapped on top.

Tyrone Booker, once an all-star quarterback in his junior years, the youngest commander on NASA's roster, and the first astronaut with Jamaican roots, had been specially selected by the previous president, who shared a similar skin color, and was now just useless baggage. His mission was to get them to the moon, scope out the crater, send in a remote probe to test for water, retrieve the samples, and report back to Houston. *Where did it all go so wrong?* Now he was in charge in name only. A secret moon base had been built, and they were driving to a mysterious item, which might be an alien space craft, at the opposite end of the crater.

He sat in a seat that overlooked the black rim, oblivious to the beauty of this rugged alien landscape. Behind him was safety, the ship, the habitats, and his friends. Ahead of him was nothing but danger. He did not trust the military men around him, and certainly not Major Carson. The lieutenants were young and looked and acted like tough thugs who would follow the major's orders with unfailing loyalty. He knew they would risk it all to get the job done, which was noble but fool hardy in this airless world for which they were not trained.

Master Sergeant Butcher was a different story. He was in his early 50s, and clearly had been military all his life. Booker figured he had probably seen some action early on in his career, and was as tough as nails. From Chicago, with a hint of an Irish accent, Butcher was bald by choice and Booker imagined that his meaty fists had broken a few noses in various bars around the world. Based on an exchange he'd shared with Shirl though, it seemed Butcher had a heart. He would follow Carson's orders, but at least he would question the ethics of them first. A nervous sweat of fear trickled down Booker's neck.

They continued to drive along the narrow ledge that surrounded the edge of the crater. Satellite pictures showed that this side of the crater had the largest ledge, upon which the SEVs could drive. At the far end, the ledge stopped at the wall. This is where the crane and elevator would be set up. Using the elevator basket, with high-strength lightweight cables, they would descend about a kilometer into the crater's depth. When they reached the shelf, they would have to walk five kilometers to the item, in total blackness and sub-zero temperatures.

They traveled beyond the track marks left by Butcher's earlier excursion, until they reached the limit of the makeshift road.

The passengers exited while Santos backed the vehicle closer to the edge to disengage the crane assembly. The crew worked together with military efficiency, setting up all the necessary equipment to facilitate their decent into the crater. Booker had been so busy watching the military men working so effortlessly that he only just then realized that the ground cover had changed. It no longer consisted of the fine dust particles he'd walked on while exiting the *Endurance,* or the pebbly surface he had encountered while walking through the cut. Instead, it was like smooth glass—melted volcanic rock to be precise. He noticed Carson hauling out two large black canvas bags, which he secured to the elevator basket frame. What struck him as odd was the color of the bags. Traditionally, everything NASA sent up with them was white.

Meanwhile, inside *Endurance,* the fourth strut warning light flashed again from green to yellow, and then momentarily flickered red before returning to green. This time, the signal was sent to Mission Control. It was overlooked once again.

"Ma'am, how should we proceed to get the solar panels working to capacity?" Pierce asked the senior crew member.

"Pierce, if we are going to work together for the next week, call me Shirley and this is Natalie. Ma'am makes me feel old."

"No ma'am. We have been given orders from the major to follow strict military protocol. You are a civilian, but still my superior, because you are the pilot. So both of you are like officers and out rank me, ma'am," the young man snapped back at attention.

"Well that doesn't work for us, Jon. So while you are working with Nat and me, you will call us by our first name. That's an order. When we are around the other guys, you may refer to us by our last names, if that makes you feel better," the matriarchal pilot commanded him in a friendly, yet firm tone. "Is that clear soldier?" She had no trouble dealing with the military, and she also had two sons of her own. This kid was not going to be a problem.

"Yes ma'am—I mean, yes Shirley, ma'am."

"Close enough, we'll work on it. So tell me—no actually tell Nat—what the problem is, because I don't understand this technology."

"Okay, first we installed six banks of panels over there in full sun." He pointed to a spot beside the last habitat, and they could clearly see the solar panel array tilted up to the sun, glinting in the sunlight as they walked over to the white habitat.

"The voltage regulator and power storage is in that white box, just behind HAB2." The box was where he indicated, easy to spot as they followed the thick orange solar-panel wires around to the back. The regulator-battery unit was in the shadow of the habitat's wall.

"The oxygen extractor draws from it and uses microwaves to heat the rock, vaporizing out the oxygen. There is a little hydrogen in the rocks, so it's vented off. We expect a higher concentration once we work with actual water-ice." The young man pointed at another larger white box, labeled O2 EX. By the smile on his face, visible through his clear face shield, and the tone of his voice, it was evident that he was proud of his work and of his learned skills.

Worthy turned to Van der Hoose. "Well Nat, how do we fix it?"

The MIT graduate, and solar-panels expert, having visually inspected the setup, had already formulated a few opinions of the critical fail areas. Walking over to the first panel, she read the amperage output off the digital display at the wire housing at the connection point on the lower right-hand side, as well as the manufacture labels stating that the optimum amp range was between 25 and 30. The display panels that she checked showed outputs ranging from 25.4 to 26.9. She noticed something strange however.

"Hey Jon, is there a reason every other panel is upside down?"

"It doesn't make a difference, ma'am, as long as we point it at the sun. These were made for a space environment, and we are on the moon, so it doesn't matter."

"And who told you that BS?"

"The technician in Houston. The one who demonstrated the setup."

"Well it *does* make a difference," Van der Hoose informed him. "The glass is polarized, and like sunglasses, it works best from a certain angle, focusing the sun on the collectors. Let's flip them around."

Using the SEV backhoe, and assistance from the women, Pierce managed to correct the orientation on the panels within a few hours.

"Jon, I also noticed dust particles on the glass, further reducing their efficiency. Our landing probably kicked up most of it, but that tractor moving around also contributed. Use the air hose to blow the dust off."

Pierce completed the cleaning task and the readout total jumped to 29.7. "Thanks ma'am, but won't they get dusty again?"

"No. There's no air movement. So unless you drive around near them or we lift off again, there is nothing to disturb it. Okay," she looked around, "last adjustment. Shirl and I will move the power box."

"Why? What's wrong with where it is?" both Worthy and Pierce asked.

"Simple. The box uses power to cool and heat the electronics and batteries. If you'll notice, the cooling section is in the sun and the heating part is in the shade. By rotating it 180 degrees, we optimize both the heating and cooling, letting the environment do the work for us, and saving on power drain." She beamed, enjoying showing off her knowledge.

"That simple." Worthy gave her a pat on the back. "Girl, you know your stuff."

"Okay Jon," Van der Hoose said, "let's check the input at the extractor."

They followed the power cable that led to a white filing-cabinet-sized box and a hopper of the same dimensions.

"Ma'am, here it is. We load the rocks that we excavated from the wall into the hopper. This grinds them down and feeds them into a pressure chamber. The chamber seals and microwaves, heat up the rocks and separates out the oxygen, which gets pumped into the tanks in HAB2. It's pretty cool, isn't it?"

Both women acknowledged the clever simplicity of the design.

"I didn't know there was oxygen in rock," the younger women admitted.

"Actually lunar soil is rich in oxides," Worthy explained to her younger crew mate. "The most common is silicon dioxide (SiO2). Like beach sand, about 20 percent of the mass of lunar soil is oxygen. *Apollo 15* proved it."

"Ma'am, I'm no scientist," Pierce said. "All I know is what the people at NASA told me: Check on it every two hours and reload the hopper."

"Check the power levels now," the engineer instructed.

"It's working perfect. We may just have tripled the output of oxygen by the end of the day. I'll check on it in an hour just to be sure."

"Excellent work, team. That only took four hours," Worthy noted, checking the time display in her visor. "Jon, why don't you show us the habitats and the mess hall; I'm famished."

***

Sergeant Butcher casually walked up to the commander, and before words could be exchanged, he held his gloved finger up to his visor, in front of his mouth—the universal signal for "shhhh". He then flashed five fingers, indicating the private frequency he wanted them to use.

Once they were in private communication, Butcher got right to it. "Sir, can I speak freely with you?"

"Yes, of course. What's up?"

"I may be wrong, but something doesn't feel right. The two lieutenants are not who they say they are. They're not engineers I mean."

"What makes you think that?"

"It's just a gut feeling. They don't seem like any of the guys I worked with before. You know how it is. And I asked them about a supply officer over there and they didn't know him."

"Come on, seriously? There has to be more than one supply officer."

"Yes, but that's just it. If you need anything from a shovel to a toothbrush, you see Major Nackers. If they hadn't seen him, they would have at least *known* about him. Hell, everyone in the regular army over there knows that, whatever you need unofficially, off the books, he gets. I don't think these guys are regular army, and they're sure as hell not with the corp."

"Have you voiced your concern with the major?"

"No, no way. I met him once in Kuwait. I was part of a team hooking up a desalination water system for one of our bases. One week into the project, the major flies in with a team of mercenaries and tells us to scram. Two days later, the first Gulf war started, and Kuwait was overrun by Saddam Hussein's army. Pierce and I get orders to come to Houston, and he shows up like we're old friends and tells us to join this detail. We didn't find out about the alien thing until Houston gave us a security code to play back a message from Carson, once we were already on the moon. So I don't know him, and I sure as hell don't trust him."

Booker paused for a long moment, considering this new information. Finally he shook his head. "I think, what with the tension of the mission and the expectations, you might be imagining things. I'll talk to him and straighten out your concerns."

"I wouldn't do that, sir." Butcher grabbed the commander's arm for emphasis.

Registering the fear in the man's eyes, Booker agreed that Carson could be an actual threat and nodded his head in understanding.

"Commander," Nuzzi's voice broke through on the command frequency, "the elevator is ready." Butcher quickly hopped over to the SEV, and started to top off his O2 levels, an action designed more to keep himself from being seen with the commander than indicative of really needing a top-up. He still had twenty-four hours of air.

"You can get on board with the sarge, Commander," Nuzzi said. "Santos and the major are already strapped in. I'll be there in a minute."

As the wire frame basket slowly descended into the abyss of the crater, Booker thought of the new information he'd learned. Any number of things could go wrong on the moon, and even more deep inside a crater. Military personal that couldn't be trusted were a problem, and added to that, there was a big unknown alien thing, which might be dead or just sleeping.

What the hell am I doing?

❧ CHAPTER 10 ☙

The warning light flashed to yellow and then quickly turned red. Senior communication technician George Messer, monitoring *Endurance,* saw the indicator light slowly flash red and heard the buzzer a millisecond later, after the second pulse. Instinct and procedures told him to reset the fault, and wait for it to trip again. It reset back to green, and then back to red as the sensor on the moon vessel re-synced with Mission Control. This time the flashing increased in frequency, indicating urgency.

As senior com tech, it was his responsibility to inform the crew about the sensor and possible strut joint failure.

"Commander Booker, this is CAPCON Houston, we are showing a warning on strut four, mid-joint. Can you confirm the status on board?" the voice message went out on the secure command frequency, and was picked up clearly by those closest to the ship. The crew members who were a kilometer down in the crater only received beeps. It was the default sound when the communication signal with Houston was degraded.

"Worthy here, copy that. The commander is out of COM range. I am EVA with Van der Hoose, and will be back at the ship in fifteen." She avoided informing Messer about Pierce and the habitat, fearing he was not cleared on that part of the mission.

"Copy that Worthy. It may be nothing, but it has to be checked."

"Understood, on my way."

"Jon, hook into the SEV radio and try reaching Booker or Carson. Inform them of the situation."

"Yes ma'am," Pierce acknowledged, as he put down his hot chocolate and ran to the airlock and his EVA suit.

"Nat, you're with me; let's go!" They followed fast behind Pierce, donning their suits and taking off for the large Odin craft *Endurance* like a herd of bounding space rabbits.

"Do you think it's just a sensor failure?" the brunette engineer asked, mid-hop.

"Let's hope," Worthy answered, sounding concerned, "but the sensors are there for a reason, and if it's reading true, then ... well I don't need to tell you about landing-strut failures, now do I?"

"Commander Booker, Major Carson, this is Pierce. Are you there? Do you copy?"

A few seconds later, the communication panel on board the SEV indicated that the signal had been received but without audio. He rotated the antenna to point into the crater through the cut, in the hopes that voice communication could be re-established. His efforts paid off when the weak, crackled sound of the commander's voice came through his helmet speakers.

"Give me a SITREP, Pierce!" Booker ordered.

"Sir, Houston informed us fifteen minutes ago that *Endurance* is showing a strut-failure warning. Worthy and Van der Hoose are checking it out now."

"Where — you?" the commander asked, his voice cutting out into bouts of static

"I'm in the SEV, using the vehicle communication network, sir." There was an undertone of fear in his voice.

"Drive through the cut. -aybe we can ge- - better signal — patch me thr— to W–thy."

"Say again. I didn't receive that last part of the transmission, sir."

Worthy reached the ship and headed towards the elevator, while Van der Hoose went directly to the strut that was the source of the warning. They both knew that if the strut was failing, the leg could give out and topple the vessel. The ship was designed with six legs, and needed all of them for stability. If one leg collapsed, the remaining five legs would not support the vessel. They also knew that, if one component failed, the others could as well. As NASA astronauts, they were trained to react to all warnings as if they were critical.

The elevator to the command module was moving at normal speed, but to Worthy it felt like the old Otis lift from an ancient department store she remembered from her youth. She was thankful for how easy the suit was to remove.

Van der Hoose keyed into the ship's frequencies as she inspected the leg strut.

"Shirl, are you showing a warning light?"

"Yes, I have a flashing red on the mid-joint of strut four. I'm going to reset the switch. Stand by, Nat."

The switch was pressed and then released. It momentarily turned green, but started flashing red seconds later.

"Houston, Worthy here; do you copy?"

"Go ahead Worthy; Messer here."

"I performed a manual reset on signal S4; no change."

"Copy that; try a hard reset on S4."

A hard reset meant turning the power off on strut four's sensors, and turning it back on. There would be a four-minute delay while the sensors powered down, back up again, and then re-calibrated. The pilot and com tech waited patiently, hoping for positive results.

The indicator light came on green and remained steady.

"Houston, I have a steady green."

"Copy that; I show a steady green as well."

"Van der Hoose, what are the visuals on strut four?" the pilot asked.

The engineer rubbed her hand over the hydraulic elbow that allowed the strut and leg to fold under the ship. Looking at her gloved hand, she noticed a light sheen of oil.

"Shirl, I'm detecting a minimal hydraulic fluid leak from the actual knuckle of strut four's mid-joint."

"Is it a hose connection, Nat?"

"Negative, it's the actual seam of the knuckle."

"CRAP! That's not good!" Com Tech Messer answered.

"No kidding!" both females responded in unison.

"I don't suppose we have a spare?" the engineer inquired.

ORION - Escape Velocity

"I don't think so," Worthy said. "Houston, do we have a spare knuckle?"

"I'm checking."

Changing frequencies from ship to command, the pilot updated Pierce, who was sitting in the SEV on the other side of the crater wall. He was to convey the information to the commander.

"Isn't that just wonderful? How the hell did that happen?" the commander bitched at the corporal, who felt the weight of the world on his shoulders just then. Booker sighed roughly. "Pierce, standby. I will get back to you."

The corporal only knew Booker by reputation; the commander was supposed to be a nice guy who worked through a problem. This mission was the first time that he actually saw the commander up close, and Pierce found him intimidating. His suit had to have been the largest ever built and that scared him.

"Major Carson, take us back up."

"Now just hold your plow horse, Commander," Carson snapped. "I don't reckon that will help. We can't just interrupt our descent."

"Reverse this elevator, damn it! That's an order," Booker barked.

Both lieutenants pulled small-arms ordinance and aimed them at the commander.

"No sir," Nuzzi said. "You heard the major. Not until we reach the bottom."

The commander turned to Sergeant Butcher to get a visual of which side he was on, and noticed that he wasn't carrying a weapon.

The commander gritted his teeth, and sent a message to the corporal in the SEV. "Pierce, get to the *Endurance* and help Worthy. Booker out." There was no need to inform the corporal about the armed confrontation in the elevator and have that information conveyed to his good friend Shirl.

Worthy re-donned her space suit and exited the ship to assess the leak herself.

Pierce was about to exit the SEV, but as an afterthought, jumped back in and maneuvered the vehicle through the crater wall to *Endurance*.

Van der Hoose was still underneath the big Odin space ship, trying to push on the knuckle to stem the leakage, when Worthy approached her from the side.

"Well, what do you think, Nat? Can we fix it?"

"No. The moon's negative pressure is pulling the hydraulic fluid out. The more the fluid escapes the lower the pressure is in the hydraulic cylinder. When the pressure equalizes, the strut folds and so does the leg."

"Come on, Nat, use that engineering brain of yours. You built this assembly. If we can't fix it, can we stop the fluid leak?"

"No. This is *not* my design. It's close but different. My MIT mock-up was of thicker gauge aluminum, with I-beam-like bends to make it stronger. Plus, I didn't use hydraulic cylinders to operate the joint; I had it spring operated, locking in place when the full weight was put on it. Don't forget, it's a one-way trip for this landing section."

"You still must have an idea."

She stopped for a moment to consider the situation. "Okay, let me wipe the oil off and maybe we can just wrap it with tape from the suit-repair kit." She hoped a MacGyver patch job would work.

Using the cloth intended to wipe her visor of moon dust, Natalie got the metal as clean of the oily substance as possible, while Shirl pulled the tape out of her repair kit. The cloth worked too well at sucking the oil from the metal and the knuckle joint. Having cleared the fine moon-dust particles from the leaking seam as well, it caused the flow to increase. The tape was quickly wrapped around the three-inch joint, but wouldn't stick because of the slickness of the fluid that was escaping. Oil was now on two sets of gloves and most of Shirl's right arm. Her own elbow joint was now covered in the slightly acidic hydraulic fluid, now mixed with the fine particles of the environment, which quickly wore down the micro-bead bearings and prevented full motion, and created a leak of pressurized air—air that was needed to maintain 4.3 pounds of pressure that prevented her body from decompressing. Her suit alarms went off in her helmet, but she held on to the knuckle joint as tightly as possible, able to deal with only one problem at a time.

Enough fluid had escaped to render the cylinder useless, and the back pressure it was providing to keep the leg out finally failed. The joint folded, catching the suit material of the engineer's arm and pinching it in the moving mechanism.

"Look out, it's got me!" Van der Hoose screamed, pulling the fabric out as if were a normal jacket, creating a rip three-inches long on her forearm and penetrating the skin beneath. A controlled panic gripped the team, as the engineer tried to seal the rip with her tape, knowing that the oil on her gloves would make it temporary at best. She didn't hear Shirl shout out her own problems. The pilot's suit pressure was now only 2.1.

Pierce exited the crater gap as fast as the tracked SEV could manage. He felt like he could have run faster, but knowing the specs on the vehicle, he made the right choice by staying in it. He could not hear the repair team, because they were on a closed-ship frequency, but based on their frenzied motions and the slant of the ship, he quickly put it together. Bringing the backhoe bucket up, he positioned it near the collapsing leg, pushing it back in place. In doing so, the leg jumped back into position, pinning Worthy's arm below the elbow. Being the on-board medic, Shirl knew that her ulna was broken, and was thankful that the low air pressure and cold made her arm numb, and the pain manageable.

The engineer and corporal hastily and resourcefully stabilized the ship, correcting the slant using the scoop and hand gestures.

"Well Shirl, we did it!" Van der Hoose exclaimed, turning to the pilot, who was now attached to the damaged strut joint, dripping blood that the moon quickly absorbed.

"SHIRL!" Van der Hoose shouted, as she raced toward the unconscious pilot.

☙ CHAPTER 11 ❧

Carson's objective, if known by his two military minions, was not disclosed to Booker, and if Butcher knew anything he wasn't talking either, at least not on the command frequency. So all was silent as the men descended. The cage stopped abruptly, or as abruptly as possible on a low-gravity moon. The men were unloading the gear when Carson pulled Booker to the side and suggested a private frequency.

"Booker, you go and fix whatever the problems are up there. Take care of the lady folks. I'll do what I gotta do down here."

The commander nodded. "I'll call you on the hour, and Carson, be careful; this environment is not forgiving." He spoke with sincerity in his voice, as the elevator started to rise, and watched the men trudge off into the black.

The elevator's ascent was surprisingly fast without the other four men. Reaching the surface, Booker disconnected the pressurized cabin with the crane and took off in the drive portion of the SEV. With the bulk gone, the light-weight stripped-down chassis moved with astounding speed and agility as he raced back to the ship.

He tried the command frequency every quarter kilometer, attempting to reach his crew. He was getting pissed now, at the communication equipment, Carson's secret agenda, being held at gunpoint, the faulty leg strut, and the mission in general. What the hell else could go wrong?

"*Endurance* do you copy? Shirley, you there?" he repeated for the umpteenth time.

"*Endurance* here; is that you Commander?" Van der Hoose responded joyfully. "Boy, we're glad to hear from you."

"What's the situation there, Nat? Talk to me," the big commander demanded, as he passed the working COM repeater.

"Jon and I got the ship stable using the back-hoe bucket. The strut did fail, but we caught it. Oh and Shirl is still unconscious."

"WHAT! You should have started with that, dammit! What happened? How is she?"

ORION - Escape Velocity   67

"She broke her arm when the strut gave way, and was bleeding pretty bad, but Jon got it under control. He thinks the low pressure and the cold saved her. We are at *Endurance* and Shirley is in stable condition."

"But still unconscious," the commander countered, before continuing. "What's Houston's opinion?"

Van der Hoose looked at Pierce for courage and strength. He only nodded, as if to say, 'you have to tell him.'

Taking a deep breath, she started. "Sir, we lost communication with Houston thirty minutes ago."

"I'm still fifteen minutes out. You keep trying to raise CAPCON, and Pierce, look after Shirley," the exasperated commander responded, with still a modicum of control in his voice. His crew was already on edge, and nothing would be accomplished by reprimanding or yelling.

Com Tech Messer called in all support personnel, as well as additional supervisors. He knew that when IT hits the fan, it's better to have a lot of bodies in front and around you, to catch it. The COM board was lit up like a Christmas tree with flashing red lights. Green sensor lights were turning to yellow and red faster than reds were turning off. The catastrophic failure alerts started as soon as the strut joint gave out. A team of engineers from manufacturing were working with simulators to come up with a solution to the structural problem. Electricians were working on their own SIMs, in an effort to isolate the fault. Supervisors, managers, and everyone up the chain of command at NASA, including generals, had excuses as to why this had happened in the first place.

Without voice communication, the medical staff could only guess as to why the pilot had an erratic heartbeat, why her breathing was shallow, and her blood pressure was low. Someone up there had hooked her up to the MED sensors. The only crew member that they had any data on was Worthy, and she was the only medical personnel up there. The biometrics on the rest of the crew was off line.

Booker leaped from the open vehicle as soon it stopped. He could see the SEV parked with the scoop bucket positioned under a strut joint. A black stain on the ground was visible, along with many footprints that led to the entrance. The stain followed. He continued to the airlock with his hand on the helmet release, ready to detach it the second the room was pressurized. Three crew suits were fastened to the suit supports, and his eyes immediately went to the one that was stained with blood. His thoughts were on his colleague and friend. It looked like a lot of blood; he didn't know what to do or how serious the injury was. Despite his fears and uncertainties, he knew that the two rookie astronauts inside the ship, and his friend, needed him to be strong.

As soon as the pressure light changed to green, he stripped off his space suit and ran to the elevator, feeling short of breath. Through sheer willpower, he forced himself to breathe slowly. *She will pull through!* He knew it. He hoped it. *Get control of yourself before that door opens or you will lose the crew's support.*

The upper doors opened and he saw the female engineer trying to reverse a wall of red lights, but his attention was diverted when he saw Shirley in a crew seat, tilted back to form a bed. This was the only chair that did that, and was to be used for just such a purpose.

"How is she?" he asked Pierce, standing next to his patient and taking her pulse for the hundredth time. He had the medical kit open and a stethoscope around his neck.

Booker didn't wait for an answer as he took her other arm and started to count her heartbeats himself, as he watched the fifteen seconds count off from the cabin digital display. He then multiplied the number by four to calculate her BPM, and arrived at 60, fifteen beats below normal. He looked at the devise attached to her arm and read off the last BP reading: 100/60. That was low too. It should have been around 135/85.

"Sir, her breathing is shallow, so I was just about to put her on oxygen. Please move." Pierce gently pushed the big man out of the way. In his hand was a portable air cylinder and a clear tube that clipped to the nostrils. The commander stared at him curiously.

"I've had some medical training," Pierce commented, without looking up. "I'm the backup first responder."

"Should you put an IV in her, to increase her blood pressure?"

"Yes, but I'm not qualified. I've tried a few times, but I couldn't hit the vein. This is the first time I've had to do it on a living person, and I'm afraid I'll hurt her."

"Give me the needle," Booker said. "I'll do it. She won't yell at me if I save her life." He smiled at Pierce, hoping to relieve the tension.

Looking at the back of her hand, he could see the signs of the young man's previous attempts. The commander tapped the veins to get them to show. Nothing. Then he remembered a seminar he'd attended on medical treatment in low-pressure environments, like the space station and the moon. He tightened the Velcro cuff back up, making it snug, and then pumped some air into it using the manual inflator, increasing the pressure in the arteries, thus increasing the pressure on the veins. The blood vessels in her wrist started to balloon up. The veins were still not visible, so he quickly loosened the cuff gain, slapped the back of her hand, and a blue vein popped up. Without wasting any time, he carefully inserted the needle and started the IV drip. Pierce took over and applied tape to secure the needle and tube.

"I'll keep an eye on the bag and check her PB every five minutes," Pierce said calmly, relieved he didn't have to jab her again.

With one crisis averted, the commander turned his attention to the young brunette, pushing keys and touching icons on the various computer monitors. He noticed that there were more green and yellow status lights now than red, which was always a good sign. He looked over the engineer's shoulder, ready to assist with whatever instructions she gave.

"Sir, I have isolated the landing platform from the rest of the ship, and have regained control of most of the sub systems," she said, feeling the commander's presence behind her.

"Do we have COM yet?"

"Not yet. When the strut joint collapsed, it shorted out that sensor, which in turn fried the primary sensor array. A stupid design, if you want my engineer's opinion. I'm sure it was cheap to build and easy to maintain, but as you can see, there are too many points to fail," she observed casually, continuing to type and touch icons.

"Okay Nat, you can build a better design, next time, but for now, get me Houston. Please."

"Done. I have the COM working. I piggybacked onto the medical frequency. Audio only. Oh, and it's not secure."

"It will have to do. Thanks. Houston do you copy? This is Booker; do you copy?" Static was the only response from the cabin speakers.

"Houston, do you copy? This is *Endurance*. Do you copy?" he repeated, looking over to the engineer who had put the small miracle together.

After the third try, a crackled reply was heard.

"*Endurance*, this – Houston. We are receiv— your transmission."

"Houston, we have a situation," the commander responded, realizing that he'd almost used the famous *Apollo 13* statement. "Worthy is unconscious; she lost a lot of blood after breaking her arm. Her suit also ripped, lowering suit pressure to critical. Her O2 levels are now under control and her BP is rising, now that she is on an IV as well as oxygen. We are still assessing ship status. The strut collapsed and my quick-thinking team stabilized it with the SEV before it could tip. Currently it is being held up with the backhoe. Van der Hoose informs me that we have a sensor-array failure, so the landing platform's electronics have been disconnected from the rest of the ship. COM is on MEDI frequency. Carson and company is EVA to primary objective. Do you copy?"

"Yes, message understood. Will advise on a COM alternative. CAPCON out."

CHAPTER 12
THE HISTORY WALKER

The shower was refreshing and invigorating, yet Simon still couldn't shake his apprehension. Should he confront Gregory? Should he call Mac back in the Bahamas to confirm that he was there? Should he demand answers from the staff and insist the housekeeper meet with him? What would Sam do?

He tried again to touch her mind using their internal voice. At first he'd been annoyed at this strange ability they had acquired after being exposed to an exploding crystal, but over the weeks, he found that he enjoyed having her in his head. Now it had been almost six months, and he missed her voice. He missed her.

Entering the kitchen, he considered re-questioning the cook, but was quickly taken aback when she pointed to the fresh brewed coffee pot, without saying a word, and then to the patio that could be seen through the garden door. Her expression was that of a mother telling her child to go outside and play. There would be no arguing with her.

Taking his black brew in a delicate bone-china cup, he exited the building quickly, half expecting a clip behind the ear for tardiness. On the right, in the distance, was a small stone cottage, presumably the cook and stable master's dwelling. Between the cottage and cobblestone patio was a wild-flower garden.

Sitting next to the stone wall that surrounded the sitting area was an old man in a wheelchair. He was sipping his morning tea and looking out over the wall at the gardens beyond. The wall blocked the north wind and kept in the warmth from the rising sun. There were two unoccupied wrought-iron glass tables with chairs that he could have chosen, but the gentleman in him dictated that he sit with the elderly man and attempt to strike up a conversation. The setting was tranquil, with the birds flitting around the low bushes looking for insects. Close to the house, he spotted a slinking black and white kitten on the hunt for whatever captured her attention.

"Lovely morning, isn't it?" the young man asked.

"It certainly does not get any better than this," the elderly man responded, without turning to face him. Instead he adjusted his wide-brim hat lower. That was when Simon noticed the senior's prosthetic hands.

"Did you sleep well after your flight?" the elderly gentleman asked.

"Yes, it's extremely quiet here; didn't hear a peep. I must have needed it, what with the flight and time change."

"Time change bothers you?"

"Yes, kind of like time travel, don't you think?" Simon asked, in a casual tone. "With a five-hour time difference?"

"What do you know about time travel?" the wheel-chaired man challenged, still with his back to him.

"I don't—I mean, nothing; not really. I guess what I'm talking about is jet lag, not time travel."

"That is correct, but Albert Einstein proved that it is possible in his space-time theory," the old man stated in a mater-of-fact manner. "If you travel in space at 300,000 kilometers an hour, you would age slower than the people you left on your home planet."

"I do recall reading something about that," Simon said. "Totally unprovable though. At least until we can achieve those speeds." He realized that he was enjoying the engaging scientific conversation.

"It is easy enough to travel back in time, if you know how."

"Oh really? And I presume you know how?" Simon wanted to ask what medication he was on, to have such crazy notions, but instead played along, enjoying the distraction.

"Yes."

"Hey, by the way, I'm Simon. My mother owned this place, before she passed." His voice lowered on the last part. The old man said nothing, and then activated a joy stick on his chair, slowly turning toward the table and his conversation partner.

He stuck out his plastic right hand in greeting.

"People around here call me Pa."

"Okay, Pa," he smiled, "so how do you travel in time?" He had to stop himself from staring at the fake limbs. He wondered what the story was behind them.

The old man removed his hat and revealed a skull completely devoid of hair. He smiled and placed Simon's reluctant hands to his old scaly scalp. Next, he removed his right prosthesis by using the left one to hold it down. Then, with the misshapen stump, he wiggled out of the last synthetic limb.

Simon had a soft spot for people, and veterans in particular, who had lost limbs due to some tragedy. One project at MIT had allowed him to work on the mechanisms that control finger movement. Although he worked with people using their new limbs, he'd never actually touched a stump. He felt embarrassed because he was a little squeamish, and didn't know where the old man was going with this.

Next, the man placed his stumps on Simon's forehead, which forced the younger man to hold back a gag. When he detected the pungent odor of putrid flesh, it was all he could do not to wretch. He looked into the old man's eyes. They had a sickly pink glow to them. The man then lowered his head, as if in prayer, and Simon followed, curious as to the ritual's outcome.

"Take a deep breath and focus on your breathing," the old man said. "Feel the air move into your nostrils, your sinus ... your windpipe ... and now your lungs. Feel them inflate. Slowly exhale through your mouth ... Again!

"Concentrate on my words; using your fingers, seek out my thought waves. Breathe in, breathe out ... focus ... listen to my words. With your eyes closed, look up into your head, to my fingers; feel my fingers on your forehead." The old man kept this up and Simon was thinking he might actually be able to feel the man's non-existent fingers.

"... Keeping your eyes closed, look into my head, past the skin, past the skull ... see the brain. Look deeper still ... look into the center of the gray matter. Focus on the synapses ... and now focus on the one that is brighter than the others. See the electrons firing ... feel the spark as they ignite. Feel the electricity move through your fingers into your hand, your arms, and shoulders. Feel them in your body; feel the electricity of my brain throughout your being. That's it … concentrate deeper, breathe in, breathe out, focus on my words, feel my thoughts flow to you in the stream of blue electrons."

Simon no longer heard the words; he felt them. Gradually an image came into focus: a large round, silver sphere, humming with high-voltage electricity, crackling blue sparks all around it as it hovered above the ground. An opening grew, first a crack, then larger and larger. A blinding white light swelled as the opening widened until the white light overwhelmed any outside light on the surface of the ball. The sphere was now glowing white, and slowly an object moved from within that light. It too was white, but looked almost black in comparison to the pureness of the interior light. The object became more visible; it began to take on a humanoid shape as it grew. Another object started to take shape beside the first; it was approximately the same size. The humanoid pair became more visible in the light. Arms, legs, torsos, and heads were clearly visible as silhouettes against the light. A third smaller humanoid figure appeared behind the pair. It clung to the second humanoid's hand.

Simon could see this in his mind, and thought he could feel the electricity from the object on the ground around him. The second form held both arms of the smaller form, and created a circle between them. They slowly moved this circle to the glowing sphere, and gradually the sphere shrank until its brightness was almost consumed. The giant ball was fading and shrinking. With the light from the sphere diminished, more of the background was visible. Trees came into focus; they were in a wooded area on a moonlit night. The brightness further softened and a dirt road became discernible. The giant sphere had now shrunk to the size of a child's toy, floating in the air between the three forms. As details became more pronounced, it was clear that the humanoid party consisted of a male, a female, and a child.

Simon watched this activity from a vantage point on top of a hill twenty yards away. The ball of light was now no more than the flicker of a firefly. The child took the firefly in its hand, and brought it to its face. From his vantage point, it appeared that the child ate it, as the light vanished.

As he was pondering the scientific possibilities of the object, and its ability to shrink, gunfire erupted, breaking the silence. Muzzle flashes from hundreds of guns fired from all around him, all seemingly aimed toward the humanoid party. Simon tried to flatten himself as low as possible on the hilltop, as bullets whizzed by him and through him. Forcing himself to raise his head enough to get a good look, he saw the female and child lying on the ground with a greenish liquid oozing from them. The male tried to shield the child and female, but was soon cut down as well.

Men in military uniforms ascended on the strange party. The uniforms held an insignia band on the right arm. Simon knew this insignia from history, as did most humans living today. It was the swastika.

He stared at the black symbol and the view faded to nothingness.

He looked into the void and saw the old man still beside him. An image gradually came into view, but remained hazy. It was a hospital room, or some type of medical facility, with an air of antiquity to it. A man in a white medical coat was tending to the patient on the bed. A second man in uniform, with the trappings of authority, entered the room.

Simon could hear them clearly. They were speaking German, which he recognized, but in his mind it was English.

"Have you finished your examination, Doctor?" the officer asked.

"Yes. The subject is severely wounded but will survive. The body composition is similar to human, with recognizable organs, more or less in the areas you would expect to find them. There are some organs I cannot identify, nor see a purpose for," the doctor stated clinically.

"Fix what you know, but don't let this thing die. Did you perform an autopsy on the other two?" the uniformed man asked in a commanding tone.

"No, Doctor Grubber did them. He says the bodies are decomposing quickly. He can confirm that they were both females, possibly mother and child. He will take some more tissue and green blood samples, and then burn the bodies."

"The creature is ugly. Are you certain it is not a trick from the Russians or British?"

"No, this creature is not Russian, British, or even American. It is not from this world."

"So our scientists were correct when they said that there is a possibility of other life forms in the universe. Our leader has been informed and wants to meet this creature. He wants to learn all he can from this thing."

"I will do what I can to keep him alive. I don't know if his skin pallor is normal, but he does not look healthy. Look how scaly he is."

"Yes hideous, and it has a foul stench." The uniformed man started to turn away and then stopped. "Why are there bags on its hands?"

"The creature skin is dry and scaly, but his hands exude an oily fluid. I am collecting as much of it as possible."

The officer pulled off the cloth bag, revealing a slimy hand with only three fingers. He quickly pulled off the bag covering the other hand, displaying another appendage with three fingers. It was not a deformity.

"The females also had only three fingers, and if you notice, he only has three toes per foot, as did the females."

"Disgusting!" the officer exclaimed, as he touched the slimy oil on the skin surface of the three-fingered hand, and held it to his nose. "Yes … disgusting indeed." He grunted in repulsion as he moved toward the door. Before he could get to the wooden door, his hand started to glow, a white glow which spread until his whole body became consumed with the light.

The doctor watched with scientific curiosity as the Nazi officer's radiance grew to blinding levels, forcing him to shield his eyes. The brightness grew and then blinked into nothingness. The officer had vanished.

Picking up a bone saw, the doctor methodically cut the hands and feet off the creature, careful not to touch the liquid, and placed each appendage in a glass jar.

Simon's emotions were reeling. He was being forced to watch a horror movie … to actually *live* the horror. He felt the pain of the man on the table as his hands were slowly cut off—a torture he'd thought he would never in his life endure.

His guide was gone and he panicked, breaking the physic bond and finding himself in the here and now again, back at the estate. The old man stared back at him with his pink eyes and scaly skin. He turned his head to see the kitten on the stone wall jumping at a bird. Both the bird and cat were frozen in time, not moving. Gravity should have taken over. He turned his head farther, following the gaze of the old man once again. The cook, exiting the door with some hot muffins and refills, was stopped in an instant, with one foot off the ground, waiting to complete the motion. Everywhere he looked, time stood still.

"You see with your eyes what your brain does not fathom," the old man said, somehow without moving his lips. "Remember, son, that place in your mind when you first started this vision ... this walk-through history. Practice and you will become stronger."

Simon broke contact with the strange man, and watched the kitten miss the bird as the cook walked over to the table.

"You are a good person, sitting with an old mute. I'm sure the conversation was stimulating," she said sarcastically, laughing as she refilled the cups.

"Who is he?" Simon asked wide-eyed, realizing the situation as the old man winked back at him, with a sickly grin that revealed a toothless, tongue-less orifice. Simon glanced down and realized he had mud on his hands.

"He has been here as long as I can remember," she said. "An old friend of your mother's that we now care for. I can't pronounce his name. It's something like 'Paa-ka-Poooheeed', but we just call him Pa."

Taking his refilled coffee, Simon left the patio. He needed another shower, and time to make some sense out of what he'd just experienced.

CHAPTER 13

"There must be a way we can fix that damn knuckle joint," Van der Hoose snapped at Pierce, as she attempted to improve the COM link with Earth. "You and I are the smartest engineers up here. We have to secure it somehow."

"I agree Natalie, ma'am. The backhoe is not the best solution for a launch support."

Worthy was now conscious and her vitals had improved with the IV drip and oxygen. The medication made the pain bearable, but it was having her friend at her side that made her feel best.

"Commander, I have a secure link with Houston!" the flight engineer excitedly announced, now that they had mostly green lights on the computer screens and only a few yellow ones.

They listened as Com Tech Messer's distant and authoritative voice filled the com line from Earth. "We can confirm that strut four's mid-joint did fail, and as a result, the sensor array went off line."

"Tell me something we don't know. Do we have a solution?" Commander Booker asked.

"We have teams working on various scenarios, including swapping out a strut from the other ship. The real problem is the sensor electronics module. It needs to be replaced, and *Inuk's* is not compatible. Without that module, you will not be able to power up the landing platform, which contains the ascent engine."

"Is there a way to bypass the module and hard-wire direct control?"

"That is one of the things we are testing," Messer answered, "but so far all simulations blow the ship up. The teams down here are working on all possible solutions. We are doing everything possible. We will get you guys home, Commander."

With the ship's fate in the hand of Houston, and Worthy in stable condition, the next undertaking was to re-establish communication with the team in the crater. They'd lost audio ten hours ago, but still had sporadic bio readings on all four men, which indicated that they were alive and not under stress.

"ARSEHOLES! All of them!" the commander shouted. "They should've aborted their descent when COM first malfunctioned, as per NASA protocol."

"You're right," Worthy said, attempting to calm him down, "but those boys are gung-ho military, with a different protocol for when COM goes down. They're a tough lot; I wouldn't worry about them. Who are you taking to the crater?"

"Not sure. Let me ask you this: Who do you want to stay?"

"Well … Pierce has the medical knowledge, which I don't need now, and Van der Hoose is a wiz with ship systems. I would have thought Pierce would be your choice."

"Yes, probably the most logical, but I'm not sure if I trust him."

"Why on earth would you not? He's a good kid."

"He may be okay; it's Carson I have trust issues with." The commander explained his suspicions and described the incident in the elevator at the crater.

"So you think, because he's military, he would blindly follow his major?"

"Yeah, something like that. I just don't want to be put in a position where the person I think has my back is working for the other team. Van der Hoose I would trust, but I'm not sure how she would handle the situation if there were a conflict down there. I would rather take you!"

"Well this old dog's not hunting today, or in the near future, so pick one. I recommend Pierce. He is on your side and not part of whatever is going on with Carson."

Nodding in agreement, he gently put his hand on her arm in a gesture of thanks.

He gestured to Pierce, who was out of earshot, getting his attention and waving him over. "Pierce, you think we can get COM working into the crater?"

"Yes sir. I have a hunch that I would like to test. The way the communication system is set up, each component repeats and amplifies the signal it receives and re-transmits it on down the network. If one fails, they all fail, but the diagnostics didn't reveal a fail. It revealed a weak intermittent signal."

Commander Booker wasn't following. "What are you suggesting?"

"I think the problem is not with the repeaters, or how far apart they are, but rather with the placement. The crater wall acts like a shield, blocking the signals. When I was trying to reach you using the SEV, I found that by pointing the directional antenna at the wall opening I received a cleaner, stronger transmission."

"So you're saying we should add more repeaters around the cut? To improve the signal strength?"

"Yes sir."

"Good; let's make that happen. You and I are heading down there, and I want a link back to the base camp."

"Yes sir!" The young man beamed with excitement at the chance to see the item up close.

Using the SEV with the stripped-down chassis, they headed back to the elevator to make their descent with additional air packs. Van der Hoose would remain with Worthy and maintain contact with Houston. Adding the extra communication equipment, plus replacing a broken antenna on a repeater, paid off, when a strong signal to *Endurance* was established.

Each man in the crater carried an extra day's worth of air and provisions. It had been thirty hours since either of the crew had slept, and checking each communication node was laborious. When they reached the crane assembly and the pressurized cabin, they topped off their air supplies, and while batteries were charging, they replenished their own energies with protein bars and water.

"We are receiving a full signal from your position commander," the flight engineer said, when the connection was made.

"Are you receiving anything from Carson's team?"

"No sir, still intermittent."

"How's Worthy doing?"

"You know what they say about doctors making the worse patients? Well so do flight medics. She told me to readjust her seat and that she wanted something to eat."

"That's good, but her bark is about the same as her bite, so be careful."

"I heard that!" Worthy snapped at the commander, generating a laugh from the two men in the crane cabin.

"Okay, Van der Hoose, we will be taking the elevator down in two hours, after our packs have fully charged. Get some rest until then, but stay on COM."

"Yes sir, stay by the radio and get some sleep, but don't sleep. Understood."

"Welcome to the wonders of space travel," Commander Booker replied with a smile in his voice.

Spirits were up and his friend was back to her old self. He had earned the respect of the young man with him, and Houston was busting their butts to solve the problem. Maybe he could salvage the mission after all.

"How's our signal now, Van der Hoose?" Booker asked, as his team successfully reached the bottom after adding a repeater halfway down.

"Still strong at 95 percent, Commander," Worthy replied, surprising him with her presence.

"Well that answers my next question about you."

"Yes, it does. Don't worry Ty, I sent Nat out to check the perimeter and make sure our temporary support hadn't shifted. While she's out, she's going to take a stroll over to *Inuk* and salvage what she can of the medical supplies."

"How are the bio readings on Carson's team?"

"Sporadic, with no change to signal strength, and we're still not receiving ID signatures. Two of them are showing elevated heart rates."

"Can you give me your best diagnoses as to why?"

"If I had to guess, I would say some form of trauma, but I wouldn't rule out stress from the extreme cold and uncertainty of what they found."

"Yeah, walking in pitch blackness, next to a ledge that drops into an abyss, toward an alien ship isn't scary at all. So how are you doing?"

"Van der Hoose has been taking good care of me, but has a lousy bedside manner."

"You do know you're on the command frequency, don't you Shirl?" Van der Hoose broke in, causing the two men to break out in a laugh.

"You two take care up there. I will contact you at mid-point in two hours. Booker out." He smiled, inwardly thankful for Worthy's camaraderie on the mission.

Half a kilometer in, and twenty minutes from last communication, the team saw a flashing light near the wall of the crater.

"It's Butcher!" Booker shouted into his headset, as he rushed to the downed astronaut.

A scan of his bio readings indicted he was barely alive, and his power reserves were almost depleted. That power was what maintained suit temperature and filtered out deadly carbon-dioxide gas.

"Worthy, we have a medical emergency with Butcher!"

"What are the vitals?"

"Low pulse, shallow breathing, and bluish skin color."

Booker noticed six numbers that had been scribbled into the dust near Butcher's right hand. While he waited on Worthy's response, he made a mental note of them in case they turned out to be relevant at some point.

"Replace his battery pack, increase his oxygen mixture, and get him back here."

Following instructions, they carried their fallen comrade out, leaving the supplies marking the spot with a communication-tone locator.

Three hours later, Booker and Pierce carried an unconscious Butcher to the med chair previously occupied by Worthy.

***

The next day, the media played up the failure of the multi-billion-dollar space program. Fingers were quickly pointed at the political players, whose interests had been placed above the safety of the crew. It was revealed that many of the parts had been outsourced to foreign countries, and that the quality of components was not up to original specs. Shortcuts had been taken on tests that should have been performed.

Houston eventually reported back to them that switching the strut assembly from the *Inuk 1* was not an option, because of a design change. It was also discovered that the heaters for the valves of their backup oxygen tank had failed, causing it to freeze in the closed position. The situation wasn't critical, yet. The crew could always stay in the habitats, and the now-working oxygen generator could keep the main tank topped up. It was just another thing that had gone wrong with this ill-fated mission.

Answers were demanded from NASA, who redirected the anger at subcontractors, who deflected it onto mandated cost cuts from the president. The White house singled out manufacturers from China, Russia, India, Japan, Italy, Israel, Mexico, and Canada—all partners in the space program—for allowing sub-par workmanship. The bullying tactics had little effect on the two other nations with manned moon missions planned. Russia and China quickly sent their regrets, but could not assist. It was a political ploy directed towards the new president.

The astronauts on the moon were not aware of the magnitude of the problem. Although anonymous sources at NASA had spoken to reporters, saying that the astronauts' chances of survival were very low, the following official statement was issued to the press on day four of their mission:

NASA: No viable solution has yet to be found for the safe return of *Endurance* crew. There is a single astronaut currently in critical condition, and another missing and out of communication, his condition unknown. The crew can survive many weeks with the food supplies and rationing.

CHAPTER 14

The feisty, curly-haired brunette paced back and forth on her mother's porch, distraught as she wiped tears from her eyes. She was angry, frustrated, and terrified that she would never see her future husband again. Why couldn't the greatest government agency in the country do anything to save him? Save all of them? She was also miffed with the other space-faring nations, making excuses instead of offering assistance. She stopped and drank from her water bottle, thinking about Tyrone and the feel of his strong arms wrapped around her. She was upset with her Jamaican-born mother, who offered her prayers and suggested that the Lord had a plan. Right now, she needed her best friend, but Samantha was unavailable in Afghanistan, doing what she did best: fighting.

Sam would know what to do—or if not her, her twin brother. Simon would have a solution, but he was at their late mother's estate without cellular reception. With all the technology he had on his boat, she questioned why his cell phone wasn't the latest in spy gear.

She wished the wild story they'd told her about Orion was true. They had tried to convince her that Orion was an alien, of the E.T. variety, and not a spy as she suspected. Although Orion did have some really cool stuff, that was way beyond her imagination, it was still a stretch to believe his claim that he had lived in his father's space ship in the ocean somewhere near the Bahamas. If it were only true, they could fly up and rescue Ty and the other astronauts.

The tall 'alien' was very convincing—almost too convincing—but so what? Even if it was all true, she had no way of getting in touch with him ... or did she?

Four months ago, she had received a congratulatory message from Orion, with the strangest address, which she had given little thought to at the time, assuming it was odd because of his secretive profession. Scanning her email history, she found it: **%Orion%**

Looking at it again, she realized that it didn't look like any social-media format she was familiar with. She supposed it could be a secure government server. *If he's using his work account for personal messages, then shame on him,* she thought. *He deserves whatever punishment they give him.*

Sitting on the swing, she composed a text message using the same format he had used.

> %Orion, I need your help. Please PLEASE reply!! Tamara.%

She read it over a few times, and then with her fingers crossed and holding her breath, she pressed send and waited. She stared at it, as if concentrating on the screen would make the reply come faster, if it came at all. Three minutes later, she got a reply.

> %Tamara, how can I help you? Orion%
>
> %Orion, it's about Ty and the other astronauts. Can you do anything?%
>
> %Where are you? Provide GPS co-ordinates.%

She texted her location and waited, again, not knowing if there was a convoy of government or military vehicles on their way to arrest her for improper use of secret government communication channels. She stood and started pacing again. Well at least he hadn't said no. In fact, he had said very little. Four minutes later, his next replay came and she shrieked. He had agreed to meet.

> %Tamara, I have been following the situation on the moon. Meet me down at the Pier Restaurant, six blocks from your mother's house, in one hour. Walk and come alone. Orion%

Come alone? Restaurant? What did he have planned?

She quickly showered and changed, throwing on a bit of makeup to hide her tears.

"Mama, I'm going out for a bit to meet a friend. I won't be home for dinner. See you later. Love ya."

"But dear, I have dinner cooking: your favorite Cajun chicken with black-bean sauce."

"Sorry Mama, something came up. Put the rest in the refrigerator; it always tastes great the next day. See you later, bye Mama." With a quick peek on her cheek, the young women left the house.

Tamara walked down the street with renewed strength and optimism in her heart. She was thankful that she'd decided on the practical little black boots with the low heels, because the route was all downhill. She had completed her look with a turquoise tee and skinny jeans, since the Pier Restaurant was more of a water-front bar with pub grub, and this was not a date.

She glanced at her watch, the only jewelry she wore other than her engagement ring, and smiled knowing that she was five minutes late. She was about to open the door when a group of guys who had obviously had too much to drink exited, holding the door for her. There were whistles and lewd comments, which she took in stride, with the knowledge and confidence that it wouldn't be a fair fight if she took them all on. Instead, she just turned and winked, giving them her famously wicked smile and sending them on their way, to be dealt with by their wives or girlfriends.

Males running in a pack are so easy, she chuckled inwardly.

Orion was easy to spot standing at the bar. At six foot five, he dwarfed the tourists and the regular patrons. That combined with his greenish-blond spiked hair and the blue floral shirt was like a flashing neon sign.

She meandered her way through the happy-hour crowd, all eager to take advantage of the cheap booze. The noise level was over the top; a mixture of voices and laughter attempted to drown out the recorded electric tunes, which was already over-modulated.

Orion was at the far end of the bar, obviously having entered from the ocean side of the pier, and when confronted with the mass of humanity, deciding to stay right where he was. She had approached from the shore side of the bar and so had to battle her way through still more drunks, as she felt her body groped in far too many places to make it exciting.

Getting angry now, and ready for a fight, she swore that the next guy to grab her butt was going to get a smack down.

"Hey Tamara, I didn't know you were in town!" a man yelled over the din, slurring his words as he confronted her, blocking her path. "Can I buy you a drink?"

"Oh, hi Logan, I'm meeting a friend. Yak later okay?" she answered, not wanting to talk to an old college acquaintance known for his volatile temper.

"No, now Tamara! No one talks to me like that. You're coming with me!" He forcefully grabbed her shoulder, preventing her from moving around him as he directed her to the door she had just entered.

Her khaki green eyes brightened, as did the color in her cheeks.

"I said NO! Beat it, Logan. I have something very important to talk to my friend about." She stared into his eyes and detected dilated pupils, a telltale sign that he was on some kind of narcotic. He had always been on the drug *de jour* in college, but she thought he had gotten clean. He continued to hold her tightly, digging his fingers into her flesh.

"Hurts, don't it? Almost like how you and your friend hurt me with your teasing."

"Logan, let go of me or I will lay a whooping on you that will make you wish you were dead. You know I can, and then everyone in the bar will know you got bested by a girl. NOW BACK OFF!" she shouted, as she prepared to break his grip.

He wouldn't release her.

She grabbed the offending hand, stepped back (forcing him off balance), and then smashed his hand down, causing his upper-body to follow, which met with her knee, connecting solidly with his nose and jaw. With a change in grip, she put a vice-like hold on his thumb, putting him on his knees with his arm twisted up behind him. With just a little pressure, she could now manipulate him like a marionette. He knelt there crying, as blood poured out of his broken nose and two teeth fell from his mouth.

"I TOLD YOU TO LET GO OF ME!" she shouted, realizing that she was no longer surrounded by the hoard of pub goers, who were now silently hugging the walls. Someone had turned the music off and a waiter rushed over with a wet cloth, offering aid.

"You okay, miss?"

"Yeah, this jerk was trying to make me go outside with him. I told him, 'no I'm meeting a friend.'" She relaxed her grip, and he rolled to his side, holding his jaw and nose.

"Tamara, are you hurt!?" Orion, noticing the commotion and realizing Tamara was involved, rushed to her side.

"No, I'm okay, just shaken up a bit."

"Come sit with me over here; I'll get you a beer." He held her hand gently, as he guided her to the bar and sat her down in a vacated stool beside him. The music was turned back on and people started talking again, mostly about the guy who got the crap beat out of him by a girl.

Logan Hall, who was two years older than Tamara, had a history of drug abuse and was no stranger to violence. He was currently out on parole and wanted nothing to do with the police. The owner of the restaurant was a friend and called the local fire house instead. They sent paramedics who were now waiting for him outside. Logan refused a ride to the hospital, but did accept minimal medical treatment. He was embarrassed, now that he was coming down from his adrenaline rush and narcotic high. They taped up his nose, making sure his nasal passages were clear, and the bartender gave him some ice wrapped in a towel to reduce the swelling of his nose and jaw.

"So, what happened buddy? Fall off your stool?" one of the paramedics asked, as he checked his pulse.

"Typical bar fight," the bar owner answered, covering up the truth. "Someone didn't like the way he looked at a girl, right Logan? No harm done."

"If you're going to press charges, you really should get checked out at the hospital and make a formal statement," the second paramedic said.

"No, I'm good, just a little too much to drink, but hey, you should have seen the other guy!" Logan joked.

"Oh, is there another person in need of medical aid?"

"No just some bruised egos, nothing more," the owner said, as he palmed them two fifties in a handshake. "Thanks guys, appreciate the quick response and your discretion."

This was tourist season, and New Orleans was just clawing itself out of a deep pit of expenses. The locals knew it and did what they could to help the businesses survive. The paramedics were no different. Katrina had devastated so much and the rebuild was slow.

Logan was seated at a table in the kitchen and given a bucket of shrimp and a pitcher of beer on the house. Tamara, the victor and the victim, was given a pitcher of beer as well, but Orion insisted on paying for the meals.

"Wow, that was some fight. I never saw moves like that before," Orion calmly remarked, making small talk.

"Seriously, and you have seen many?"

"Well no, not really. I did see a human sacrifice once!"

"That's gross and sick." She shook her head in revulsion as she downed the remainder of her glass, then refilled hers and topped up her friend's barely touched one. It was obvious beer was not his drink, but it did help to cool down the establishment's famous Cajun chicken wings.

"Orion, I have a problem. Tyrone and the others are trapped on the moon. If you are who Sam and Simon say you are..." she leaned in and whispered in his ear, "... *an alien* ..." she pulled back and looked him in the eye, "then you can help. Please." She held her breath.

He said nothing, only stared at her and thought about what she was asking. She interpreted his lack of response as indicative of a wrong assumption on her part.

"Look if you're a spy after all, then maybe you can get word to your superiors to possibly send one of those top-secret shuttles you guys have."

Still no response; he was still processing and formulating a plan. This was not the place to discuss a rescue, nor his alien heritage.

"Let's finish eating, and then we can talk outside. Too many ears."

"You said in your text that you were following the situation up there. Do you have more information than what was released to the public?" She spoke just above a whisper, ensuring that only he could hear her, regardless of whether he was a spy or an extraterrestrial. It didn't matter. Her only concern was for the safety of Ty.

"Yes," he answered. "I have some ideas, but I don't know how the two of us could pull this off without being discovered."

She nodded, considering the situation. "I tried to get a hold of Simon, but he's in Scotland at his mom's estate and there's no cell signal. Sam is on a mission in Afghanistan and won't be back to the base for a few more days. If we can get to them, I know the four of us could come up with a plan to rescue them without revealing your secrets ... whatever they are."

Orion remained quiet and looked away. He didn't want to talk about it. Instead he wanted to enjoy being out in the fresh air with people and to just be normal, not dragged into a situation where his alien technology was needed.

He let out a deep breath, realizing his spirited friend was not going to let him enjoy the moment. "Okay, we should go and talk more outside."

Catching the bartender's eye, he dropped two twenties on the bar and stood up to leave. Tamara was already standing and straightening her hair, raring to go. She was ready to get the truth and the help she needed. Orion on the other hand was resolved in the knowledge that their little game of alien or spy was about to be over. He felt comfortable knowing that she already had doubts.

They exited the bar on the ocean side and started walking down the old wooden pier. The sun was low in the water and the bugs were out. Most of the old timers casting their fishing lines had departed, as had the tourists. The pier was silent now except for the sounds of the ocean beneath them and the sea birds squawking above. These sounds of nature drowned out the noise of humanity as they walked farther away from the restaurant. These sounds also drowned out the running footsteps of Logan.

"You little bitch, how dare you embarrass me like that!" He spun Tamara around.

Before she could react, she felt a shooting pain in her side, then the warm ooze of her blood.

"Hey, leave her alone!" Orion yelled when he saw Tamara double over, from what he believed to be a punch. "Get out of here, before we call the authorities!"

"Oh Mr. Tough Guy, you want to get involved?" the now sober-ish Logan sneered, as he punched the tall man in the gut.

The unexpected blow caught Orion just below the rib cage, knocking the air out of him. Startled and winded, he moved his arm up to protect his face, which he believed would be attacked next. That was the move Logan expected, and with Orion's left side exposed, it was easy to give two quick jabs of his knife into the vulnerable flesh. The first jab penetrated his liver, and the second nicked his intestines.

It all happened in slow motion. Tamara, still standing doubled over in pain, was holding her stomach and watching her blood leak out between her fingers, when she noticed her friend on his knees, with the wood below him turning dark crimson. Out of the corner of her eye, she saw it coming but was too late to react as a size-twelve boot caught her on the side of the head, sending her crashing to the deck. With her eyes closed, she heard Orion cry out in pain as he was kicked in the ribs. Then she heard the sounds of their attacker running away and laughing.

Military training told her to get her own bleeding under control first and then to help her friend, but she had nothing to use as a tourniquet. Orion did.

"Orion, take off your shirt!" she forcefully commanded.

She helped as he struggled to remove it; then she ripped it in half. She removed her own and tore that as well. She packed it into her wound and tied Orion's shirt around her waist to hold it tight.

Orion, figuring out what she was doing, attempted to mimic her actions, but the broken ribs restricted his motions, and he was relieved when Tamara came to his aid.

"Okay, that should help so we won't bleed out too much. Can you walk and make it back to the restaurant?" she asked, once the triage was complete.

Standing on shaky legs, she tried to pull her big friend back to the building, but the act of standing caused a drop in blood pressure and her head injury started to throb. It was a familiar feeling she had felt once before, when an overzealous training partner had taken her down in boot camp. Her instructor kept talking to her as she faded into unconsciousness. She remembered his words: "Tamara, can you hear me? Don't let it take you to dreamland; fight it."

She tried to heed those words now, as she drifted in and out. Then she felt someone effortlessly take her to the railing, where he held her tight. It was Orion. She recognized the musty smell of his clothes.

She felt a warmth wrap around her; then a strange glow enveloped them. Through hazy eyes and possible delirium, she felt him lift her up over the protective railing, and together they fell into the ocean. She watched as she slowly approached the water. Waves were visible but cloudy, as if she were viewing the world through a silk curtain. She waited to feel the wetness on her skin, and to feel the sinking sensation as she submerged, but neither was felt as she gently drifted to the bottom.

The pier's supports were now only shadows in the fading light. She guessed that they were in twenty-five feet of water, under the pier, when a round blue light appeared, hovering above the sea bottom and coming for them.

They tumbled through the strange light, and she felt Orion fall against her, limp and unconscious. In her concussed state, she knew her friend was in worse shape than she was. Raising her hand, she felt for a pulse on his neck and was sickened to find blood on her hand. In the strange dim light, she realized that they were sitting in a pool of their co-mingled blood. A wave of nausea overcame her, and she slowly slipped completely into nothingness.

CHAPTER 15

In her dream state, she felt herself being lifted and held securely in a reclined chair—the most luxurious chair she could imagine—which conformed to her body shape and radiated warmth. Out of the corner of her eye, she detected motion. With extreme effort, she slowly turned her head and watched her friend being elevated on a column. She realized that it was the floor itself creating this supporting device and chair.

Where am I? she asked herself, feeling like Alice down the rabbit hole. Her dream-world fantasy was intensified when a beam of light came down from the ceiling, bathing her friend. It pulsed slowly, changing colors until it had cycled through the entire spectrum, and then repeated. After two of these cycles, a similar beam of light activated above her.

She fought hard, but its gentle pulses lulled her to a deep and dreamless sleep.

Tamara fluttered her eyelids, and then licked her lips. She sensed the beam above her pulsing with a greater intensity. Her headache was gone, as was the pain in her gut. Moving her hand carefully over her stomach, she felt for the stab wound and realized it was gone. She felt remarkable—rejuvenated.

The gloom-and-doom news broadcast, the weird texts with Orion, the bar fight and the stabbing, and of course the hallucinations … all that felt like days ago. She would ask the nurse or doctor how long she had been out. Slowly she opened her eyes, and it was obvious she was in a different room. There was the same drab gray, futuristic and organic-feeling chair bed, but she was in a larger space than she remembered, and definitely not a hospital room.

Looking around, she noticed that Orion was about ten feet away, still unconscious under the strange pulsing light, and lying on a similar bed. She continued to look around, trying to figure out where they were and hoping she could meet the person in charge of her care.

There was a sound from above that startled her, or rather, the sudden lack of sound. The humming associated with the beam had stopped, as had the light itself. Taking that as her clue, she got off the bed to really look around and discovered that she still had her boots and jeans on. The medical staff should have removed them and dressed her in one of those backless all-flattering gowns associated with hospitals. She was thankful that she had chosen to wear a black bathing-suit top under her t-shirt, or she would be walking around in a lacy Victoria Secret.

She found a reflective surface and discovered that her wound was clean. There were no stitches and no blood. There was a slight redness where the blade had penetrated her skin, but very little else. Her pants, directly under the wound, were covered in dried blood though, and that bothered her.

The feeling of being Alice in Wonderland resurfaced.

"Hello? Anyone home?" she shouted. "Nurse? Doctor? Anybody?" No reply. Only silence.

"That's strange," she said out loud, for no other reason than to hear a voice. "No sounds ... as if the room itself is absorbing all noise. There should be the sounds of machinery, air ventilation fans, phones, and people. Where's all the normal clatter of a medical facility? Where am I?" She wished Orion would wake up. *As weird as he is, he would be company.*

Continuing her exploration of the room, she stumbled upon a row of clothes laid out on an odd shelf extending from the wall. It was the same drab gray as the rest of the place. The clothes were flat and crisp, as if they had been heavily starched and pressed by an industrial steamer.

The first item of clothing was a cream-colored pair of men's shorts; they looked tattered around the cuff, not like the current trend but thread-worn from use. Beside them was a smaller pair of shorts. Picking them up, she checked the label and judged they would fit her. Looking back at Orion sleeping on the table, she turned her back to him and kicked off her boots and her skinny jeans before slipping into the stiff shorts. Leaning on the shelf for support, she noticed how spongy the surface was. She casually tossed her jeans in the spot where the shorts had been and continued her exploration of the clothes.

She saw a few men's shirts, all with the floral patterns Orion was prone to wearing. Next to them were women's long-sleeve blouses, and then t-shirts of various sizes and colors. She decided on the one at the end of the shelf that had a faded logo of Janis Joplin's *Me and Bobby McGee* album cover. It was tight but she managed to get into it. It was then that she realized that the stiffness in her shorts was gone, as if the cleaning solution had reacted to her body heat. Her t-short quickly softened as well. Her new attire was clean and wrinkle free, with a casual feel to it, like jeans worn for the second day.

She turned and went back to where she'd left her boots. Using the shelf for support, she slipped them on and realized that her blood-stained jeans were gone. She did a quick search of the floor, but they were nowhere to be seen.

"Orion! Did you take my jeans?" she yelled accusingly, as she turned back to her friend.

He was still lying on the table, bathed in a pulsing beam of blue light, motionless and with his eyes closed. Walking up to him, she checked his pulse and inspected his wounds for the first time.

Unlike her injury, his was still weeping a bit of blood and the bruising on his rib cage was painful looking.

She touched his cheek. "Buddy, I'm going to snoop around a bit more, but I will come back to check on you in about ten minutes. Okay?"

The room was oval-shaped with the two healing tables off towards one end, and the weird clothing shelf running along one of the longer sides. The ceiling was domed, following the contours of the walls, and every surface looked to be made of the same spongy rubber material. In the middle of the room, centered between the two long walls, was a structure about ten-feet wide—about half the length of the room—that extended from floor to ceiling. On the side of the structure that faced her were thin threads of lights, crisscrossing randomly.

The changing patterns of light looked like modern or even futuristic art, but was there a purpose to it?

As she rounded the side of the art-wall structure, she discovered the only man-made looking object in the area: an old, heavy oak table with six matching chairs.

Tamara casually walked up to the table and pulled the nearest chair away from the table in preparation for sitting. The sound of liquid being poured onto a hard surface alerted her. It came from the art structure. On this side of it were a series of holes or pockets, evenly spaced in rows and columns. Each pocket was about twelve inches by twelve inches, with uncertain depths. Each pocket's interior was darkened, and she couldn't see inside. The sound was coming from a pocket left of center, in the middle row. She walked cautiously to it and was about to reach inside when the sound stopped and the pocket illuminated. A small shelf slowly extended from inside it, holding a simple clay mug of a hot steaming fluid. She hesitated, then reached for the mug when she picked up on the aroma of coffee.

Without a reason to question the liquid, she took a big gulp. It was thicker than expected and tasted more like coffee-flavored hot chocolate or tea. It was weird but delicious, and just what her body needed.

She stared at the structure, with its little compartments, sipping her coffee-like drink and thinking.

"Now how could a gal get a plate of nachos?" she asked out loud.

No sooner had the words escaped her lips than a pocket to the right of center started to glow red, one row above where her drink had come from. Barely perceptible at first, the glowing light intensified and started to pulse. After no more than a minute, a little shelf extended with a plate of what looked like handmade nacho chips, covered with a creamy white sauce. It too was delivered on a simple clay plate.

She looked at this marvel of technology—a futuristic, automated vending machine—for a few seconds and then grabbed the plate, turned, and settled down to eat.

They kind of tasted like the corn chips she was familiar with, but these had an earthy quality to them, and the topping was similar to cheese, but not. It was as though whoever had designed this machine had read what coffee and nachos were, but had never tasted either.

Is this Orion's spy headquarters? And if so, where are the other spies ... and the medial personnel?

This place was getting weirder by the second.

"So what do you think of my coffee and nacho chips?" Orion said from behind her, making her jump. "Taste pretty good, right?"

"Oh my gawd, Orion, you startled me! Are you okay?"

"Yes, of course, but I would not wish to repeat the experience. How are your injuries? Feeling better?"

"Yeah, that table with the weird light did an amazing job at fixing me. This is an incredible place. Is it spy HQ?"

Orion chuckled as he turned to the 'automated vending machine' to retrieve a warm drink. "Tamara, we have gone over this already. Sam and Simon explained the first time we met." Taking a sip of the coffee-flavored beverage, he sat down opposite her and continued.

"You know I'm half alien, or you wouldn't have contacted me; you said as much in the restaurant. This is my home, if you can call my father's space ship, resting on the ocean floor, home."

Shock and fear suddenly overwhelmed her. Was it possible that she had make contact with an alien and was now in a spaceship? She remained silent staring at him. The impossible was possible, as far-fetched as it was.

"Orion, I don't know what to say. I'm amazed, confused, and scared." She tried to appear calm but her body language indicated fright.

"There is nothing to be scared about. You know me, and I have never lied to you or put you in danger. If you recall, it was I who wanted to tell you the truth, to alleviate the tension between Samantha and you. Simon and Sam were just protecting my secret, just as I hope you will." He reached over and held her hand, in what Tamara thought was the first time she had seen him show any sign of real emotion.

"Well Orion, I'm just overwhelmed now that I see and believe the truth. You can trust me, but I have one question: What the heck is this I'm eating?" She smiled and squeezed his hand.

"I programmed the flavor and texture into the ship after I had some with Simon. They taste good, do they not?"

"Well the corn taste isn't right. I can't put my finger on it, but it just doesn't quite taste the way it should."

"Oh I see. Well it is the best the ship can do; after all, it is a secretion of proteins and nutrients."

"Eeww!" She pushed the rest of the plate away as she wiped her mouth off with the back of her hand.

This initiated a deep belly laugh from her host.

"It is perfectly safe and good for you. I have been eating it for centuries."

"Yuk. Where is my bag? I have a bottle of water in it."

"Come with me, and we will get it, and I can give you a tour of the ship. It really is a marvelous creature." The look on Tamara's face was a combination of shock and understanding. It was beginning to make sense.

They walked to the end of the oval room, to a smaller column structure that grew out of the floor to the ceiling. She hadn't noticed it before, thinking it was part of the wall. It was in fact about ten feet from the wall, where a large blue oval light radiated. She hesitated at first, but Orion held her hand firmly and guided her through the shimmering blue light.

Her body tingled all over as the electrons flickered around her. On the other side of the blue-light doorway, he released his hold of her.

"Go ahead; put your hand through it," Orion challenged her.

Cautiously, she extended her index finger and touched the glowing doorway. The sizzle of electricity coursed over the surface and danced on her fingertip. She tried to push her finger through, but the electric field prevented her. With a curious expression, she looked to Orion for answers.

"I guess you could call it a force field. Ships and submarines have water-tight doors, as do space crafts. The doors on this vessel are a little more alien." He smiled, hoping that if he explained things to her, she wouldn't be confused and scared. The fear in her eyes that he'd seen earlier was starting to mellow.

"Oh don't worry, Tamara; it opens to anyone carrying one of these crystals." He withdrew his black crystal pendant from beneath his shirt.

"That reminds me, we should get you one right away, just like Sam and Simon. Come, follow me."

Tamara followed her tall friend as he walked down the curved passageway, which was made of the same spongy material, until they came to a wall with the same randomly flashing light threads.

"What is this? I saw something similar in that medical room?"

"There are many of these panels; they are junction nodes for the sensors—an integration of engineering and organic. My father's people added these components and attached them to the living ship. Think of them as an interface. They provide communication, environmental controls, protection, and things like that."

Tamara began to understand thing now. She was in a living alien ship, created or bio-engineered by another alien race. All this time she had believed her friends were just joking with her. The books she read (and the movies she saw) about aliens were just writers' imagination. She was experiencing the real thing, and was officially blown away.

Orion touched the panel, pressing a few lights, and a compartment opened up on the side, revealing about a dozen black crystals hanging on the inner wall of the little cabinet. He reached in and pulled one out.

"Here, Tamara you need this to get around the ship, and honestly, it is about time you had one and learned about what it can do for you."

She accepted it without saying a word. The crystal was black and shiny, with the light reflecting off its crystalline structure. It was about two inches in diameter, thicker in the middle and tapering to the edge. Around the edge was a thin thread of silver that extended to form a necklace. She felt the weight in her hand and judged it to be lighter than any stone its size, having almost no weight at all.

"How does it work?" she asked, reverently holding it in her open palm.

"There is nothing you have to do to make it work; it just does. Let me show you. Scratch my arm with a fingernail, deep so it bleeds." He presented his arm.

"No, I don't want to hurt you."

"Remember we were both stabbed earlier. You will hurt me, and I will feel some pain, but I will heal very quickly. Please do it, so you will understand."

Not being a stranger to using her nails on a guy, she knew she could do it. But she did feel a bit guilty. Those other men had deserved the scratches (more like claw marks) but Orion didn't. He was one of the good guys, even if he was part alien.

"Okay pal, you asked for it." She held his wrist tightly with one hand, while she gripped his forearm with the nails of her other hand, making sure to dig in. His skin was soft and punctured easily. Retracting her painted talons, they inspected the wound. She had definitely hurt him; there were tears in his eyes.

"Oh, I'm sorry, Orion. I didn't mean to hurt you too much."

"That is all right. I asked you to. Now place your crystal over the puncture marks."

She did as instructed, and was surprised as the wounds healed over. The blood on the surface was reabsorbed into the flesh. After a minute, the punctures were gone. She touched the area gently and Orion showed no discomfort.

"How did it do that?"

"The crystals emit a certain frequency of radiation that works with your body to speed up the natural healing process. The beams of lights we were under use the same principal, but were designed for more serious injuries. Damaged organs are particularly difficult to heal and take time. Wear the crystal all the time and you will soon notice all the little aches and pains you get throughout the day will be fewer and fewer. You might even discover those little wrinkles around your eyes disappearing. Look at me! I'm 980 years old." He laughed at his own statement.

They continued down the passageway and rounded a sharp bend, only to be stopped by another wall structure with random flashing lights.

"Okay, what now?" she asked.

"We are going into the hanger bay, where the stingray probes and the shuttle craft are." He pressed his crystal into an indentation and touched the light below it.

The wall beside the console, which she had previously thought was solid, vanished, revealing a small round room. He gestured for her to enter. The room was about twelve feet in diameter. Once they were inside, the wall re-materialized, and she felt a slight sensation of motion.

"Is this an elevator?"

He grinned, nodding his head. Tamara was the first person he had shown this part of the ship. Simon and Sam had a tour when he first met them, but that was the upper deck, which was the only floor he lived on or knew about. Before his father died, in the Mayan village in Guatemala, he had told Orion about the rest of the ship and how to access the other decks.

He wanted to show Simon, but the opportunity had never presented itself. Whenever they met it was at the marina or on Simon's trawler, *Dragon Spirit*. As proud as he was of his discoveries aboard this ship, he was more anxious to get out and explore the world—a world that he had hidden from for so many centuries.

The elevator door vanished and opened up to a large room, similar in shape to the medical room but bigger. The room was lit, a soft muted glow, from the wall opposite to where they were entering. After her eyes adjusted to the dim, she realized that the illumination was the ocean's water reflecting sunlight from above.

She ran across the floor towards it and accidentally stepped on a resting stingray drone. It quickly rose up and assumed a defensive position, while scanning her with a narrow beam of light. Within seconds, it discontinued the beam and retreated into the shadows.

"What was that all about?"

"You have met the drones before. It was scanning you, and determined you were not a threat because you had a crystal."

"Oh." She looked around into the shadows with apprehension returning to her eyes.

Reaching the wall of water, she touched it and quickly pulled her hand back, as it had penetrated the force field and gotten wet.

"I assume the same type of force field keeps the water out."

"Yes, but from the outside it would look solid and unrecognizable as an entrance."

"Camouflage, cool."

As her eyes adjusted further to the low light, she noticed shapes on the wall. Closer scrutiny showed them to be drones attached to the wall, resting and recharging.

"How many drones do you have?"

"I don't really know; they come and go routinely and monitor the planet. At any one time, there may be a hundred in here."

"Wow." She wondered why none had ever been reported. She continued to explore, with Orion at her side answering her questions.

At the far end, in a dark alcove, she detected an object. It barely reflected light off its glossy surface. As they approached, small pin lights from the ceiling and floor lit up, illuminating the object.

In this alcove was the largest stingray drone she had ever seen. It was the size of a small executive jet but sleeker and faster looking. It was beautiful in a futuristic way.

"This is one of the short-range flying creatures my uncle and father used to fly when they wanted to travel on the planet. It will not reach light speed, so exiting this solar system might take a few weeks, but it will get us to the moon fast enough, if we need to go there."

"So we *are* going to rescue Ty!" She hugged her friend excitedly.

"If we have to, but I would rather not expose who I am, and this vessel, if I can avoid it."

"But Orion, it's a humanitarian act. We have to."

"I would rather we discuss this with Sam and Simon. They will bring a middle position to this debate."

"Well, Sam is in Afghanistan, probably on a mission, and Simon is in Scotland at his mom's estate. Who do you want to get first? If we are voting, I say let's get Sam."

"Were you a good pilot when you flew with Sam?"

"Yeah, why do you ask?"

"Well, I can fly this drone, but it takes a skill that I do not possess. The ship does not like me and will not bond with me. Possibly you could control it with your pilot knowledge."

"I've flown many helicopters in Afghanistan, delivering supplies, and was trained on fixed wings in a simulator for a few weeks. Which one would you say it flies like?"

"I would think neither; after all, it is an organic spacecraft with speeds exceeding that of your fastest jets."

❧ CHAPTER 16 ☙

The two boarded the sleek craft and "flew" out into the ocean, staying close to the bottom. When they reached the midpoint of the Atlantic, Orion reviewed the sensors, activated a control, and the ship surfaced.

"I hope there are no ships or planes around," Tamara said.

"No, we are all clear. Besides, I activated the ship's stealth mode."

"Stealth mode? I'm liking this ship." She smiled, settling back in her seat.

Orion activated a display that projected on the front wall. It was a topographical outline of the coasts, showing rivers and roads.

"It is time for you to take over." He released the strangely shaped joystick and stood. As he did so, a duplicate set of controls emerged from the console in front of his new co-pilot.

"But I don't know how!" she said, alarmed

"You will manage. Besides, you could not do any worse than me."

"Well can you give me a windshield, so I can see outside? I need to see the horizon to get the feel of it." Orion struggled with the controls at a rear console, and eventually the front wall of the ship de-materialized and a clear force field took its place.

"Thanks, that helps, but you have to react faster if this mission is going to succeed."

"I will do what I can, but I fear the ship does not wish to help me," Orion mumbled. "It appears it does not trust you yet either."

"Okay, now overlay the map on the windshield, show our position, and plot a course to where Sam might be," Tamara instructed him, ignoring his complaints.

Orion stared at the control console with its hundreds of lights, which doubled as switches. He knew what half of them could do, which was one of the reasons he wanted his friend to pilot the ship. He knew that he was not a good pilot, and his secret fear of flying didn't help. Tamara, with as little experience as she had with this ship, had been trained professionally and knew the basics of flight. He did not.

Randomly choosing one of the buttons he had never used before did the trick and gave Tamara what she'd asked for.

"Thanks buddy. Why did you plot a destination point out in the middle of nowhere? There isn't a US base close to it."

"I did not decide on the destination. I believe the ship chose that area, based on our satellite data."

"Cool, can you enlarge this area on the screen? I want to get a better look at where we're going." As before, the request slowly materialized. The destination area was enlarged and moved off to the side.

Little dots began to appear across the map, moving at different speeds.

"Orion, what do the colored dots mean?"

"Blue dots are above the ground and green are on the ground."

"So we can assume the blue ones are planes or choppers and the green are ground troops. Do we know who the friendlies are? The US troops? I need—wait, you said our satellite data. There should be an encrypted ID signal transmitted from their helmets. You should be able to hack it."

"We are not using a US satellite; we are using one of mine."

"Are you freakin' kidding me? You have satellites? This is really cool. Can it pick up the ID signals?"

"I will attempt to retrieve the ID signals."

Minutes later, white rings appeared around the flying blue dots, and around a small group of green dots as well. The rest of the green dots had black rings. The black rings were advancing toward the whites.

"Can you overlay buildings and terrain?"

Orion picked another button, and miraculously, buildings and terrain appeared.

"You're good at this. And you said the ship didn't like you," she said, teasing him.

The tall alien hybrid just smiled, not wishing to speak for fear that his luck would run out.

"Now," Tamara said, studying the display, "if we only knew which of those birds was Sam's."

Before Orion could guess, one of the blue flying dots started to pulse. It was off to the side, away from the action, and maintaining an overwatch position. The other blue dots were trying to provide cover fire for the ground troops. Beneath Sam's pulsing dot were a few black rings, moving in and out of a covered position.

"Can I get a live feed, with real-time video and zoom capability?"

Orion started to push buttons, but the desired outcome didn't transpire.

"Damn, that's not good. We don't know if those are just civilians peeking out or if they have a shoulder-mounted surface-to-air rocket." She cursed, hitting the console in frustration. In doing so, she took her eyes off the enlarged battle area and stared at the big picture.

They seemed to be moving faster than they were before, covering more ground.

"Oh, have we gained speed?"

Orion touched a small circle in the corner of the screen and a series of numbers popped up in rows.

"The first row is our speed, the second is distance to target, and the third is distance traveled."

"What unit of measure is it displayed in?"

"It would be the unit of measure that my father's people used. Would you like me to have it converted?"

"Yes, please. Can you make it metric? Give me kilometers for distance and kph for speed."

Orion knew how to satisfy that request. Entering the conversion calculation at a small side console resulted in the display changing to her requested readout.

"So according to the readout, we are going 2000 kph. Holy crap! That's faster than our fastest! Wow! Is that the speed you programmed in?"

"No, I set it for around 1500."

"How did it gain speed? Do you think there's a problem?"

"There are no indications of a malfunction. I believe the ship increased speed after Sam's helicopter was identified. Why? Would you like to slow down?"

"No, I want to go faster. Can we go to 2500?"

"Yes, that is not a problem."

The ship's jumped to 2500 kph was barely noticeable to its crew.

"Can you show me, in minutes, when we will reach our destination?"

No sooner had she said this than a fourth row of numbers appeared, indicating thirty minutes.

"I don't think Sam has that much time. Can you get us there in like five minutes?"

Before Orion could respond, the speed indicator quickly accelerated to 10,000 kph. This time she felt a slight jolt.

The map quickly refreshed, showing a steady line representing their position, which had once been a flashing triangle. They were putting distance behind them, but more important, they were getting closer to Sam.

"Are we close enough to get eyes on her?"

Orion thought for a few seconds.

"Yes, we could launch drones, which could give us a clear picture, but they cannot travel as fast as we are now. I suggest we wait a minute more and launch them when we have reached the target."

"Oh, that makes sense. Is there something we have to do to slow the ship down or does the auto pilot handle that?"

Almost as soon as she asked this, the ship decelerated and took up a hover position above Sam.

Orion launched three stingray drones and positioned them around the various combatants. He also converted the viewing screen to a 3D-imaging display. Data points from the drones, overhead satellite, and their own ship, built a realistic live model of the combat zone. The screen had the ability to zoom, if an object was touched.

Tamara zoomed in on Sam's helicopter, and continued to zoom until an extreme close-up of her friend filled the screen. Sam was looking down at an instrument. Then she looked up to scan the skies as she spoke into her radio.

"Can we tap into their communication?" Tamara asked.

Orion executed the request, and Sam's voice could be heard booming through the cockpit of the stealth spaceship.

"...Copy that, Commander. I can confirm two hostiles on the hospital roof. They have what appears to be a missile launcher, but they have not taken any aggressive action."

"Can you tell what they are waiting for?" an authoritative voice asked on the other end.

"No sir, but they appear to be young boys, 11 or 12 years old. Maybe they're afraid or don't know how to use it?"

"Do not, repeat do not, take action against them or fire on the building. There are civilians in there, as well as the senator and some of her people. Why the hell they chose this time to re-open the hospital, I'll never know."

"Could a drone take a direct hit from a missile?" Tamara asked, absorbed in the unfolding drama.

"Yes possibly. May I suggest we use it to deflect the weapon somewhere it could explode without harming anyone?"

"Good idea, make that happen if one is launched."

"Should we attempt to communicate with Sam?" Orion asked, as he entered commands into his console.

"We can do that? Then yes, but only for her to hear."

With a few commands, the tall man executed the communication request.

"Okay Tamara, you can talk to her."

"Sam, it's me, Tamara. I'm with Orion in a stealth ship above you. We have you covered."

"What? T? How—never mind actually; you can tell me later. Boy, am I glad you guys are here! Can you check out the two people on the roof and tell me if they're just kids ... and also if they're alone?"

Hearing the request, Orion dispatched the closest drone to the combatants on the roof, and within seconds a clear feed came back to their ship. The drone panned the area and only two boys were up there, hiding near a large air-conditioning unit. The drone also took close-up images of the missile launcher.

"Sam, you were right. They are just boys, maybe 10 … if that. The launcher still has the safety on, if that helps."

"Thanks T."

"Do you have forces inside the building?" Tamara asked, excited to be back fighting alongside her friend.

"Yes, we have a SEAL team—protection detail for a senator and her people. Some hostiles stormed the building and attacked them earlier. Right now our guys are trapped but have stopped the advance of the terrorists. Tamara, we are waiting for reinforcements and those guys are pinned down fifteen clicks southwest of here. Do you guys have any suggestions?"

"We can confirm that they're taking heavy fire, and it looks like two birds are down."

"Bloody hell! Do you guys have any weapons?"

"Sam, Orion here, we do not carry any weapons. It was not part of the original mission, and it would be against my morals to use this technology to shoot humans."

"Yeah, I get it, but don't drones have the ability to blow up rocks?"

"Yes, why do you ask? What are you thinking?"

"Put down a barrage of explosions all around the hostiles, so our guys can get moving."

"Consider it done," Tamara said. "What about you? Do you want us to do something about the boys?"

"Maybe. Simon told me a while ago that a drone picked him up off the ocean floor and placed him in a protective air bubble. Could a drone do the same here? Snatch up the boys and hold them, so they don't do something stupid?"

"Yes, that is possible," Orion said, sounding concerned, "but the drone would have to become visible and the boys would see it and tell others."

"Orion, they are boys. If they tell anyone a wild story about being kidnapped by a monster-sized stingray, no one will believe them. More likely they will think the boys were too afraid and hid."

"Yes, that is a logical conclusion. I will instruct the drone."

"Orion, please make sure it doesn't hurt them."

Sam watched from her helicopter position as a large fifteen-foot stingray materialized in front of the boys, rearing up to show its full size, instilling fear. She watched as a beam of light centered on the frightened young lads and drew them to it, where a bubble formed under the creature, holding the boys fast. The drone moved away to the other side of the building, away from the door, and shimmered out of sight with its human cargo.

"What happened?" Sam asked frantically. "Where did it go?"

"It is still there, Sam," Orion said calmly, "only invisible to the naked eye. I activated its stealth mode."

"Oh of course; that makes sense. T, how are the guys on the ground doing?"

"The barrage worked," Tamara answered, checking her screens. "The terrorists started to retreat, but the drones stopped them by exploding the ground behind them. Damn, those guys must be freaking out. Looks like some of them are surrendering. Your boys are convincing the others to drop their weapons."

"Angel Eyes, do you copy?" Sam's commander hailed.

"Yes sir, go ahead."

"We have contained the situation and are on the move again. We lost two ships, and the third is out of armaments. They are EVACing our wounded and returning to base. You are our only cover. How are you with ammo?"

"Full payload, sir."

"Good, we may need them if we meet up with any more unfriendlies. What is the situation there?"

"All good sir, the boys bugged out and left the missile launcher unfired. I guess I intimidated them. There are still hostiles watching the skies from the front door. They aim in my direction every time I get too close."

"Not good. Stay out of their range. We will be there in fifteen."

"Yes sir. Angel Eyes out." She re-adjusted the ship's video camera zoom and watched in the distance as a cloud of dust was kicked up by her team, exiting the area in their Humvees.

"When did you get that sweet call sign?" Tamara asked her best friend.

"The boys gave it to me a few months ago, when I was assigned to combat missions." Sam's smile was visible to all in the stealth cockpit.

"Sam, there is a small group of black ring dots converging on the road the green dots are taking. Do you want us to intervene?" Orion interrupted.

"What on earth are you talking about?" Sam asked, confused.

"It's how the good guys and bad guys show up on our display," Tamara explained.

"Oh, okay," Sam nodded, "but try not to hurt them, and don't let our guys know what's happening."

"Orion, explain this stealth technology," Tamara asked as they moved towards the enemy position. "What do people see when they look in our direction?"

"The technology is actually biological. The creature's outer skin has photoelectric properties, which reflect back its surroundings, making it disappear into any environment it inhabits."

"So if we were to fly between the convoy and the bad guys, could we reflect back a blank canvas, making the trucks disappear?"

"Yes, and we could blow dust back towards the hostile party, further masking our image and the vehicles. In fact, I believe we could have a drone follow us, making a small dust cloud, creating the illusion that the convoy is twenty or thirty meters behind their actually position."

"Yes, and since Sam is the only one in the air, no one will notice something strange going on. I like it, good thinking Orion."

Orion put the plan into motion as Tamara watched on the big screen. They took up a position between the convoy of US Marines and the enemy fighters positioned on a rocky ridge parallel to the road. The ship slowed and the stealth projection adjusted to blank out the trucks racing by.

As the first of the Humvees sped into the trap, the sounds of its engine reverberated against the ridge, alerting the disorganized fighters. They heard but saw nothing on the road. All the men were on alert, ready to start firing and ridding their country of the western occupiers.

The commander in the Humvee was on the alert for an attack, and the ridge would have been the perfect spot for the trap. That was where he would have attacked from, if the situation was reversed. He saw a head pop up wearing a *keffiyeh,* the traditional head scarf worn by the locals. "They must be able to see our trucks; why aren't they firing?" he said out loud, to no one in particular. The marines just held their collective breath and said silent prayers as they raced through the potential killing field.

They waited as the last of the vehicles left the ridge area; the drone/decoy convoy created an impressive dust cloud, following right after, and was attacked with a fury. Every man and boy took aim and fired on the middle of the cloud. Some bullets even struck the invisible drone, echoing back to the fighters, who re-doubled their efforts to take out their foe.

"They made it Sam," Tamara told her, "and there are no more hostiles in their way."

"Copy that, T. Now if you guys could do a little RECON, and tell me exactly where the bad guys are in the building, that would be most appreciated."

The ship flew sluggishly as Tamara piloted it to the far side of the health facility, then descended to the sandy soil where they could look into a row of ground-floor windows. Using a technology akin to infrared vision, x-rays, and sonar, they slowly scanned the building, moving up one floor at a time. Gradually a 3D model of the interior started to form before them on the big screen. When they'd checked almost half the building, little green dots started to appear in various rooms and corridors. At first there were no rings to identify the good guys, but it was soon revealed that the white-ringed guys were spread out on the second floor, guarding stairwells and a small group of green dots in a central room. The first floor had just plain green dots, without the black ring to identify them as the enemy. Through careful observation, they realized that some of these green dots had taken up position opposite the white rings on the second floor. These men were guarding the stairwells, preventing the people on the second floor from leaving. The first floor also had a group of people in an inner-room, huddled together in the center with a few green dots patrolling the hallway outside.

"Looks like they may have hostages." Tamara pointed to the first-floor room.

The third floor was vacant but the fourth, which was the top floor, showed almost fifty green dots, six in each of the eight hospital rooms. In the hallways, there were five others moving back and forth between rooms, possibly doctors and nurses checking on the patients.

Tamara explained the situation to her friend, and gave her opinion of where the bad guys were.

"Sam, do you think you could land on the roof and extract the senator and her staff?"

"Maybe, but I can only carry two passengers. Most would be left behind. The bigger problem is them starting to shoot at me if I get any closer to the hospital. We need to wait for the marines. Besides, a couple of transport choppers and a squadron of Apaches have been dispatched. They should be here in about twenty minutes. The commander will do whatever it takes to rescue the senator and her people, regardless of civilian casualties. I'm afraid there's going to be bloodshed when they get here."

"Sam, I feel an insane idea percolating in that mind of yours. What are you planning?" Tamara asked, knowing her friend.

"I'm going to fly away from the building. Can you guys move between me and the building, hide my approach, and maybe mask the sound, so I can land on the roof?"

"Yes we can," Orion said. "Just like we did with the convoy."

"Good, and Orion, do you have any of those EVA belts to give us protective shields and allow us to float?"

"Yes, I have six in this vessel."

"What do you have planned, Sam?" her friend asked, having used the technology once before.

"I'm going to land my helicopter, float down the side of the building, sneak into a first-floor window, and force them out the front door, right into the hands of the marines."

"Won't they see you?" Tamara asked.

"The EVA belts can be adjusted to provide the same stealth cover as the ship," Orion explained.

"Even better," Sam added. "We know the force shield will stop bullets, because Simon was shot at, and protected, back in the jungles of Guatemala last year."

"I'm going with you girl," Tamara said, "and I want one of those drones as backup." She made it clear that this was not a request.

"Tamara, this could be dangerous, and you know you don't like people shooting at you."

"Serious girl? Like you do?"

"Yeah, but this isn't your mission. Besides, don't you have a wedding to plan for?"

"That's one of the reasons why we're here. We need your help, and Simon's too."

Sam expertly landed the Apache helicopter on the roof and shut down the engines, just as the space ship landed and materialized a short distance away.

The girls hugged each other, each silhouetted with their respective flying machine behind them. Noticing the sleek vessel, Sam broke her embrace and ran over to the large stingray-winged ship and ran her hand over the ultra-smooth wing.

"Where did you find this beauty?" Sam cooed, caressing the vessel. She could feel little shivers radiating from her touch as she embraced the beautiful ship.

"Remember how I said that I only lived on one deck of my ship, and that I couldn't get into the others, because I thought they were flooded? Well my father gave me the codes, with instructions to open them."

"Oh, how is your father? He wasn't doing so well when we last talked to him. Did the crystals help?"

"He passed away. He was holding on I think ... waiting to see me again to share what knowledge he had. We spent his last few months together. He was the wise teacher once again. My father lived a long and courageous life, the way he wanted. It was too bad he never got to return to his planet, but now his spirit has been returned to the universe." The remorse was clear in his voice.

"Orion, I'm so sorry." Sam hugged him, knowing that, although he was more than 900 years old, he was still that 10-year-old who had been left all alone in a space ship on the ocean floor, for centuries.

"Hello?" Tamara jumped in, interrupting the reunion. "Remember me? We need to deal with the bad guys on the first floor, and then talk about helping Ty."

"Yes, of course." Before she could ask, Orion presented the girls with the EVA belts. He started to give Tamara a demonstration of how it worked, when Sam summarized it in simple terms.

"Basically, it will do what you tell it to with your thoughts."

"Can we communicate with this ship and you, Orion?" Tamara asked, with a hint of fear in her voice.

"Yes," he nodded. "Talk in a normal voice when you are in the protective shield and you will be heard in the ship."

"If we are in stealth mode, will others hear us?"

"No, it is both audio and visual stealth, as well as infrared, so you both will be invisible to any electronic devices that may be used."

Sam checked her Beretta nine-millimeter sidearm and re-holstered it in her flight suit's chest harness.

"Do you have one for me?" her spunky friend asked.

"Sorry girlfriend, it's the only one I have."

"Don't you carry a backup?"

"Yeah I do; it's called an Apache gunship."

"Just a little too heavy to carry, but no worries; I'll borrow a weapon when we get there." She chuckled as they floated down from the roof, controlling the gravity around them using the EVA belts, with their big drone companion leading the way.

CHAPTER 17

Orion had explained earlier that thinking about being invisible would trigger the belt to pick up on their request and generate the necessary camouflage. To an observer watching the building, only a slight shimmer would be visible as the girls quickly descended the wall. Orion stayed in the ship, closely monitoring his friends and all other parties in the conflict. If this were to work, timing was critical. Too early and the bad guys would run out and vanish into the surrounding buildings and desert. Too late and the marine commander would come in shooting.

They needed to execute Sam's plan, where there would be no causalities.

Reaching the ground, Orion gave the all-clear signal. The room they were going to enter was free of any biological signatures. The probe attached itself to the window, and using only sound waves, silently blew the window out, turning the glass to microscopic dust.

The room was a waiting area with a large admitting desk. Patients would come into the hospital either via the rudimentary ambulance system or (more often) carried by relatives on makeshift gurneys. The large double doors leading to this room from the outside of the building was chained and armed with explosives. If they had attempted to sneak in that way, the resulting explosion would have alerted the terrorists and threatened the lives of the first-floor hostages and possibly the rest of the building.

Past the admitting desk, usually staffed by nurses and clerical personnel, was a short hallway leading to triage—a room full of curtained cubicles and examination beds. This room would usually have doctors and nurses rushing between patients, determining if a swollen ankle was sprained or broken, or if chest pains were a heart attack or simply indigestion.

Although the people of Afghanistan were no strangers to war, this was neither a combat hospital, nor a big city hospital, but rather a rural medical facility for the local villages. It catered to people who grew apricots and figs—Afghanis who were devoted to their faith and loved their families.

Sam and Tamara crept through the triage room, which was clearly where the carnage had started. Blood splatter and bullet holes riddled the room, as did the stench of death. Four bodies were lying on the floor, left where they had fallen. They were Americans, part of the protection detail, and cut down for wearing a shoulder patch with stars and stripes while in the region as part of a humanitarian effort.

Tamara reverently searched the closest soldier, and relieved him of his service revolver and ammo clips.

"Okay, now I'm armed and dangerous."

"Hey T, I have an idea," Sam whispered to her friend. "Give me a hand over here."

There was a body partially covered with a blood-stained white sheet in one of the curtained cubicles.

"What's your idea, girl?" Tamara asked, walking up to her friend, who was standing over the body of a young man. He looked to be in his late teens, showing early signs of facial hair—his first tribal beard. His clothes, complete with wool head scarf in the colors of the region, were that of a peasant sheep herder. He still wore a gun belt with AK47 rounds, and was most likely the younger brother of one of the other men who had taken over the hospital, probably influenced to join the fight, just like his sibling.

The two girls lifted the young soldier and put him face-down on the floor.

"Okay," Sam said, "I will push him up to the door, and it will slide open. The guard at the end of the hall will see him and investigate. When he gets here, and leans over the boy, you knock him out with the butt of your gun."

"Wait, I have a better way to get him to sleep. I saw a drug cabinet over there. There has to be something in there that would be safer and less painful."

The two walked over to the cabinet and found it smashed. Most of the bottles were broken. Beneath the cabinet was a small refrigerator. Tamara opened it quickly and searched its contents.

"Here, this will work." She held up a bottle of propofol, used in IV injections.

"How do you know this will work?"

"I helped out in a field hospital a few years ago. This is a general anesthetic and will put him under in seconds. Now let's look for some syringes."

"Do you know how much to give him?" Sam handed her a box with a dozen new syringes.

"No not really. I'm not a doctor, but I was told to give a patient 10 ml prior to surgery, and the guard looks about the same size as that guy. It will be enough to knock him out for about fifteen minutes, I think. When he wakes, he shouldn't have a clue what happened."

"Okay, Nurse T, let's do it."

Sam slowly pushed the teenager to the door, and Tamara extended his lifeless hand. The motion sensors triggered and the door slid open with the typically mechanical swishing sound. With as deep a voice as she could generate, Tamara moaned out into the hallway, alerting the guard.

The door closed but was stopped by Tamara, holding the dead boy's hand in the doorway, triggering it to reopen. She moaned again, and Sam pushed the body farther into the opening.

Cautiously, and with his rifle in position, the guard slowly approached the doorway, ready to shoot whomever he saw.

Sam lifted the body by the shoulders, giving the impression that the teen was struggling to get up.

The guard saw the head scarf and rushed to the boy's side, with little regards to his own safety. Looking through the glass doors, all he saw was the boy lying on the floor with a trail of blood behind him. The women's EVA belts worked, making them invisible. Sam held her gun on the approaching man as a precaution.

"Aarman!" he whispered excitedly, grateful that his brother-in-arms was alive and not even feeling the pin prick of the syringe. "We thought you were dead!" He dropped to his knees next to the young man, running his hands over the boy's head and chest. "The doctor confirmed it. Your cousin will be pleased. How ... do you..?"

He slumped over the dead boy, the drug having taken effect.

Tamara disabled his weapon by removing the firing pin.

"Okay, let's go find some more bad guys." With their stingray drone following, the two left the emergency room and ventured into the rest of the hospital.

"There is another person with a weapon around the next corner," Orion said, watching from the space ship's monitor, "ten meters to your left."

"Copy that."

Invisible, and floating above the floor tiles, they approached their target silently. Tamara already had another syringe prepared.

The women moved to either side of the sentry, as he rested his head back against the wall. Sam put her hand over his mouth as Tamara injected him in the neck. They held him until he stopped moving and went limp, sliding down to the floor.

As before, Tamara disabled his weapon by removing the firing pin.

Orion gave them an update. "Three more men are around the next corner, six meters from your position. They are guarding the door to the hostages, but you will have to go through a swinging door to get to them."

Sam frowned at that. "As soon as the door opens, they will see it move and start shooting. Any ideas?"

"Yes, if I may suggest, the two of you could stand behind the door and pull it towards you. As you do so, I will instruct the drone to project an image of the door still closed. Let it move in front of you, while you hold the door open, and then slowly close it behind you."

Sam grinned. "Good idea buddy. Thanks."

If the guards saw the door move, or a slight shimmer in the hallway, they never showed it. Two men were talking in low tones while the third stared down the empty hall in their direction. The illusion was working perfectly.

"Orion, do you have any more good ideas?" Sam asked, in an unnecessary whisper. "Like how we can overpower these three big guys?"

"Yes, you could use the drone again. It could get in front of them and push them to the wall, while creating a bubble around them. I can change the bubble's air mixture to nitrous oxide, rendering them unconscious."

"Smart and easy."

"One moment, Sam..." After a brief hesitation, Orion continued speaking, his voice tense. "There is another man in an office on the right, five meters from your position. He is walking towards the door. Sam, he has an electronic devise in his right hand. It may be a detonator switch for the explosives."

The two held their breath as they watched the office door open and an older man exit, walking towards the guards. Unlike the scruffy clothing the combatants wore, he was dressed in a clean shirt and pressed European-styled pants. His boots were polished leather, his head scarf was of a fine material, and his beard was trimmed neatly, rather than shaggy as was the local custom. He carried himself with the authority of a leader and did not seem to be from the region.

"Your friends from the ridge just informed me that the Americans slipped past them and are almost here," he said, in a strong and commanding voice. "I have friends close behind them, however; they will stop the infidels before they get here. Allah will make sure of that. The Americans hiding on the second floor, protecting their female senator, will not escape. I will blow the building up before I allow that to happen." He turned then and retreated towards the office.

Sam and Tamara looked at each other, shocked that he would go that far.

"Orion, you have to help our guys or this rescue will never work."

Before entering the office, the leader stopped and turned back. "One of you, check on the men by the emergency room. They are not answering their radios."

One of the guards shrugged his shoulders and mumbled something in Arabic, heading down the hall towards the invisible women and stingray.

"If he comes down the hall, he will break the illusion," Tamara said.

"Hug the wall. No wait ... let's float up to the ceiling. The drone too."

They watched as the guard passed beneath them.

"Tamara, go with him through the door and give him an injection when he gets to the other side. I'll take care of these guys, with the help of our drone."

"Okay, but be careful."

Tamara slipped through the doors, in her invisible state, just as it was closing. Neither the guard she was following nor those posted at the other end of the hall noticed.

Sam and the drone floated down from the ceiling and advanced towards the gathered men.

The big stingray drone executed the plan they had discussed earlier, surrounding the men with its large wings and pulling them into a gas bubble of anesthetic laughing gas. The men were rendered unconscious in minutes.

Sam turned quickly, seeing motion out of the corner or her eye. The door swung open and her friend Tamara walked through, smiling.

"Okay, now we only have the guys at the front door left," Tamara said. "Oh, and Mr. Fancy Clothes. Any ideas on how we can get the detonator off him before he uses it?"

"Not sure," Sam said. "Hey Orion, can the drone block radio signals coming from the room? We want to deactivate the detonator he has with him."

"Yes of course. Considered it done."

"Excellent. Now one other thing. Can we make ourselves glow, and the drone too, so he'll think we're spirits? I've got an idea."

"The EVA belts work off your thoughts. In theory, if you can think it, the belts will attempt to achieve it. I would suggest that you test it out before you enter the room though."

She explained what she had in mind, and her allies loved it. Sam was the first to test out her glowing apparition form, and with a few suggestions from Tamara, she managed to pull off a frightening vision of a Hollywood ghost. Tamara and the drone duplicated the effect and were ready.

"We need a spectacular entrance if this is going to work," Tamara said. "What if the drone pumped in a smoky vapor under the door, and then blew it open? Then we could materialize through the mist and scare the bahjezzers out of him."

"I speak the local dialect; maybe I can convince him to repent his evil ways." Sam chuckled lightly.

The drone did as instructed and a white mist poured under the door. After a few seconds, the door was blown inwards. The stingray, still holding its unconscious captors, floated into the room as a bright white apparition with two dead men in its grasp.

The girls took this opportunity to become visible, and shimmered into sight a few feet from the terrified man.

Sam held out her hand and asked for the detonator. The man knew it was not a request and relinquished it, while pushing the red button. As expected, the electronic signal never reached the explosives. He had failed. He reached into the open desk drawer and retrieved an old nine-millimeter Makarov, from the 1950's Soviet era, and pointed it at Sam.

"I'm not afraid of you. You are a trick!"

"Oh you should be afraid of me." She whispered in a deep voice, as she rose higher off the floor and extended her arms, in a classic pose that clearly said, 'I'm a ghost.'

Sam then quoted a line from the Koran, which made the man turn white with fear. He slowly backed away as the female spirits approached, until he was stopped by the wall. He was trapped and had nowhere to run. He fired a round at Sam and then Tamara. Their force shields absorbed the kinetic energy of the bullets, which fell harmlessly to the floor.

"We are just two of the spirits of the many women you have brutalized and killed over the years. You will not be joining Allah. You will instead be sent to Jahanam."

Tamara had never heard of this Islamic version of hell, but could easily follow the threat based on context.

He fired round after round at them, until all ten were spent. He didn't stop pulling the trigger for a few impotent seconds afterward. Finally giving up, he threw the useless weapon at Sam, making her laugh.

The stingray drone had been slowly floating along the ceiling as the girls kept the man busy. When it was within reach, it dropped down and encased him in another bubble of nitrous oxide and held him as he slipped into unconsciousness.

"Orion, how many guards left in the building?"

"Only two remain at the front door."

"Where are our guys?"

"They are pulling up now."

"Good, we have a final performance, and then we are out of here. I don't want to stick around when our guys show up asking questions."

Sam and Tamara headed to the front doors and could see the remaining men hiding behind a large wooden reception desk, waiting for the imminent attack. Using the same tactics once more, they approached them silently, still invisible. At about the three-foot mark, they shimmered into view as ghostly specters. On instinct, the men screamed in unison and ran out the front door. They were looking behind them with terror in their eyes and literally stumbled into the marines who had been sneaking up on their position.

It took the commander and his men about ten minutes to secure the hospital and carry out the unconscious terrorists. The protective detail assisted the mop up but confirmed that they knew nothing about what had happened downstairs. They had sealed off the stairway doors, and after a brief exchange of gunfire earlier, it had remained quiet. Both sides had been waiting for reinforcements.

Sam and Tamara, using their EVA belts, floated invisibly to the roof during the cleanup commotion. When asked, Sam confirmed that she was not aware of the activities inside and had waited on the roof for the commander and his men.

As the drugs wore off, the terrorists babbled that the place was haunted and cursed, which sparked laughter from the elite American forces.

Senator Debra Stevens thanked the team, but wanted to get back to "civilization" as soon as possible.

Sam trailed the senator and the escort helicopters as they headed towards the base.

"Well that was fun." Tamara's voice broke the silence as she materialized in the co-pilot's seat of Sam's helicopter. "Now can we get down to business?"

Startled, Sam had accidentally banked her craft, and then quickly corrected.

"Bloody hell! You scared the crap out of me! How did you get in here?"

"I snuck in while you were doing your pre-flight check. I thought I would wait until you were airborne before I spoke to you."

"I thought I felt someone in the cockpit. I should've known it was you. Thanks for your help back there. It was kinda crazy, but still … an interesting mission, wasn't it? Not sure if I would label it fun, though. More like playing with high-tech toys."

"Oh yeah, really high-tech toys."

"So, what is so important that you came all the way to Afghanistan? You said something about saving Tyrone?"

Tamara nodded. "He and the other astronauts are trapped on the moon and we've got to help them."

"Sorry, T. I've been out of touch in terms of international news events. I didn't know. What happened?"

Tamara briefed her friend about the moon-mission problems and NASA's response. By the time they were fifty kilometers from the base, Sam was up to speed on the situation and in agreement with Tamara that a moon mission was needed. She was also in total agreement with Orion though. They couldn't just expose themselves. Simon would have a plan.

"Okay, girlfriend, so all we need to do is get you out of here for maybe a week. Guess you can't just ask your CO for a week off?" Tamara asked, knowing the answer.

Sam smiled and slowly shook her head.

"Well the only other solution is to get you time off for medical reasons. If you crash this chopper, and maybe break a few bones, would they let you recoup in Germany, like you did before?"

"OH MY GAWD! That is an insane idea! I am NOT going to crash this *very* expensive machine." Sam was aghast at the suggestion.

"Oh don't worry, Orion can heal you. I was in his alien ship and let me just say…. wow!"

"T, I know about the crystals and how they heal." She chuckled as she shook her head knowingly. "Remember the boat?"

"Well you leave me no choice then," Tamara said, sighing in frustration. "I'll have to shoot you. Not fatally, just a flesh wound to get out of work."

"NO!"

"Sam, quit being a baby. We need your help to save Ty."

"Well if you can just keep quiet for a minute, I can tell you that my tour was up before this mission. Senator Stevens asked me personally if I would stay on until after her visit. My CO has me shipping out as soon as I land. I'll be in Athens in just under six hours, and I'll meet you at the Hilton, but not before I take a long hot shower. Now get out of here."

Tamara leaned over and hugged her best friend, then activated her EVA belt and floated out of the moving helicopter, making sure to secure the hatch behind her. Orion and the invisible ship were flying next to them, waiting to retrieve her.

CHAPTER 18

"Oh baby girl, I was so worried when you didn't return home last night." The voice of Tamara's anxious mother cut through the poor cell reception.

"Mama, I'm fine. I met a friend and talked about Ty. We're going to Houston; he has contacts at NASA Mission Control, so we'll be able to find out more information about what's going on." She felt a twinge of guilt over the little white lie.

"Did you hear that there was a fight down at the Pier? That is a dangerous bar. You didn't go there, did you?"

"I met my friend there, but it was crowded and we couldn't get in, so we went to that new Cajun place in the French quarter," she lied, feeling guiltier than ever but knowing that her mother would not understand the truth. She was having enough trouble understanding it herself. She was just beginning to really grasp the truth about Orion, and accept the responsibilities of knowing about him, and the mysteries surrounding him.

"Will you be home tonight, child?" Her mother's voice reverberated through the little cell phone's speaker, interrupting her internal struggle.

"No I won't. We're actually flying to Houston right now." Guilt surged through her now, as the lies accumulated.

"Oh my ... and they let you use your phone on the plane?"

"Yes, it's a private jet. I have to go now, Mama. Love you."

"I love you too, dear; be careful."

"Sure, I'll be careful," she whispered to herself, as the connection terminated. *After all, I nearly died from being stabbed, was in a gun fight with terrorists, and now I'm planning to go to the moon. I'm careful,* she thought, staring out into the clear waters as she sat on a white sandy beach near Athens, Greece. *Right.* She wiped away a tear that had formed.

"I love you, Ty," she said, looking up at the sky. "Am I doing the right thing? My friends may get hurt. Orion and his technology might get discovered. Could the world handle the knowledge of his existence? Talk to me, Ty!" She wiped away another tear, as she battled her inner conflict. "Are you worth it?" Curling up on the beach, she fell into a deep sleep—due in part to her collapsing adrenaline rush—while an invisible drone watched over her protectively.

"Tamara wake up, I brought us some food." Orion gently shook his friend, sleeping on the beach.

Damn, it's not a dream. How long was I out and when was the last time I had a good night's sleep? She rubbed the sleep from her eyes and sat up.

"Thanks Orion, wait ... is this like the weird food I had on your ship?"

"No it is not. It is called souvlaki, with a yogurt-based sauce called tzatziki. This food comes served on wooden skewers. I also got you a salad with goat cheese and black olives. Apparently it is a local dish and quite tasty."

"Orion, you have a strange sense of humor. They're called 'kabobs'. For a guy who has been around as long as you have, I'm surprised you never tried them. You should teach your ship how to make them." Tamara laughed as she was handed a Styrofoam container of the popular Greek fast food.

"That is a wonderful idea. I believe I will."

"Hey, where did you get them? I thought you said that this was an isolated cove with no beach access?" She started eating, enjoying every mouthful.

"I used my EVA belt and took a 'walk' into town. Friendly and interesting people. They love to talk about their history. It gave me an opportunity to practice my Greek. I also bought us a change of clothes. What do you think of these?" he asked, retrieving a couple of shirts in the traditional blue and white Greek colors.

"I hope no one spotted you on your 'walk'."

"Thank you for your concern, but I used the stealth mode. I materialized in an empty dressing room. That is where I purchased the shirts."

Silence fell between them as they devoured the delicious meal, enjoying the view and each other's quiet company.

When the last morsels had been polished off, Tamara inhaled a deep breath and let it out slow, smiling at her friend. "That was wonderful; thanks for the food. I didn't think I was hungry, but I guess I was." She stood and stretched, feeling refreshed.

"Orion, do the crystals help combat fatigue or hunger?"

"I am not sure, but I have gone weeks without food or sleep."

"Oh yeah? What were you doing?" Tamara inquired.

"Researching something on the internet."

"You do know that you can't always believe what you read on the internet, right? Besides its not healthy for you."

He nodded calmly, standing up and brushing sand from his clothes and gathering up the mess from their meal. "In the early years, it was called ARCNET. Universities and some government departments used it to share information. With my technology, I easily connected with the new network and teamed up with early programmers, giving them the base code that built the backbone. Now I have full access to what is now referred to as the 'world-wide web'."

"Wow, really? But still, like I said, you can't trust the crap out there." Holding her new clothes, she started to walk back towards the invisible ship, nestled up against the rocky bluff overlooking one of the many fingers of the Aegean Sea.

"Tamara, what you, as a normal user, sees on the web is the proverbial tip of the iceberg." He followed casually behind her. "There are many layers that most people do not know exist. It was in one of these deep layers that I was making a code adjustment ... to improve efficiency." He said this with a quirky grin, walking up beside her with the gathered-up food containers.

"I forget that you are really old," she joked, as they approached the ship.

He responded with a rarely heard chuckle. "I would like to think of it is as experienced."

"No Orion, not experienced. Let's go with wise." She laughed, receiving another big grin from her friend, who touched the outer skin of the invisible ship and activated the bluish oval portal so they could enter.

Following him through the lighted entrance, without any of the fear and hesitation she'd felt when she first stepped through a similar door back on the big ship, she watched him touch a panel near the back of the ship. A compartment opened up, into which he deposited the trash.

"Is that the garbage disposal?" she asked curiously.

"Yes, I suppose you could call it that, but it is more like a feeding chute."

"I forget sometimes that this thing is alive. Is there a shower in here?" she asked, looking around. "Some place I can get cleaned up?"

"Oh yes, but it is not a water shower like you are familiar with. It is a shower of light particles that scrub your skin. When you are ready, stand in that alcove and place your hands on the walls, like this." He demonstrated.

"I assume I have to remove my clothes?"

"Yes of course, and if there is anything you want cleaned, place them in here." He showed her what looked like a large thin drawer. "All biological residues will be removed, leaving it sanitized and fresh. I will leave you, to give you privacy."

He opened another drawer and retrieved a pair of worn shorts. Walking back to the water's edge, Orion changed into his swim shorts and dove into the cool clear waters. He enjoyed the way the water felt on his skin as he immersed himself. He reflected on the fact that it was only recently that he was able to do this. Prior to meeting Sam and Simon, he had been terrified of the water, even though his home was surrounded by it. He was forever indebted to them for showing him how to swim.

He swam for a while, occasionally diving down the four meters to the bottom to scare a crab. He was amazed at his lung capacity, and his ability to hold his breath. He would discuss this with Simon, and between the two of them, they would determine if this was a result of his hybrid DNA.

Getting out of the water, he saw Tamara standing and holding a towel, which she tossed to him.

"That was an amazing shower. I didn't think I would like it, but now I want one."

"I agree; it is refreshing."

"Okay buddy, throw some clothes on and let's get Sam; the moon is waiting and so is my sweetheart."

The two departed for the hotel in the sleek alien craft.

CHAPTER 19

Lieutenant Samantha Harding slept soundly on the flight to Athens. Senator Stevens had arranged for the young helicopter pilot to accompany her on the private jet. Stevens, from a wealthy mining family in Oregon, was still in her first year of a six-year term. She had been elected on her stand for women's equality, not only in the workplace but also the household. The Middle East was a hot-bed of women's rights issues, and was where she planned to launch her global campaign. Lieutenant Harding stood out because of her accomplishments, and was an ideal candidate to represent the face of the senator's movement. Sam had little interest in politics, and even less in the public spotlight, but was willing to accept the free ride in luxury and listen to the offer.

When they landed at Athens International, Sam informed the senator that she would not be accompanying her on the rest of the circuit to Turkey and Syria, but thanked her for the ride and the offer.

"I could use a woman like you on my team," the senator said, graciously. "I know you said you were through with the military and just wanted to sit on a beach and enjoy the peace and quiet, sipping on a margarita, but Sam ... that's not you. You won't be happy unless you're flying around in the clouds on some dangerous mission. Uncle Sam is not done with you yet. Sleep on my offer; take a few months, and when you finally get stateside, give me a call."

The Hilton Hotel lobby was very modern, yet still captured the classic feel of ancient Greece. It was good to be back in civilization, and what better place than the birthplace of civilization and democracy? As she waited for her room to be ready, Sam sat at the outdoor café and enjoyed a strong cup of American coffee. She was lost in thought, thinking about her life, her father (the general), the military family she felt safe with, and her brother (Simon) and her feeling towards him. She thought about Orion, and what he'd said about her DNA. Apparently, it was not like a normal human's double helix, nor like his alien hybrid's triple, but rather something stranger—more alien. It was a five-strand helix. What did it all mean?

"Lieutenant, ma'am, your room is ready," said the young women from the front desk, interrupting her thoughts. *Why can't I be more like that girl,* she thought, *carefree and oblivious to the world's problems.*

One of the reasons she liked this hotel was that it was a favorite stop-over for military personnel, resting and relaxing before they returned home—a party place to detoxify from the poisons of war. It also had one of the best showers in the world, with twelve hot jets, blasting at her from all directions, numbing her senses and washing her problems away.

The last and best reason for staying at the Hilton was the bed. The barracks had okay mattresses, but the Hilton had mattresses fit for a princess. *This princess still has two more hours before Tamara's going to start calling, and I'm going to make the most of it.*

The piano riff started in C and then a C-major chord progression repeated. The soft, lilting voice of John Lennon filled the room, singing "Imagine", one of Sam's all-time favorite songs. She savored the lyrics and melody for a long moment before registering its relevance and cursing.

She rolled over in the king-sized bed, and growling, reached for her phone on the nightstand.

"Ugh, Tamara, give me five more minutes. Please!" Shutting off the music alarm, she read her friend's text.

'Orion and I are on the roof. All clear, see you ASAP.'

Sam sighed and texted back:

'I'll be there in 15.'

Jumping into the shower again, with one nozzle active, she quickly washed away the sleep, wondering when she would enjoy such elegance again.

She ran a comb through her blonde hair and put it into a ponytail, then slipped on a pair of simple black slacks and a taupe blouse. She picked up her only carry-on bag: a green military-issued duffel. The rest of her belongings were to be shipped from the base in Kabul to an address in the Bahamas. Having made arrangements for express checkout with Michelle at the front desk, she dropped the key card on the dresser and headed for the stairs.

Roof access was from the fifteenth floor. Quietly Sam opened the door marked 'Employees Only' in both Greek and English. The roof housed the normal heating and ventilating utilities, as well as elevator-lift motors. The roof was also a poor man's lounge for off-duty employees. A worn table and chairs, as well as faded pool lounge chairs, were scattered around so that employees could enjoy a quiet lunch while still enjoying the Grecian sun and the Athens skyline. Sam had discovered this secret retreat when she befriended a bartender a year prior.

Looking around, she almost missed her friend Tamara, lying on a lounger. Her black tights, blue top, and dark skin made her almost invisible in the early twilight. Orion was easy to spot, wearing baggy shorts and a floral shirt, as well as a big silly grin.

"I should have asked for another few hours; I'm exhausted. You didn't by chance get me a coffee, did you?"

Tamara laughed, turning to Orion who was walking towards them carrying a large cup of coffee from the restaurant. "I told you that would be the first thing she'd ask for."

"Am I that predicable?"

"Yep." She grinned at her friend. "So what's it like being a free woman? No more flying gunships!"

"Not sure. I *am* going to miss flying those cool helicopters and the missions, but I'm not going to miss the shooting and the bloodshed," she replied between sips of the brew. "You know what I'm talking about; that's the reason you got out."

"I hear you, girl. But the Coast Guard still has guns."

"If I may interrupt this emotional bonding of sisters in arms," Orion said calmly, "may I suggest we leave Athens and talk to Simon?"

"Yes, good idea. Where are you hiding that beautiful space ship of yours?" Sam looked around, just as the craft shimmered into view between an AC compressor and the roof edge.

"There you are, my girl. Don't you look lovely?" Sam swooned as she ran up to hug the ship. Slowly, she ran her fingers over the sleek surface, the skin of which rippled with little goose bumps as the shiny black surface darkened and then shone brighter, as if happy to see the human.

"Wow, it never did that with me?" Orion and Tamara said in unison.

"It likes me," Sam said simply, gently rubbing the cool skin.

"Yes well ..." Orion watched the display of affection and felt the need to fill the silence that followed. "This is one of the short-range ships my father and uncles used. It will get us to the moon, if that is the plan we decide on."

Sam traced her fingernail around an oval patch on the vessel's outer shell, and a glowing blue hatch appeared, allowing them access to the interior.

"How'd she do that?" Tamara asked a dumbfounded Orion.

"Sam has a gift for my technology." Orion chuckled, following the girls through the portal.

"As you can see, it offers us comfort for long trips," Tamara said.

"How fast can it go?" Sam asked Orion, as she sat in the form-fitting command chair.

"It can travel at a half of one percent of the speed of light."

"Sorry, I'm not Simon; how fast is that?"

"Don't they teach that at the Air Force? Speed of light is 1,800 million kilometers per hour; therefore a half of a percent is 540,000 kph. Since the moon's current distance is 384,400 km, at maximum speed we could be at the moon in about forty-five minutes. Is that fast enough?"

"Damn straight. That's fast," Sam said, stating the obvious, "but will we be okay? I mean, that's some serious G-forces?"

"Sam, we will not feel the forces against us. It was designed for that purpose, but … I do not believe it has achieved those speeds before. I certainly would not want to control it at that speed."

"I want to take this baby out for a test drive. How do I drive it?"

"Don't you think we should lift off before someone comes out on the roof?" Tamara asked.

"There is no need for concern, Tamara. I programmed it to automatically fly us out on a pre-planned route, as soon as the hatch was closed. We are now at the bottom of the Mediterranean Sea."

"Can we see that?" Sam asked. The vessel became transparent before she'd even finished speaking.

"As I was about to say, you control it with your thoughts, like the EVA belts. I am not that good at it, but Tamara is better. This vessel is similar to the ship that is my home at the bottom of the Caribbean; both are living creatures with augmentations of technology. You must create a bond with it, and I would conclude that you have accomplished just that."

"I didn't do too badly, did I?" Tamera asked, moping.

"No, Tamara, you and I managed an adequate attempt at flying, but Sam has created a symbiotic bond with the ship that we were not able to do. What we had to do with manual controls, Sam is able to do with her thoughts."

"That's not fair; I could do that with more time."

"Sam and Simon both have the DNA in them to control our technology; I do not believe you possess that ability to bond with it. Do not feel bad about it, Tamara. I have the gene and the ship will not accept me." As Orion spoke, the vessel creature slowly moved forward under Sam's mental guidance.

She changed the internal illumination level to full brightness, then returned it to the original setting and stopped the vessel.

"The creature obviously likes you and responses instantly to your thoughts. With me it was sluggish," Orion complained.

"I think the creature is female and we gals stick together." Sam grinned as the interior took on a curvier, more feminine style. Interior edges became softer and smoother. The control chair changed from a utilitarian gray to a dusty pink, as did the control station.

"Are you doing this?" Tamara asked.

"I'm not sure ... maybe."

Over the next hour, Sam experimented with underwater 'flying' and soon the creature could anticipate her thoughts. Little colored circles appeared around them, similar to the 3D display Orion wore as a wristband.

"The black circles with a line through them are inert objects, that are not natural and yet pose no threat."

"Oh, like sunken ships."

"Yes, green are biological, and the yellow circles are objects in the water that were made on this planet."

"So the blue circles are above the water," Sam added learning the symbols quickly.

Tamara touched a blue circle and a display formed beside it, identifying it as a plane and registering its speed.

"Orion, why is the display in English?" Tamara asked

"The creature has picked up on the common language being used around it."

"Okay, let's go and rescue my Ty," Tamara said, getting impatient.

"We cannot just show up and bring them back," Orion said. "There will be too many questions that we cannot explain without exposing my existence and this technology. I am sorry Tamara, but we need a plan."

"T, you know he's right. We need a plan." She turned to Orion. "Is there anything on board your big ship that we need?"

"Possibly, but let us first meet with Simon."

Breaking the ocean surface somewhere west of the Gibraltar Strait, Sam expertly flew her new creature friend in the direction of Scotland. She varied her altitude and speed, while maintaining stealth mode. It would be complicated, if not impossible, to explain a stingray-shaped craft flying faster than the most advanced military jet. Most likely, if they were seen, it would be labeled a UFO, which is exactly what it was.

"How do we contact him," Tamara asked, "if there is no cell signal in his area?"

"I have tried using our inside voice," Sam said, "but have been unable to reach him. Truth be told, I have been unable to feel his presence for some time now."

Orion smiled. "Leave that with me."

CHAPTER 20

Simon sat at the table outside, drinking coffee and soaking up the scenery. He had thoroughly enjoyed the delicious breakfast prepared by the house chef. The old mute he'd met earlier, whom everyone referred to as Pa, had been taken back to his room by the nurse. The mental images he had pushed into Simon's head must have weakened the elderly guest. The housekeeper, the woman who ran the estate now that his mother had died, was going to meet with him. Lost in thought, he didn't hear her approaching.

"Good morning, Simon; I trust breakfast was to your liking?"

The elderly schoolmarm-looking woman had gray hair pulled back into a tight bun. The wrinkles on her face, neck, and hands showed her age. She wore a conservative black dress, befitting her position and advanced years and successfully hiding any curves she may have had.

"Yes, quite wonderful," he said. Standing up, he pointed to the opposite chair. "Please join me." Despite her stern appearance and ridged mannerisms, there was something likable about her. He thought she seemed familiar, as though he had met her someplace else. Her voice was husky, lacking the higher vocal tones of youth, yet he could imagine a light feminine laugh accompanied by a song in her voice. The more he studied her face, the more he realized that her nose and eyes were similar to his sister's. That must have been why she looked so familiar.

The woman sat there quietly, waiting for the young man to speak first.

"Do I know you?" he finally gave in and asked.

"That depends. Why are you here?"

"I'm here because my mother left her two children a letter saying that this land, this estate, would explain everything. I also want to know why she was aloof with me and why she abandoned her daughter. I'm here because Sam is not as forgiving as I am. So … do you have answers for me or is there someone else who can help?"

"I see. Do you hold hostility towards your mother?"

"A little, yes."

"What would you say to her if you could?"

"I would want answers. I'm not concerned about her relationship with my father, or how they separated. That is none of my business. Why she abandoned Sam, however, would be another question entirely. I also would want to know who she really was. I mean, I knew her my whole life and didn't know she had this beautiful land. She must have had some money."

The housekeeper smiled sheepishly at him. "I do suppose there were some things she kept from you."

He was about to ask for details about those secrets, when his cell phone beeped, indicating a message from Orion.

"Excuse me."

> *'Can you get away to a secluded area where we can talk?'*
>
> *'Not really, why?'*
>
> *'It is important. I'm above the grounds near the old ruins. Meet me there quickly. Sam and Tamara are with me.'*

"That was my friends. They want to meet me."

"Before you leave, maybe the easiest way to explain your mother is to show you." Touching a hidden belt, she slowly shimmered and altered her image, becoming a beautiful forty-something, woman wearing a trendy wool tartan skirt and a mauve turtleneck sweater, which complimented the gingham colors. The now-beautiful woman, sitting in front of him without disguise—the woman whom he thought looked so much like his twin sister, Samantha—was his mother.

Wide-eyed and in shock, he said nothing, unable to form a cohesive thought. *What? How? Why?*

She placed her hand on his, and held it as a mother would to console her child. It was an all-too familiar gesture. Fear and anger slowly ebbed, being replaced with comfort and trust.

"So you faked your death?"

She nodded.

"Why? What could possibly be happening in your life that you would need to disappear like that?" His phone beeped again.

"Mother, I have so many questions that I don't even know where to begin." He was perplexed and drawn in two directions. His emotions begged him to stay and learn the truth, but his curiosity about Sam and Orion's presence won out. "Mom, it is good to have you back, but I have to take off for a bit. I will explain later. It's good to see you." He rose from his seat.

Before she could respond, a scruffy red-haired man with an unkempt red beard entered the patio area.

"Stay. Sit. What your mother has to say concerns everyone on the orbiter as well," Mac said, with barely a hint of an accent. "Have them land over there." The old Scotsman pointed authoritatively to the open field in front of their sitting area. "No need to walk all the way to the ruins."

As Simon texted them the message, Mac turned towards Simon's mother. "Maybe the staff could bring out a fresh pot of coffee?"

Simon stared at his longtime companion, and for the first time in his life, wondered who he was. He trusted Mac as much, if not more, than he trusted his own mother. Whatever was going on, he knew it would be better if Sam, Tamara, and Orion were with him. Dazed and mystified as he was, he knew that all the questions he'd had in his life were about to be answered. The black crystals with the strange radiation, Orion, his alien-technology creatures, the hallucination he had with the strange tongue-less man earlier that day … all of it would hopefully soon make sense. He looked at his old Scottish friend, and now wondered if he was really even Scottish, or a friend. His dead mother was still alive, and Mac had clearly known. Yes, he would get answers.

Mac and his mother looked up into the sky and waved the invisible ship down.

Sam exited the craft first and embraced her brother. "Simon? You told Mac and this woman about us?"

"No, they told me … and this woman is our mother, Lynda. She was about to explain everything when Orion texted." Orion and Tamara joined the group, just as confused as Sam.

"Good to see all the family together?" the Scotsman asked, directing his words primarily to Lynda.

"Yes it is. Now shall we sit and enjoy a coffee or would you prefer something stronger?"

Simon was the first to answer. "Well when in Scotland drink like a Scotsman. I'll have a scotch." Sam and Tamara both asked for rum and coke.

"Is scotch like tequila?" Orion inquired.

"No it's better," Lynda answered, taking his hand.

"I am sure I will regret this decision. Okay I will have scotch."

Tamara joined in. "What the heck, me too."

Mac left the group and returned with his favorite single malt and a tray of glasses. With sips taken and tensions reduced, Mac addressed the group.

"First, let me welcome you all to the family estate. *Our* family estate. I am one of three travelers that came to this planet long ago, on a mission to mine a rare meteor that impacted the earth a few million years ago. But this you know. I had a daughter with my human mate. That daughter, 'LinUna', is your mother, whom you call Lynda Ferguson. Orion—or should I call you 'Little One'—knows her as his cousin." Mac looked calmly at Orion and the rest of his audience. Smiles started to appear and thoughts and memories slowly surfaced.

"Orion told us his story," Sam jumped in, directing her comments to her estranged mother, "and how he was in a ship when the mine exploded; he thought you had died in the accident."

"I was trapped and hurt badly," Lynda said matter-of-factly. "A mining drone found me, and while it had the healing beam active on me, the tunnel roof collapsed, trapping us both. With fresh air cut off, and both of us hurt, it locked us both in a stasis bubble. I don't know when, but some time later, we freed ourselves and I headed for the coast with my drone. About this time, the Spanish came to Guatemala and overran the Mayans. I was captured before I could give instructions to the drone. I was put to work as a slave and sold three times before I was fifteen. I was eventually sold to a Viking captain who bought me to be his daughter. We sailed to Scotland, where he and his wife raised me. This is the original property." Lynda concluded her story with her palms up and arms out stretched, indicated their surroundings.

"Lovely story," Sam remarked bitterly. "Now fast forward nine hundred years to when you abandoned me."

"Don't take that kind of tone with you mother!" Mac commanded.

"Oh don't get me started with you!" Sam said angrily berating him. "My so-called uncle Mac, and me, your 'wee lass'. You two have been lying to us since ... well, since forever."

"Samantha—I mean Sam," Lynda interrupted, "it's not what it seems. You were never abandoned."

Sam gave her a look that said, "Hell yes, I was!" better than anything she could have said with words. Simon came up beside her and hugged her. *'Calm down Sam,'* he whispered in their special inner voice. *'This is not helping.'*

"Why did you not try to find me?" Orion asked his cousin and uncle, with questions of his own to unravel.

"I did, but you will recall that I was not at the mines. I was in the asteroid belt near Mars, scanning for more of the crystal ore. When I got back, everything was either destroyed or overrun by the Spanish. I thought my travel companions were either dead or had left Earth without me. I salvaged all the processed crystals I could find, but I could not get a reading on the big ore ship or the smaller passenger vessel that you were on. That was one of the reasons why I moved to the Bahamas. I knew you were out there somewhere, because I would get the occasional sensor reading of a drone in the area. Your father programmed the ship so that even our own technology wouldn't discover it. He feared that our planet would send more ships to take the crystals and arrest us. If they knew we had children with the locals, they probably would have had you killed and destroyed anything we had touched. 'Contamination cleansing' is what it was called."

"So that's what we are?" Sam shouted in anger. "A contamination?"

"No honey, far from it," the matriarch tried to explain, but her words fell on deaf ears.

"This is a lovely family reunion," Tamara interrupted, "but where the hell do I fit into this alien jumble?"

"You are my grand-daughter," Lynda said straightforwardly, looking affectionately at the spunky brunette, and getting blank stares from the young people in return. "Simon and Sam are not my only children, you know."

"I never met my father," Tamara said. "Who is he? Can I see him?"

"Yes, but not now. He is out of town on business. I will make arrangements."

Mac looked at the group. "So, was there a reason you came here to get Simon?"

"Oh my god, I'm so sorry, T," Sam said. "We almost forgot in all the confusion. We have to rescue her fiancé. He is one of the NASA astronauts in trouble."

"Do you have a plan?" Mac asked.

In light of this greater purpose, the rest of the discussions were tabled for the moment. All agreed that they couldn't just fly up to the moon, looking the way they did, in an alien spaceship. The proof of extraterrestrials might blow the minds of the average human, but the existence of alien hybrids living on earth, with advanced alien technology, would likely trigger a massive manhunt that would rival any blockbuster alien movie. If they were to be discovered in space, it would be better they were mistaken for true aliens. Mac and Lynda, assuming the role of mentors, strongly suggested that the team keep their human identities a secret, and demonstrated how the EVA belts could create a mask, projecting a false image as a byproduct of the protective force field, a feature that they had discovered when they projected the ghost images earlier.

They toyed with the idea of showing the humans a traditional movie alien, with gray skin, big head, and black oval eyes, but this guise was voted down. The gray alien persona held too many negative connotations. Instead they would stretch the truth a bit and present themselves as their true blood ancestors: Mac's people, from the eighth planet around the star Alnilam, in the Orion constellation, with their large bright green eyes and long green-toned hair. They worked on their disguises for a long time, finally altering the skin color to pale white and making the head slightly larger and elongated enough to ensure that Tamara's fiancé would never recognize her.

"What should we wear?" Tamara asked the group.

"Yeah," Sam said. "Whatever we choose can't look like it came from Earth. What did you guys wear when you first came here?"

"Let me think," Mac said. "That was a long time ago." After a long pause, he shook his head uncertainly. "We just had on a white bio-coating. It gave us some protection and kept our bodies clean and warm. It was actually very helpful when we went into the mines."

"I do not believe my ship could create such coatings," Orion stated.

"Come with me lad, and I'll show you. There is still a lot you need to know about these ships, particularly in the personal grooming area." Mac and Orion went to the ship, returning later with Orion coated from neck to toes in a white, futuristic, latex-like polymer.

"OH MY GAWD!" Sam exclaimed. "We can't wear that! It's way too revealing."

"Can you make the coating thicker," Tamara asked. "Less skin-like?"

"We can, but it would be less flexible and restrict movement," Mac answered, scratching his head.

"What if you made it thicker in the chest area," Lynda suggested, maternally protective of the girls, "down the front and around their hips?"

Orion nodded. "I *would* like to see if you could give me some built-in boxers." This prompted a round of laughter from the group.

Mac took the group back to the ship, and with Lynda's help, reconfigured the skin-tight coating to be more modest in certain areas, by adding additional layers that would hang like cloth.

"What about a toga wrap?" Lynda offered.

"Too boring," Sam and Tamara replied in unison.

"Let me check the image archive from the home planet." Seconds later, 3D images of women's clothing floated in the air above Mac's arm bracelet.

"I like that one," Lynda exclaimed, pointing at a sleek over-the-shoulder wrap.

"They look like something a teenager would wear," Tamara said, shaking her head.

"What about this one?" Sam interrupted, pointing to an elegant version. The material covered one shoulder and crossed the upper bodice, before sweeping down to the thigh on the opposite side.

Tamara liked it. "That's kind of sexy-looking, without being too revealing."

"I agree. It's cute." Lynda expanded the image. "I wish I could still pull that look off."

"It looks perfect and futuristic. I'll take one in my size."

The guys decided on a simple boxer-brief design built into their coating. Fashion, function, and modesty united to create a futuristic alien look.

"Uncle Mac, how did the women of your planet—I mean *our* planet—wear their hair?" Sam asked, anxiously wanting to complete her look, as she admired her new outfit.

"Women of your age tended to wear their hair long, about to the middle of the back. They also varied the hair color, similar to what girls do here, but wilder, with intricate braiding." He smiled, pleased that his favorite granddaughter had embraced his culture. Using his arm bracelet again, he projected various images of hairstyles.

Mac taught the group some words from his native language, which they could intersperse with English to maintain the ruse—simple words that were easy for the team to pronounce, and within the vocal and audible range of humans. They picked up the language phonics quickly, and well enough to fool the astronauts and anyone else who might be listening.

After a long brainstorming session, they worked out the fake back story for their small group of alien rescuers. A teacher, Professor Noi Ro (Orion spelled backwards) and his three students, Nom Iz (Simon), Ma Z (Sam), and Aram At (Tamara), were on a senior field trip in planetary archaeology, in a large school ship that traveled the galaxy, and had been dropped off in this solar system for a semester of field studies. Their assignment was to explore the outer planets, avoiding contact with indigenous life if any was discovered. The principle protocol was to keep away from the third planet, which had a thriving, sentient space-active civilization that was prone to violence, but when the distress signal went out from the moon, the group felt they had to attempt a rescue.

"I still don't understand why you left me," Sam asked as Lynda braided her fake alien hair. She was struggling to accept her maternal attention and be civil for the sake of the mission, and politeness, but a lifetime of resentment is not easy to erase.

"Sam, dear, I was always with you, just not part of your life. It's complicated and you and Simon deserve an explanation. I know that. I promise you, once this rescue mission is over, we will have a heart-to-heart talk." Lynda hugged her daughter for the first time since she was a baby, as tears rolled down her cheek.

After a special dinner of Chef Annie's famous butter chicken, they departed into a moonless night, disguised as extraterrestrials on an alien ship, a disguise that was far more fact than fiction.

Engaging stealth mode, making them invisible to both radar and star gazers, Sam coaxed the vessel to sub-light speed, easily achieving escape velocity within seconds and breaking free of Earth's gravity. Fear and excitement consumed them all, as they approached the unknown.

CHAPTER 21

The sleek craft approached the crater and set down fifty meters from the Odin space crafts.

"Good lord!" Booker shouted out to the crew. "Guys get over here! You are not going to believe this!"

"What is it, Ty?" Worthy asked.

"I'm not sure," he replied, still staring out the window, "but I think we have company. Let's hope they're friendly!"

The flight engineer assisted the pilot to another port window, while Pierce left the unconscious sergeant, and found another one to look from.

"That doesn't look like NASA sent it," Worthy said quietly, to whoever was listening, "or Earth either for that matter?"

"Holy Crap!" Van der Hoose exclaimed. "Is that what I think it is?"

Booker nodded. "It's outside the camera range; cut the public feed and get Houston."

Pierce just stared out the window, mesmerized by the black alien ship.

George Messer, on CAPCON, was already trying to re-establish a communication link after the public feed was cut.

"CAPCON Messer here; what's happening up there?" he asked, staring at a blank screen that just moments before had presented a live panoramic view of the moon, with the earth on the horizon and the American and Canadian flags standing proudly together in the open area in front of *Endurance*.

"Messer, switch to secure COM," Booker requested. Once that was done, he smiled and shook his head. "Take a deep breath, and have a seat. Watch as I pan the camera."

A few hundred people in Mission Control watched as the alien ship came into view. Controlled panic took over the room. Wide eyes stared at the big screen, witnessing an event that was a first for mankind.

The signal was put through to the White House, marked ULTRA TOP SECRET: FIRST CONTACT PROTOCOL.

"Have they declared their intent?" Messer asked nervously.

"No, it just came in slow and set down a safe distance from us. There has been no activity since."

Slowly a bluish white opening started to appear on the side of the large black craft. The opening grew, and a glowing white humanoid shape exited the vessel. It was only a bright profile, without detail. It made no contact with the surface. Instead, it hovered just above it. Orion slowly floated to the flag and stood facing the NASA space craft, with his arms casually at his side, which he hoped would be taken as a universal gesture for neutrality.

"What's it waiting for?" Booker asked quietly, as the others watched in amazement.

Orion activated his arm bracelet, summoning a drone and initiating a pre-programmed command. A smaller version of the mother ship exited from its back and hovered closer, only inches above the surface, stopping every few seconds, until it moved a few feet away and the name 'BOOKER' was revealed, etched into the moon's soil. The drone continued its work for another few seconds, stopped, and then slid out of the way, revealing its next word: 'HELP'.

"Booker help," Messer read out loud.

"Houston, you getting this?" Booker asked.

"Oh yeah. Do you think it flew all this way for your help?" Messer asked. "Or is it offering? Does the situation look hostile? Are you in danger?"

"Negative. I don't see any signs of weapons ... but who knows what they have? If they wanted us dead, or off *their* moon, I don't think they would have waited for us to cut the feed, let alone attempt to communicate with us." Booker was still trying to process everything. "Either way, Messer, I don't know what could you do to help us from there."

"True enough. Well, it's your call, Commander. We are now on FIRST CONTACT PROTOCOL. Stay sharp."

The PROTOCOL, created by the Truman administration shortly after the Roswell incident of 1947, and updated by every president that followed, was a long-winded legal document written by stuffy-shirt lawyers and politicians. In short, it stated that, if contact were ever made with extraterrestrials, "*the US representatives are to show superiority and not weakness. Do not attack unless in imminent danger. Do not divulge any information about yourself, your vessel, your nation, or your planet. Gather as much data as possible, either visually or electronically, of the alien and its vessel. Above all, show no FEAR.*"

Every astronaut, starting with Alan Shepard and the first Mercury flight in 1961, memorized the PROTOCOL and hoped they would never have a need to exercise it.

Booker and Pierce donned their suits and exited the space ship. Today they were not just astronauts representing Canada and the US but also humans representing Earth.

"Stand by Pierce, I'm going to make contact alone," the commander announced. Earlier Booker had Pierce remove the Beretta M9 from Sergeant Butcher and secure it on his own suit.

"Please don't let anything happen to him, Jon," Worthy whispered nervously.

"I have him covered, Shirley ma'am," he replied, removing the weapon from its utility pocket and holding it with the muzzle pointing down. He thought of the last line of the Protocol document: 'Show no fear.' He was sweating and nervous. He was either the first line of defense or the one who would start an intergalactic war. 'Show no fear.'

Never in his wildest dreams could Commander Booker have imagined walking up to an alien on the moon. Even walking on the moon had never been a dream of his.

Keep calm. Show no fear. He recited this over and over again in his head. He wanted to believe that the aliens could not access his bio readings; if they did, and interpreted it correctly, they would learn that fear was foremost in his thoughts. He was about to become the first man to contact a living alien. Not a hoax.

He held his hand up as a greeting. "Hello." No response.

He extended his hand to touch the humanoid's hand, initiating a handshake.

Orion purposely acted hesitant before completing the greeting.

The American and Canadian flags stood proudly beside human and alien, silent witnesses to the exchange—a greeting of friendship on the moon, with a message of peace etched into the ground and the earth staring back from the horizon.

"I want a copy of that picture!" the president of the United States said to one of his advisers, gathered in the oval office and watching the secure feed. "It's a keeper!" The prime minister of Canada was there beside him, visiting the White House in order to discuss the upcoming trilateral trade deal with Mexico, or so the media believed. As events unfolded, they both watched with youthful enthusiasm.

Orion touched more buttons on his arm band, and the bluish white light enveloped the commander. The bio signal for Booker went off line. Pierce started to run towards them, aiming his gun at the alien target. The drone that was hovering peacefully nearby suddenly reared up to protect its master. Alarms instantly started going off on the ship and at Houston's Mission Control, as the commander's life signals were snuffed out.

In the cocoon of Orion's force field, the commander was still shaking the tall alien's hand and unaware of what his crew perceived as danger.

"I am Commander Booker. Do you understand me? Do you speak?" he spoke carefully, enunciating each word slowly.

"Yes, we speak human. My name is Professor Noi Ro. My students and I offer assistance. Your communication devices will not penetrate this protective shield; I will release you from it. Inform your crew that you are not harmed." Orion said all this calmly, as rehearsed. He added just enough hesitation to his speech pattern to imply that English was a recently learned language.

When the force field was released, Booker turned and faced his crew and the cameras, raising his hands slightly in what he hoped was a reassuring gesture.

"I'm good everyone. Everything's cool. We were just talking. His protective force-field blocks our signal. I'm going to continue talking with Professor Noi Ro; he and his students will help us, but there is much to talk about. So I will be out of COM for a few minutes."

The commander reached out, touched the glowing alien on the arm, and was once again enveloped. Thinking quickly, he released the arm and was instantly visible again, his bio signs clear. He hoped this would show his crew and Houston that he had control of the communication blackouts.

"Please inform your crew that we mean you no harm, and that weapons are not necessary."

Booker withdrew from the shield and advised Pierce to stand down. With the M9 safely back in its pocket, the drone took on its former peaceful posture.

Alone with Booker once more within the force-field, Orion started to speak. "I am certain you have many questions, but first ... are there any injured crew members?"

"Yes, our pilot. A female, approximately 50 of our earth years old, is conscious with a broken bone in her right arm and has suffered from decompression-like sickness. We also have a male, approximately 45, still unconscious from having too much carbon dioxide in his air mixture." Booker just realized that he had given the alien important information about the health of his crew, as well as several potential weaknesses of the species; so much for following the PROTOCOL.

"Are these injuries that threaten life?"

"No, not life-threatening now, but we do need our pilot healthy enough to get us off the moon and take us home." He made a gesture toward the blue-white planet overhead. *Damn, I broke the rules again.* "We have a mechanical failure that is preventing us from leaving. Can you assist us?"

"Yes, we can assist. I would like my students to come from our ship so that they may also help and learn."

"Sure, of course," he said, not knowing if he had any choice in the matter, as he extracted himself from the shield.

"Booker stand by, the president is being patched in," CAPCON Messer announced, as soon as COM was restored.

"Commander Booker, this is the president and the Canadian prime minister. We want to speak to the alien."

"Professor, the leaders of two of our earth nations would like to speak with you: the president of the United States and the prime minister of Canada."

Orion had not expected this. "I do not know how we can make that possible with my shield active. Perhaps after we start repairs we could attempt a dialogue. I will summon my students now." It had already been decided that he would maintain the subterfuge by speaking in the alien tongue when talking to the rest of his crew. Booker listened as strange words and sounds were transmitted to the students.

Moments later, three alien students in identical bluish-white force-fields exited the craft, and hovering above the soil, moved over to stand beside Orion. They lined up in order of height, starting with Nom Iz, then Ma Z, and Aram At. They had agreed earlier not to give Tamara access to communications, proving justified when she waltzed up to her fiancé and gave him a passionate embrace that lasted several surprising moments.

"I see they have females," Messer commented dryly on the open COM.

"And friendly too," the president added, on the same frequency.

"Let me present my students." The professor introduced each of his crew to Booker, once Aram At had withdrawn from the embrace, using their fake reversed names with just enough alien tone to make it a bit of a challenge for the human tongue to repeat. After each name, the commander broke the force-field bond and tried to repeat the name to his crew and the camera.

As he did so, there was some back chatter from Houston, asking how the females looked without the force field. Booker declined to respond.

CHAPTER 22

The professor, the student Ma Z, and Booker entered the *Endurance* to offer medical assistance to the injured. The military advisers for NASA strongly rejected the idea of aliens entering a US space ship, but were over-ruled by the president. Once on board in a pressured environment, the force-fields were lowered, revealing the camouflaged alien forms of humanoids similar to humans but with larger heads and larger eyes. Noi Ro had long, lush, dark green hair that fell halfway down his back, like it had when he'd first met his human friends. Ma Z had multi-tinted green hair in a complex five-strand braid. Without the protection of the field, she felt exposed in the crew cabin and wished they had made the crocheted cover-ups less transparent.

"This crystal will mend the bone and tissue around it," Noi Ro said softly to Worthy, as he moved the object lightly over her injured arm.

"Is it dangerous?"

"No, it is a type of radiation, but it will not harm you."

The student Ma Z went to the side of the injured male crew member and held her crystal on his chest, moving it slowly over his lungs.

"Hi, I'm Jon Pierce. Nice to meet you," he said, extending his hand, excited to be meeting an alien—an exquisite one at that. "Do you speak English?"

Ma Z paused what she was doing and thought of how she should speak.

"Yes, I know words." She emphasized this by holding her fingers apart. "≈⊃☐*ʧ~" she added in alien, unable to remember if it meant 'carpet' or 'bathroom'. It didn't matter, as she tried to come across as a shy school girl, which was a persona she'd never had. "More talk. I learn words fast."

"I am a specialist on board," Jon said. "That means I am responsible for the stuff we bring. You are quite pretty."

"Stuff. Pretty." She giggled a bit, playing the role.

'Laying it on a little thick, don't you think?' Simon internalized to her, as he listened to her thoughts.

ORION - Escape Velocity

'This is fun. He is totally flirting with me.'

With the addition of the aliens, the ship's confines were tight. Booker suggested that Van der Hoose and Pierce leave. Noi Ro suggested that there was no need for everyone to be there, including himself and Booker, but Ma Z decided to stay with Worthy.

"Did you have a long flight getting here?" Worthy asked Ma Z, who had been identified as a pilot, like herself. "You must be tired."

"Long flight from ringed planet, yes. Tired, no." Ma Z replied, stretching. What she needed was a coffee. Her caffeine levels were low, and the last one in Scotland hadn't done the trick.

"Would you like a hot beverage?" Worthy asked, only to get a strange look from the alien woman. "I was just going to make a tea for myself. Would you like to join me?" If anything, the alien's look grew more uncertain, and so Worthy took a deep breath and let it out slow.

"I'm sorry dear; you probably have no idea what I am talking about. Here, let me show you what your choices are." She explained the benefits and joys of various Earth drinks, showing her a pouch of tea bags, to which Ma Z scrunched up her nose, hoping another choice would be offered. After all, in her alien disguise, how could she possibly explain that she was craving a good hot cup of Joe. The chocolate mud drink that Orion had offered her on the flight hadn't worked. It might have had all the nutrients and electrolytes her body needed, but it was not what she wanted.

"Tea is not your drink? What about coffee?" She offered the alien a chance to smell the aromatic dark brown grounds.

In her excitement, she had to remind herself to struggle with her words. "This have a … flavor … that I would … enjoy, if hot. Thank you."

"Just give me a sec and I will have a cup brewed for you. I don't think Natalie will object if I use some of her special blend." She prepared the one-cup dispenser.

"Why is special?"

"Oh I don't think it is. She just says that because it's from her country. A small local coffee shop she calls 'Timmy's'."

As the two women drank their drinks, Ma Z kept moving the black crystal over the unconscious sergeant, stopping every so often to move the healing crystal over to Worthy's injured arm.

"This school of yours sounds interesting. Is this normal? For students to fly around the galaxy helping others?"

"Yes, it is interesting, but not normal. Excitement." Ma Z laughed, pleased that she could tell the truth.

"This outfit you are wearing, is it a fabric from your planet?"

When Worthy didn't get a response, she explained her question. "Fabric, a woven material to make clothes you can wear." She emphasized this by giving her sleeve to the alien. The hesitation from Ma Z was not because she didn't understand what the word meant but rather that she didn't know how to describe the rubbery coating she was enclosed in.

"Not fabric, like this." She held the cotton flight suit material. "It is a … a skin coat for space travel."

"Very lovely. Is it hot?" Worthy asked, touching Ma Z's arm.

"Not hot. Cold with no shield. Cold wrong word … Less cold?"

"I think you are looking for the word 'chilly'." Worthy and Ma Z laughed as they discussed the various degrees of temperature and how to describe the feelings.

***

"Your teacher tells me you are studying engineering on your planet," Van der Hoose said to the student Nom Iz outside, taking his arm and directing him to the damaged strut.

"I do not know this word, 'e-n-g-i-n-e-e-r-i-n-g'."

"Mechanical things and how they work."

"Yes, non-biological. I can help."

'Don't act like a moron,' Sam internalized to him, laughing.

As they walked, Nom Iz noticed Van der Hoose's damaged suit and the temporary taped patch.

"Yes, I ripped it. On Earth, that's what we call 'a MacGyver'. A quick fix." She laughed as she held tightly to the alien man's arm. She was both excited and scared, but would not have missed this opportunity for anything. *Who would?*

"This is the joint that is damaged. See? It is leaking hydraulic fluid. Can you fix it?"

Simon, who had worked on the same strut assembly project with this same woman five years prior, at MIT, knew exactly what the problem was but decided to confirm his beliefs. Activating his bracelet control, he set about scanning the metal object with a focused beam of energy, which displayed the results in 3D.

Van der Hoose touched the floating image at the point she saw as the failure. Simon in return expanded the image to ten times the actual size, giving detailed imagery.

"Can you show me an x-ray? An interior view?" She attempted to show the alien what an x-ray was.

He laughed internally, realizing how tough it was and the problems his sister was having.

'Told you.'

'Bite me, sis.'

"This internal join ... of the two metals ...they were connected by intense heating. It is flawed," Nom Iz stated his interpretation of the data logically.

"Yes, I see what you mean," said the human engineer. "The weld has deteriorated. Crap job."

"Yes, crap job," he mimicked, careful not to sound too natural.

She chuckled. "Can you fix the crap job?"

"No. Crap job. Replace. Need parts."

"We don't have the part up here on the moon, but we do back on Earth." She was still holding his arm. She was not sure if the tingle she was feeling inside was from his force field or something else.

"No part, I cannot fix."

"Can you temporarily repair? Like the tape on my suit."

I.JAMES FORREST

"MacGyver?"

She laughed and chuckled. "Yes, exactly."

"No. This more ... complex?" She nodded. "More complex than hole in suit. Need *&~ɔ□≈ ⏋*ŧ^& *~ɔℭ₹." He threw in some alien words, not remembering what they meant.

She dragged him over to the commander, who was in conversation with Noi Ro.

Touching his arm, the four of them were engulfed in the field and could talk.

"Sir, he says repairs are not possible. We have to get NASA to send the part up, and even with the part, it will be difficult to install it without the proper equipment."

"We can fix with part," Nom Iz explained, moving his hand back and forth between his chest and his new friend, indicating a collaborative team effort.

Booker shook his head. "They won't send a hundred-dollar part on a billion-dollar rocket." Turning to Noi Ro, he asked, "Can you pick the part up from Earth?" He pointing to his planet.

"I will discuss with my students." With that, he broke the connection of the field and walked to the side, taking his students with him.

Back inside the shield alone, they could talk easily among themselves. Simon notified Sam on the ship, using their internal voice, telling her to activate her force shield.

"They want us to fly back and get the part? We never talked about revealing ourselves to anyone other than the astronauts. I do not like the direction this is heading!" Orion said with a seriousness that the others had never heard before.

"What other option do we have?" Tamara asked.

"From the scans I took, they also can't ignite the rocket engines," Simon added.

"We cannot reveal any more of ourselves to the humans," Orion continued, voicing his concerns.

"Are you listening to yourselves?" Tamara asked. "We are not really aliens; we are just like them and they need our help. I say let's do it."

ORION - Escape Velocity

"T is right," Sam said. "She and I will go. Orion, you go make some big speech about breaking a big alien rule, blah blah blah."

"If I may remind you, we really *are* aliens living on Earth," Orion pointed out.

"Yeah, but we're hybrids. We do have human parents, so that doesn't count. Besides we, and that includes *you*, were all born as earthlings." Sam was beginning to embrace her alien side.

"Sam, listen," Simon said. "Orion's right. It will be scary down there, what with a first contact and the chance to meet real extraterrestrials. We will be in danger. Think about it, if they won't send a billion-dollar rocket with a hundred-dollar part, what makes you think they will let you leave? As an alien, you are worth much more to them than any ship."

"Good point, when you put it like that. I guess we have to get assurances that we won't be taken captive. T can stay in the ship, and if they don't let me go, I will say she will blow up the planet." They looked shocked at the suggestion. "Come on guys, think like aliens. We are supposed to be smarter than they are, with advanced technology. Let's use that."

"I'm with Sam," Tamara agreed. "We can pull this off."

"I'm going with you then," Simon added.

"No. Remember back in the Bahamas, when you wanted to sneak onto the island to take back what those pirates stole, I convinced you that feminine charms and wit were better."

"I remember. I didn't like it then and I don't like it now."

"But you know I'm right."

"Fine. Orion make the speech."

Breaking their huddle, Noi Ro and Nom Iz walked over to the commander and flight engineer and touched their arms.

"Commander Booker, it is against all our rules, against all our planetary principles to do what you are asking."

"I understand that, and appreciate what you have done, but we still need your help."

"As I was saying, our rules say not to land on your planet and definitely not to associate with inhabitants. Even now, being here, talking to you, showing our technology, could bring about punishment. There are special teams of emissaries that have been trained to make contact with people. We are not qualified for such a task."

"Professor Noi Ro, I too am unqualified to meet with your people, but I think we are doing a pretty good job, both of us."

"Yes, and I have students who wish to become future ambassadors. They argued the same sentiments. Against all my strong beliefs, I have agreed to let them go, but I will need assurances that they will not be harmed."

"I give you my word."

"You Commander Booker, I trust, but what of your people? How do I know my students will not be captured and experimented on?"

"I have to believe they wouldn't be," Booker said. "The mere fact that we know of your existence, and the fact that you're willing to risk everything to help us, says a lot about you and your people. I suggest we go to the habitat, where there is more room, and we can talk with Houston together."

"The people in charge, who wanted to speak with me earlier, I will speak with them now."

'Orion's good,' Simon internalized to Sam. *'He missed his calling as a diplomat.'*

"Yeah not bad, but I think he has played this scenario in his mind many times before.'

With the three aliens and most of the astronauts settled in the large pressurized habitat, Nom Iz suggested that Ma Z bring the rest of the crew over.

"We should go to the others. I will assist you with the injured man," Ma Z informed Worthy.

"Sorry hon, I don't have a space suit. It got damaged and it would be difficult to get Sergeant Butcher into his. Besides you don't look strong enough to carry him."

"How is your arm? Working now? No damage?" She smiled, knowing the answers.

"Yes much better; it also corrected my decompression problem. Why do you ask?"

"We go walk and get ℂ₹&^₹ℒ to carry." She smiled, because this time she was sure she said 'black thing', as she used two fingers to indicate walking.

"Really, we can do that?" Worthy felt giddy at the chance to walk on the moon without a bulky suit; doing so with this friendly young alien woman was an added bonus. For a brief moment, she thought about her own daughter and grandchildren and the story she would tell them.

Hand in hand, with a drone following and transporting the unconscious sergeant, they walked leisurely to HAB1. They found everyone around the communication station talking to CAPCON.

"Yes, we have the parts," Messer replied to their question. "It's here in Houston."

"I think they should have a more secluded and secure site," Booker said.

"Where do you suggest?"

"I wish to speak to the person you call President," Noi Ro said, interrupting.

Messer looked at his supervisor, who was following the conversation, and nodded his head while activating a second communication link to Washington.

Booker made the introduction to the men visible on the large television monitor. "Mr. President, Mr. Prime Minister, this is Professor Noi Ro." Since the first contact hours before, the men in the oval office had been briefed by all government departments on this historic event, and had been personally reviewing all COM transcripts.

"Are you the rulers of your planet?" Noi Ro had the nerve to ask.

'Ballsy asking a question like that. He does know who they are, doesn't he?' Sam internalized to Simon, sitting on the other side of the room.

'I sometimes wonder what he knows, holed up in that space ship of his.'

"Well other countries may think so, but no. I hold the position of president of the United States, leader of the most powerful country on this planet." He chuckled nervously, and smiling, he offered the microphone to the Canadian dignitary.

"I am the leader of Canada, the country in the northern part of this land mass. As our host has implied, we are just two of the many countries on this planet. It is an honor to meet you, sir."

The president politely reached for the microphone. "Professor Noi Ro, thank you for rendering aid to our people. It is great to finally have confirmation that there is life out there. I always suspected we were not alone. The scientific communities have many questions—"

"Offering assistance to another sentient species has serious consequences on our planet," Noi Ro stated calmly, cutting the president short, "if not handled properly."

"Why did you do it then?" the president asked, genuinely curious.

"Our moral principles would not allow us to ignore your pleas. We offer aid to a few individuals, not to a planet. It is the degree that we felt was justified."

"For that we are forever grateful," the prime minister offered, leaning in to the mic.

"Yes, we are very very grateful," the president agreed. "Noi Ro, I would like to extend an invitation to you and your students to come to the US, my country."

Noi Ro considered this for a moment. "Your people on this moon need a piece of your technology in order to leave. It has been asked that we send our vessel and crew to your planet to retrieve it. My concern is for their safety."

"I can assure you they will be safe; there will be no action taken against you or your crew. You have my word as the president of the United States, of the planet Earth." He added the last part impulsively, and thought he must be the first to ever use that full title.

Twenty minutes later, Noi Ro, the president, the prime minister and numerous government departments from both countries, including NASA—and against the military's objections—created a flight plan for the aliens. It was agreed by all parties that no other country, or the general public, should be aware of this historical mission of mercy. The parts were to be flown from Houston to Area 51, for retrieval by the aliens.

The professor informed them that he would not go to earth, until after he consulted with the school ship and his home planet. Because of his position at the school, his people could have him arrested for violating his planet's main directive. The crew, being students, would only be reprimanded without consequence. He and Nom Iz would remain on the moon to assist with preparing the vessel for repairs and continuing assistance. He added that he and his students would remain in this sector of the solar system, exploring the other planets, for another Earth year, and if he received permission from the school and his planet's government, he would welcome the opportunity to be part of an official first-contact meeting.

"How long will it take you to reach Earth?" a top astrophysicist asked.

Not wanting to give too much detail about the ship's capacity to the humans, Ma Z answered carefully.

"It will take two of your hours to reach the co-ordinates given."

"Can you make your vessel invisible, so people can't see it, with or without technology?"

"We have no such capabilities." They figured it was best to keep some things a secret.

"Our Deep Space Observation did not track you coming to the moon. How did you manage that?" a gentleman from the NSA asked.

"We were exploring the large ice moon around the planet with rings. The rings contain radiation particles that may have masked our approach," Nom Iz interjected, with a plausible scientific explanation.

"We can enter orbit at speed to look like a comet burning up, or enter more slow, so there is no heat trail," Ma Z added.

"Come in hot, then drop like a rock," the same astrophysicist answered.

More questions were asked over the next half hour, while Houston had the parts flown to the secret desert airbase.

When the departure time arrived, Simon and Orion gave last-minute instructions to Sam and Tamara in private, mostly about being careful and not saying much.

Before leaving, Aram At gave Booker one last long hug. Not knowing what to do, he returned the embrace, thinking of his worried fiancée back on Earth.

CHAPTER 23

There were only two stipulations that the air force would not bend on: No deviation from the flight path outlined would be tolerated, and the alien ship was to be escorted at all time while in Earth's air space. The consequences of these items not being adhered to were only implied, but it was made clear that their space craft *must not* be seen by civilians or the governments of any other nation. They were to enter the atmosphere at co-ordinates over the Pacific Ocean, exactly 200 kilometers due west of San Diego.

Assuming the pilot's seat, Sam took control of the ship again, as the creature had bonded with her. The feeling of this creature, with its size and power, was almost overwhelming. They maintained only an intermittent stealth shield, giving those who were monitoring them a signal that validated their *lack* of invisibility. With the timeline they had been given, they were able to take their time.

Tamara sighed happily. "Isn't this beautiful up here?"

"Yes, it truly is," Sam agreed. "I love it. I also love this ship. It's an amazing being, with all the things it can do. I could stay up here forever and just fly with it."

Tamara couldn't have agreed more. "I never noticed the stars being this bright ... this *close*. Look at the Milky Way. It's just begging for us to travel there. Can you make the canopy transparent?" No sooner had she asked than the ship responded, giving them the feeling of traveling fast in a convertible.

"Wow!" Sam laughed. "Now if we could only have the feeling of wind blowing through our hair."

The creature, realizing that opening the canopy to the vacuum of space would not have given them the effect they were looking for, and would have been detrimental to their health, did the next best thing and increased the air flow directed at their heads.

"Cool, I love it," Tamara said, grinning hugely. "Next we should get some tunes and go crazy."

"I think you're already crazy, girlfriend."

"Hey, which one of those stars are our people from?" Tamara asked, humming a tune in her head.

"The middle star in Orion's Belt. It's called Alnilam. Our people are from the eighth planet, the name of which I can't pronounce."

"Sam, do we know what's really going on?"

She turned to face her. "What do you mean?"

"Think about it; six months ago, you left the war for medical reasons. You never showed me, but I heard you got whipped pretty bad. A few weeks later, you're hanging out in the Bahamas with a nerdy guy in an old secret trawler."

"And this is leading where?"

"Well that's not like you, to sleep with him, I mean. We don't do that. Yes, we flirt and tease, but we don't get serious with guys."

"T, it's not like that. I fell in love, and … maybe I still am. Can I help it if I found out later that he's my biological brother and twin?" She shook her head, still unable to quite wrap her mind around it.

"Yeah about that … what was that our freakishly tall, alien hybrid friend was saying about your DNA? That it's human/alien and with still *another* alien DNA thrown in for good measure?"

"What do you want to hear? That's who I am. Who Simon and I both are apparently."

"But you have to admit, that weird twin thing you two do, with that silent telepathy, has *got* to be the strangest part of the whole thing."

"Oh really? Girl, look around. Does flying in an alien space craft look normal?"

"That's kind of what I'm talking about. You went from getting your wings as fighter pilot to packing it all in, and for what? To fly around pretending to be an alien and taking on the world's problems?"

"Tamara, I don't know what I want, or where this is all going, but I do know that, as of right now, becoming connected to this powerful creature has been the greatest achievement in my whole life." She paused thoughtfully and then continued. "Besides, what about you? Five months ago, you had never heard of Tyrone Booker, and now you're getting married in five weeks. Assuming you can rescue him from the moon. Whose life is stranger?"

Without even hesitating, Tamara laughed. "Yours!" She leaned over and hugged her best friend. "But nice try."

To hit the co-ordinates, they had to enter at high speed on a steep re-entry angle, creating enough friction to feel the heat inside and create a spectacular fireball to any star gazers, who would assume it was simply a meteor.

"Sam, don't you think you're going too fast?" the brunette asked in a panic, as the ocean loomed closer. Pull up or you'll hit the water!"

"T, don't forget, this thing is amphibious and alive. At times, like now, I'm not really in control. It is. I also get the feeling that *she* enjoys this speed, this rush, as much as I do."

The vessel came in hard and fast, and pulled up at the last second, passing through a wave crest that cooled the outer shell; it also took on some water to lower the internal heat for itself and its crew. A few minutes later, they screamed towards the mainland to meet their armed guides.

Four blue circles appeared on the canopy screen, indicating aircrafts approaching.

Tamara watched their approach. "Slow down, our escorts are coming fast." *Never mind, you've flown by the F22s.* She was about to repeat this thought aloud, but realized that Sam had already heard her, in her head, as had the ship, which stopped instantly.

'Can you hear me?' Sam asked Tamara in the same internal voice she used with Simon, as they waited for the aircrafts to bank around and approach.

'Yes; how are we doing this?'

'I think because we are both linked to the ship, and it's more efficient.'

The supersonic, ultra-maneuverable F22 Raptors, were fifth-generation stealth fighters, with air-to-air and air-to-ground missiles, as well as electronic gathering and jamming capabilities. For this mission, the fighter jets were piloted by the best of the best, and heavily loaded with a full complement of armaments and scanning equipment, all of which were targeting the alien ship.

Sam easily adjusted speed to match the jets. Simon had recommended that they avoid verbal communication with the aircrafts. Sam agreed and suggested that, as aliens, they could pick up the human signals but that earth technology couldn't receive theirs. This had been explained to Booker and the Air Force.

"Alpha 1 Aircraft, you will take up position on my starboard side," the flight leader for the earth forces, whose call sign was Badger, intoned mechanically, with an air of superiority in his tone. Alpha 1 Aircraft was the alien space ship's predetermined call sign. Badger smoothly opened up a hole in their formation. "Follow us precisely. Acknowledge."

Sam wiggled her craft's wings, which was the universal (and now intergalactic) sign for 'Yes, I acknowledge your command and will comply.'

"Alpha 1, close formation," Badger confirmed, sounding even more condescending, "and try to keep up."

"He wants us to keep up?!" Sam yelled, in their much superior vessel. "What an ass!"

"Approaching Carmel," Badger announced. "Back it down to cruise, acknowledge."

The jets had been flying at their maximum speed of Mach 2.25 (2,410 kph), until they made land south of Carmel State Park, where they dropped to cruising speed, which was just below the speed of sound, to comply with a California noise by-law.

"Magic Man acknowledges," the fighter on Sam's left replied

"Hawk acknowledges," one of the fighters trailing within missile range replied.

"Foxxy acknowledges," a friendly female voice replied, behind and above the others.

Alpha 1 wiggled her wings and waited for the jets to bleed off speed so that she could match them.

"Do we know them?" Tamara asked her military-pilot friend, controlling the most powerful flying machine now in the air.

"Badger's voice is familiar, but we never met. I've flown with Magic Man and shared a few drinks with him at a bar; he's a real nice guy. Hawk I've heard of, but I've never met him. And Foxxy gave a talk once to our squad. Good speaker. She motivated me to become a 'fighter jock' instead of a 'baggage handler'."

They continued east, in formation, until they reached a barren strip of land south of King City, where they vectored northeast to the San Benito Mountain nature area. The five flying crafts avoided populated areas as they maneuvered their way east. They crossed into Nevada at Death Valley National Park.

Flying through the Betty Wash Canyon air space was tight.

"Badger, don't you think you are squeezing our guests a little too much?" Magic Man questioned his leader. "You're close enough to touch their wing, or whatever it is."

Alpha 1 could hear the chatter between the two ships, but Sam and the ship were already aware of the lead jets aggressive posturing. Sam reassured the host creature that they were in no danger and received a strange image that she did not understand in return.

"Let's see if this alien pilot has a pair. I'm going to tip his wing," Badger announced to his flight team.

"Don't do it Badger," Foxxy replied intently. "We don't want to offend the visitors."

"Hell, this may be the only time we get this close to a UFO," Badger said. "If they come back and attack us, we may be the only four people who know what their ship and flying skills are like."

"For the record, I don't like it. They may have bigger ones than you," Hawk replied, getting a chuckle from their encrypted closed frequency.

"Oh, if he only knew," Sam laughed, hearing the comments.

"Don't worry, Sam; he can't hurt us," Tamara said. "Besides he's only going to give us a little tip. I hear they do it all the time as a form of respect."

"Oh heck, I'm not worried about us; this thing can fly in space and take re-entry heat. And it doesn't matter if he disrupts the air under its wings, because they don't provide lift. I'm worried about the F22. At this speed, he could break a wing, and they're going to blame 'the aliens'."

"Is there something you can do?"

"Well if I don't, *she* will," Sam said, patting the control station.

"Huh?"

"Remember I told you it's a living creature. It's female, and referring to herself as 'she' ... and *she* just might interpret these actions as aggression, and I don't know how she will react or if she will retaliate."

As the lead jet touched their wing, Sam skillfully maneuvered her craft, tilting it and flying sideways, which was possible because her craft was not a traditional flight frame, dependent on air flow for thrust, lift, and drag ratios.

"Ha!" Sam laughed. "Let him try that."

"That's pretty cool. Are you doing it or is she?" Tamara asked, patting the control station in front of her.

"It's all me, babe, one hundred percent manual control."

"Guess the alien pilot can fly okay," Magic Man remarked. "Probably could fly circles around us."

"We'll see," Badger challenged.

The flight leader maneuvered in closer so that his wing tip was inches from the space craft's underbelly. Air turbulence on his wing caused his plane to veer into Alpha 1, with enough force to cause significant damage to his jet if it hit with full force. With split-second timing, the space craft took control, rolling out of the way and on top of the leader's F22, mere inches away from its wind screen and the human pilot's head.

The vessel creature somehow sensed that her own pilot did not want the other pilot or his plane hurt. Her pilot was good, but *she* was better, and could out-fly these primitive smelly aircrafts. If her pilot did not want to retaliate, then *she* would at least teach him a lesson on flying etiquette. Opening her intake valve, she extended the fluid-exchange tube near the tail of her underbelly and released a couple of hundred gallons of hot ocean water over the aggressive pilot's plane.

"OH MY GAWD! Are you doing this?" Tamara asked in shock, as they watched the activity unfold on the 3D imager.

"Not me, *she* took over as soon as Badger touched us."

The F22 port engine flamed out, forcing the pilot to increase power to starboard in an attempt to compensate with the remaining engine.

"You okay there, Badger? Let's give him some air space," Magic Man announced as he and the rest of the jets backed away.

Badger's cockpit alarms blared and lights flashed. The on-board computer-generated voice, which was female, was calm but insistent on telling him to restart the port engine. "Duh, state the obvious," Badger mumbled to himself.

Sam watched helplessly as the lead pilot struggled with his craft. She gave him space as well.

The vessel creature did not understand the problem with the plane, but knew from its heat signature that one power source was rapidly cooling while the other had increased. To her, it seemed to be an object struggling to stay in the air, due to something that she had instigated. Taking control once again, she flew above Badger's plane, and with a beam of light designed to move large objects, surrounded the plane with a yellow glow, stabilizing its air flow. With clean and stable air, the F22 engine was easily restarted.

Badger slid over in the formation, allowing Sam to move their vessel back into the hole he created, and then moved over even more to give her lots of space and respect.

"Looks like their ship peed on you, Badger," Hawk observed, now that the crisis appeared to be over.

"Who knows? Maybe that was *alien* pee," Foxy suggested, with a smirk in her voice.

"Okay, enough chatter," Badger said gruffly. "Keep this frequency open. Alpha1, don't pull a stunt like that again. Acknowledge?"

Sam and Tamara had a hard time controlling their laughter, so the ship made the acknowledgment for them. She wiggled her wings up and down, and then pitched them back and forth. To the F22 squad, it looked like a touchdown dance.

They approached another set of canyons, and she flipped on her side again to give the inferior planes room to maneuver. At a tight bend with an overhanging rock cliff, the pilots flew above the rocky outcrop while she flew under it, hugging the ground and kicking up stones before rejoining formation and matching their speed seconds later.

"Alpha 1, how much air space do you need to stop? Can you show us?" Foxxy asked, probing for performance answers, after watching the alien pilot show off.

"Don't do it, Sam. They want you to give away some of our baby's secrets."

"I know, but why not? I won't hurt anyone, and they might just show us some respect."

"Oh girl, they respect you already. Who wouldn't? What you are flying is more powerful than anything they have, and they're scared, so don't provoke the nice humans."

'Ha ha, listen to us; a couple of days ago, I was flying one of the fastest helicopters every made and I thought that was the greatest thing, as a human,' Sam said softly to Tamara with her inner voice. *'Now, pretending to be an alien and flying this beautiful machine creature, being something I am not, is overwhelming and exciting. We are humans, we must never forget that.'*

To answer Foxxy's challenge, Sam wiggled her wings in a slow exaggerated manner, but did not execute a sudden stop. Soon they were flying over a large section of land without lights; it was as if someone had sprayed the area with black paint.

"Alpha 1, we are approaching Groom Lake, our destination. Prepare to land. Do you understand?" Badger received back a wing wiggle. Suddenly runway lights appeared on their flight path.

Scans of the area indicated a row of buildings, possibly hangars, but there were no heat signatures inside. Either there was no machinery or the buildings were heavily shielded. Additional scans did pick up the heat signature of a group of people clustered in an open area. Viewing the 3D imager, eight faint dots appeared on the ground. Zooming in revealed snipers, but before Sam could react, *she* spotlighted them with an intense beam of light. Sam had to calm her down by telling her it was okay, and that they were not in danger.

The alien spotlights were slowly switched off, one at a time, as Sam set the space craft down next to the group of gathered people and waited for her escort pilots to land and exit their planes.

Foxxy and Hawk remained airborne, watching from above, for both protection and defense, while Badger and Magic Man landed and taxied to a stop at her edge of the tarmac.

"Oh my gawd! Sam, this is Area 51! This is so freaking fantastic! I never dreamed I would ever be here."

"Me neither, unless of course, I was escorted by a squadron of fighter jets while flying an alien space ship." Sam chuckled, lightly petting the control console.

CHAPTER 24

Badger and Magic Man took off running as soon as they climbed out of their planes; they were not going to miss this opportunity to actually greet the alien beings. As excited as he was to meet the visitors, Badger really wanted to check out the black space craft. He slowly ran his hands over the wing edge and found no noticeable avionic flight control surfaces. It was hot to the touch and incredibly smooth. As soon as he touched the vessel, the area was suddenly bathed in an industrial halogen glow.

"SON! Keep away from that craft! It could be radioactive!" a technician shouted through a megaphone, as a group of men wearing white hazmat protective gear cautiously approached from the shadows, pointing various instruments at the big ship. Behind them, advancing forward, were a team of scientists wearing white lab coats, medical masks, and gloves. Around the lit perimeter, people scurried about setting up cameras, knowing that the images captured would never be made public. Parked next to each light stand was a flat black Humvee, each with a team of four heavily armed marines.

Sam and Tamara watched all this as a 3D image floating above the console, which included little circles of light around each threat target. The military positions were marked with pulsing red bands.

"Oh my gawd! Sam, they have weapons trained on us! I don't like this."

"It's okay, T. Think about it, to them we are aliens with unknown intentions or diseases. They are probably following some rule that was written just for occasions like this. The question is how we should respond. Any ideas?"

Forgetting briefly that there were three entities in the conversation, she was surprised when the 3D image shimmered and displayed everything in a glowing blue hue. They watched as six small drones exited the back and took up position over each armed vehicle, aiming a powerful beam of light on them. Sam and Tamara realized that this was a simulation, illustrating a suggestion from the ship.

'Continue simulation as if this was an extreme threat against us,' Sam thought.

The blue glow pulsed three times, and then each drone fired a pulse through the light and the vehicles melted as the ship sped through the atmosphere with the drones following.

'Good to know we have an escape plan. NO THREAT. Just lights to scare. But ONLY when I say!' Sam spoke to the ship again sternly. The blue glow pulsed three times again, before returning to normal colors.

"What just happened here, Sam?"

"*She* offered some ideas. We'll call it Plan B."

"Okay. So what do you think the procedure is? Do we just open the door and walk out or do we wait for someone to knock and invite us out?"

"You got me there." Sam shrugged. "Too soon and we may startle them. Let's give them a few more minutes to set up and declare us safe."

They watched and waited as the Area 51 personnel set up various instruments, presumably to gather data on them passively.

"Sir, there's nothing readable on the infrared," a nearby technician transmitted. "The ship is giving off too much heat."

Another technician transmitted that the x-rays were not penetrating.

The girls watched as a scientist in a HASMAT suit clumsily crept around the back and attempted to scrape the surface of the ship. They wondered if he had drawn the short straw. A small popup shelter was erected in front of the ship, complete with table and chairs, while a few men in uniform gathered around it. Those in protective suits slowly faded into the background, presumably giving the all clear.

Feeling like enough time had elapsed, and that sufficient probes and scrapes had been taken, Sam instructed the ship to open the hatch with a force shield in effect, so the interior could not be scanned or photographed.

Colonel W.R. Hill, an easygoing guy with a quick wit and a vocabulary laced with colorful colloquial expressions, talked quietly to his second in command, a civilian scientist named Courtney Williamson.

'Court', as he was referred to by friends, was a large, athletic, bald man. He loved his morning jogs and pushed his tall, 48-year-old body hard. Sometimes, working in isolation at a top-secret facility could consume you. Running was a way to relax his brain and not allow his 300-plus IQ to overpower him. After twenty years at Area 51, he'd found out what worked best, for him. He also found that working in the underground city had faded the darker skin of his Jamaican childhood to a light perpetual tan.

"Well isn't this exciting?" the white-haired cherub-faced colonel exclaimed.

"I can't believe it, Wayne," Court whispered back, rubbing his hands in the cool night air. "E.T. on our watch!" He had quite a lot of experience with oddities, working in Area 51, including caring for—and eventually losing—a creature that had resembled a stingray, at least on a superficial level. It had definitely been of alien origin, but this was an entirely different situation. These aliens were sentient, intelligent, and technologically advanced. This was the real deal.

Sam tucked her faux green hair behind her ears, feeling the shape of the alien face Mac had created for her. "Okay, let's put on our game face; it's show time." She watched her friend adjust the long braid in her blue-green hair.

"Should we exit with our force shields on?" Tamara asked.

"Yes, let's. It will be more dramatic, and remember, we have to talk slower and use proper grammar, like Orion. And we can't swear. You good to go, T?" Sam asked, turning on her glowing white force shield.

'This should be interesting,' Tamara responded, silently.

Ma Z stepped through the glowing blue hatch of the sleek craft, with Aram At following close behind. They decided to leave their force shields active until they reached the tent. They were both excited and scared as they hesitantly walked towards the shelter, while Hill and Williamson approached them. Sam stopped suddenly in front of an armed guard, with an un-slung M4 assault rifle pointing down. Her motions caused his reflexes to jerk the weapon up, creating a defensive posture. Realizing his error, he froze as the alien being walked over and slowly moved the lethal barrel down and out of the way.

'Sam, what are you doing?'

'Cool it, T ... just getting a close look to see if the safety's on.'

She lowered her force shield from her head as she held the weapon's barrel and stared at the panic on the young soldier's face, with a new kind of superiority that frightened her.

The soldier swallowed hard and felt fear for the first time in his life. He gazed at this glowing being that looked decidedly female, as a wave of nausea swept over him. He felt a mix of emotions: duty, joy, and shame. They studied each other, as an unsettling hush crept over the gathered group; then she turned and continued walking, with much coaxing from her companion. The point had been made without words.

'*Sam, that's Badger over there,*' Tamara whispered internally, pointing in the direction of the pilot who had harassed them on the flight in.

Taking the lead again, Ma Z pointed to the airman with her finger, and made a 'come here' motion. He quickly separated himself from the row of spectators and approached her. He was thrilled to meet this other pilot, with the unearthly flying abilities. He mentally reviewed what he would say.

She gestured for him to come closer and he complied, ready to burst out with words of honor and gratitude for having flown with her.

When he was at arm's length, she lowered the protective force shield completely, fully aware of the effect her outfit would have on him. She followed his eyes as he reviewed her body from top to bottom and back again. He was about to offer a greeting, when she slapped him in the face.

More than one soldier raised their rifles at this obvious attack on one of their own. Badger rubbed his face, all too familiar with a sensation inflicted on him by more than one upset women. Why should his reputation *not* be extended to off-world females? At least he hoped the being was female.

"You call yourself a pilot! You are a poor excuse for—"

Aram At grabbed her arm and stopped the lecture.

'Hey cool it! You sound more like Sam than Orion.'

"Sorry Ma'am. Just testing your flying skills and that of your craft. Thanks for the assist out there. Really sorry. MY BAD."

"Well, I'll be buck naked in a briar patch, with mosquitoes using my arse as target practice! What the hell is going on, son?" Colonel Hill yelled, storming over with Williamson in tow. "I apologize for this jackass," he continued, separating the airman from the aliens, "and for any embarrassment he caused."

"What the hell were you thinking, fool?" Courtney snapped back at Badger, throwing him back into the on-lookers. The pilot looked around sheepishly for support; after all, he'd just been slapped by an alien chick. That had to be a first.

The colonel extended his hand. "Welcome to earth. I'm Colonel Hill, the commander of this base. Sorry again, ma'am. I will take him out back and shoot him, if that's what you want. Twice just to make sure."

The colonel's approach and comment was unexpected, and caught them both off guard. When they heard his name, they looked at each other.

'Is that the same Colonel Hill who was looking for me earlier this year, because my face showed up on a screen shot from one of our drones?' Sam silently asked her friend, who just nodded in response.

"Thank you." She reached out and shook the colonel's hand, ensuring to make it as awkward as possible, and then stepped back. "My name is Ma Z. I am student of culture and diplomacy." She turned to look at her friend, as though to confirm that her statement had been voiced correctly. Again, Aram At nodded affirmatively.

"My outburst ... I also am sorry. That male ... irritated me with his poor flying."

"Did he hurt you?" the patriarchal colonel asked, genuinely concerned.

"His inferior machine and abilities would never h u r t me," she said, hesitantly. "He placed his own being and team in danger, by being ... j a c k a s s?" She paused, realizing that she was feeling more alien than human at that moment, and wondered if her bond with the ship was causing the effect.

Magic Man came forward. "Sir, in all fairness to Badger, he was just messing with Alpha 1. No harm was intended. I'm sure if the roles were reversed, and a superior air power entered her air space, she would have executed similar moves."

'He's right, Sam. Apologize to them before you start an inter-galactic war.'

"My … there is no word … my א*שׁ לקׁ☐ has reminded me that I have taken similar actions with visitors to our planet."

The colonel's expression was comically surprised. "Well I'll be flat-footed in a gopher hole! You telling me there are other alien beings out there?"

Ma Z was trying hard not to laugh, but failed. She chuckled silently at the cherub-faced colonel and his language. She really wanted to meet him as Sam. He was funny, for a military guy, and not like her step-dad, the general.

He saw her reaction and was pleased. "Well, don't that beat all. You find me funny?"

"Colonel Hill, you … use language that … makes me smile inside. I hope I get chance to be part of the team to greet you officially."

"Well young lady, I would be honored at that meeting, and I hope by then you've learned that diplomats don't poke their pinkies into guns. You knew damn well that object was a weapon, and may have been capable of shooting that pretty little butt of yours off. You came strutting into my house like a peacock looking for a fight."

'Oh Snap! He schooled you real good,' Tamara laughed, using their inside voice. *'You deserved it too. Now say you're sorry to the funny human.'* She gently nudged her friend in Hill's direction.

Ma Z turned and glared at her friend, feeling her face flush.

When it was clear that no apology was forthcoming, Aram At lowered her own force shield, standing before the colonel and extended her hands briefly before lowering them to her sides. "Greetings, I am Aram At, student not diplomat. I study stars. We are from the star system you call Alnilam, the center star in what you call Orion's Belt. My א *שׁל☐

did not mean disrespect. We are sorry. She is p☐☐☐... how to explain … like a tame female animal, showing it is fierce…?" She pretended to struggle.

In a serious voice, trying to keep it together, Court suggested, "Are you trying to tell us your friend is a bit of a bitch?"

'I am not!' Sam interjected silently.

Aram At tried to look innocent and uncertain of the translation. She shook her head. "I could not say." She looked at Ma Z and then back at the colonel. "Our *ɥ&^*ẅ hear distress and we come. We help. We do *not* hurt. No weapons. You point weapons at us. Hurt." She gestured towards the soldiers and the armed vehicles.

Ma Z watched this exchange and saw shame settle over the colonel's features. Her irritation softened, and without thinking, she took the colonel's right hand in her two hands and held it to her chest, to her heart, as she lowered her forehead to his arm. She held that position for a long minute. She had no idea know why she did it. It just felt right, and alien enough to pass as a bonding gesture, and perhaps, as an apology.

❧ CHAPTER 25 ❦

"Well, we certainly have been poor hosts. Can I offer you some refreshments? A drink perhaps to toast this historic occasion?" Hill asked, breaking gently from her heartfelt embrace. He turned to the young soldier who'd been involved in the earlier standoff with Ma Z. "Son, put the gun away. Everyone stand-down!"

"Yes. A drink is nice. Please?" Ma Z asked, holding her cupped hand up to her lips.

Courtney quickly picked up on the request and quietly spoke on his radio. Moments later, a group of men dressed in kitchen whites entered, carrying trays of drinks, fruit, cheeses, sausages, and sticks of carrots and celery.

Seeing the selection, Aram AT started to reach for a bottle of beer, with which she was familiar, but was quickly stopped.

'Wait! We're supposed to act like aliens, T. Remember? We shouldn't know what these things are. Let me scan the items, and you and I can talk back and forth in alien words, like we are deciding.'

'Oops! Yeah, good thinking.'

Activating her arm bracelet and 3D display, she methodically moved the scanning beam over each item on the table, getting a curious reaction from Courtney beside her.

"Not hurt you." She pointed the beam at her hand, displaying the interior structure results and diagnostics, then pointed the beam at the older white-haired male, getting similar data results.

"Hey," the colonel said nervously. "This old hunting dog isn't crazy about getting his inners microwaved."

"Look Wayne," Courtney joked, pointing to the deep-red ugly sore on his friend's stomach lining. "There's the ulcer you've been complaining about for as long as I can remember." He then raised Ma Z's arm and aimed the beam at the older man's heart, before turning the beam on his own.

"I may not be able to read this alien language, but Wayne, my old friend, you need to take better care of yourself. You and I are going to start jogging together."

"Listen here, Court, I didn't get to be a silver-haired fox without picking up some scratches."

"Now you're more like a gray goat, sitting on your ass all day behind a desk."

No one but his longtime friend could talk to him like that, not even his wife of forty years. Courtney always had a way of making the senior base commander relax and shake off some of the daily stress the position created.

"You make me smile inside," Ma Z said again as she laughed, holding her stomach. Aiming her beam at the colonel's heart once more, she paused for a moment and then nodded. "I fix."

"How?" Colonel Hill asked dismissively. "Alien open-heart surgery right here on the table?"

"No." Ma Z shook her head, laughing again, really liking her host and wondering why her own father was not more like him. While continuing to laugh, she slowly retrieved her black crystal necklace from under the lace cover up. Without saying a word, she walked around to stand behind the colonel, slowly moved the pendant around over his heart and then the area of his ulcer.

Aram At held her own diagnostic beam on Hill, as Courtney looked on. A few scientists gathered around and watched as the arteries slowly cleared of plaque and the red blistering ulcer faded to normal pink.

The colonel could feel the effects right away. Even without looking at the display, he could tell his blood flow had improved and that the nagging little pain in his gut was gone.

"While I'll be damned. Don't that beat a cat's purr. Thank ya, ma'am." He was amazed at these beings' medical abilities, and for the first time in a long time, he was at a loss for words. He hoped that what she did had really worked, and suspected that a few tests from the base doctors in the morning would confirm what he could feel.

Not sure how to proceed, but feeling the need to get the meeting back onto a less personal track, he straightened his increasingly relaxed posture and gestured towards the table. "Was there anything here you would like to drink?" He pointed to the variety of beverages, alcoholic and non- alcoholic.

Ma Z pointed the scanner at the champagne bottle then, and then turned to Aram At.

"σ%*@#*ξ ... &^@θΩ ... Þ*@3Λ." She had no idea what she'd actually said, but thought one of the words meant drink. She turned her attention back to the men at the table.

"We drink this. O k a y ... safe." She gestured to the tall bottle, speaking to Courtney, who had assumed the role of bartender. The Moet & Chandon was served. Both girls were familiar with its well-known bubbling effect, but acted surprised for their audience.

"Good. ʃ*¬ʕɰ~6 *!" Aram AT responded, pointing to her nose and giggling. She would have to remember this brand, but somehow knew it was out of her budget. She then gestured to Ma Z, directing her to direct the beam at some of the food.

"What we have here is fruit," Courtney said, pointing to each item as he identified them. "This is pineapple, melon, and strawberries ... all healthy and delicious."

Both girls daintily selected a strawberry and popped it into their mouths, then clapped their hands together as a child would, tasting something enjoyable for the first time.

"You will enjoy this, try it," Colonel Hill suggested as he placed a berry into each of the women's glasses. They tried it, tentatively, and agreed that it was wonderful with the enthusiastic mannerisms of first timers. This time the feelings were genuine, as neither had tried strawberries and champagne together.

Courtney cut a few slices off one of the hot Polish sausages, dipped it into a brown sauce, then added a piece of cheese to it before devouring the combination. Ma Z watched, and wondering what the sauce was, delicately stuck her pinky into the mix and then sucked her finger. The heat of the spice quickly overwhelmed her lips and tongue, causing her to fan her mouth. This caused everyone at the table to break out laughing.

"What the hell is that stuff, Court!?" the colonel asked in anger.

"Just a little Jamaican jerk sauce, man," he said, exaggerating his island accent. Aram At laughed as Ma Z took another gulp of her drink.

Spotted a tray of jalapeno poppers, Aram At selected one and dipped it into the fiery sauce that had taken down her friend. Before she could eat it, Court grabbed her arm.

"Whoa, slow down, girl. That's adding fire on top of lava. Burn your tongue off and blister those lips."

"Hot. Yes, good hot." Aram At smiled as she popped the crazy hot mixture into her mouth and chewed it without breaking a sweat.

"Girls, got game!" Courtney exclaimed, duplicating her moves.

Hill and Ma Z looked at each other and shook their heads.

'Bitch,' Sam internalized to her show-off friend.

"You should check if *he's* got an ulcer," Hill joked, "or better yet, see if he has a brain."

Activating the scanning beam again, she waved it over his stomach and then his head, which generated a chuckle from both the men and some of the scientist looking on.

'Sam, can you hear me?' Simon asked, using their twin telepathy from the moon.

'Wow, so this has to be the farthest our abilities have ever reached,' she replied.

'Great, isn't it? Hey, can you see if they have an extra right arm for Worthy's space suit? From the elbow down, plus two pairs of gloves?'

Stepping back from the table, and nodding as though satisfied, Ma Z faced the colonel. "We must go now. You are good people. Enjoying new friends. You have the parts needed for our return to the moon. We also need arm for space suit." She pointed to the section of the arm she needed, and held her own hand up. "And … hand? For woman-pilot suit."

Houston had already been informed of the added request, although Simon hadn't known that, and had sent the pieces, as well as an entire spare suit, in case there were any other mishaps.

"A glove," Hill corrected. "Yes Ma Z, we have the parts." Two uniformed but unarmed men entered the shelter, each wheeling a steel crate containing the necessary launch equipment, plus survival-suit parts.

"Not hurt ... not harm," Ma Z responded smiling, seeing the weaponless men enter.

"Ma Z, there is just one little thing." Receiving puzzled looks from the women and his commanding officer, Courtney continued. "I have to install the parts." He pointed to the moon, visible on the horizon. "Up there."

"What in blooming hell are you jabbering on about, son? You don't need to go with them," Hill snapped, while both girls stared at each other.

"The launch parts need to be specially calibrated, and I'm the only one who knows how to use the special tools."

Colonel Hill knew bullshit when he heard it, but remained silent. Hell, if he had thought about it before Courtney, he would have tried to pull the same stunt.

All eyes were on the two alien females, waiting for their answer.

'This is going to be difficult,' Sam said.

'You think!? Tell him no!'

"No. You get hurt," Ma Z stated.

"I'll take my chances and sign whatever intergalactic waver forms you have. You saw from your scans that I'm fit, in good shape." He emphasized the last part by flexing his muscles. Aram At resisted the temptation of checking out the offered bicep.

"Not go like that. Need protection suit for the moon," Ma Z explained, tugging on his sleeve.

"Got that covered too," he said with a large smile, as another soldier placed a large suitcase at his feet. "But can I fly up there in what I'm wearing now or can you lend me one of those fancy onesies?"

Aram At had to stop from cracking up, listening to her Jamaican countryman try to simultaneously charm and bull his way onto their ship

'Your call Sam. I'm good either way.'

ORION - Escape Velocity   197

Shaking her head in amazement, and trying to look angry, Ma Z said, "Not touch stuff!"

"All right then, that settles it!" Courtney shouted, excited. "I'm going to the moon on an alien ship!"

"Ma Z," Hill said, shaking his head and offering his hand to the alien pilot, "you have my permission to throw him out an airlock the first time he gives you a problem."

'Hey T, I would have done the same thing if I were in his position.'

'Yeah, me too. He is quite the player.'

"Okay, can I ask just one more little tiny favor?" Court said, holding up two fingers very close together.

Hill rolled his eyes and the two alien girls put their hands on their hips, all seeming to be silently asking if he was kidding them.

Not waiting for a negative response, he spoke a few words into his radio, and then looked up at them.

"Okay ladies, you have enjoyed Earth, our hospitality, our food, and our drink? Well, that's what we call 'a party'." As he spoke, the staff chef entered the tented shelter, carrying a large thermal bag, which he opened to reveal six plain white pizza boxes. Another staff member carried a thermal case containing twenty-four Red Stripe beers. "Well now the pizza and beer are on me," he said excitedly, as the two girls looked on, stunned.

Misinterpreting their reactions to mean that the aliens didn't know about his favorite food group, rather than their utter disbelief at his antics, he quickly explained. "Pizza is a popular human food and easy to eat in a group. I had the chef make up six party platters, with everything from plain cheese pizzas to all dressed pizzas with the works. Are aliens allergic to mushrooms or anchovies?"

Colonel Hill couldn't believe what was happening on his watch. He had known Court for years, and all evidence to the contrary, he kept expecting the man to grow up someday. He was nearing 50 after all. "Son, if brains were leather, you wouldn't have enough to saddle a cricket." He sighed loudly and looked at his guests. They didn't seem upset, just confused.

"Oh hell, you're a crazy man," Hill said, slapping his friend on the back, "but seeing that you're grinnin' like a possum eatin' a sweet tater, you best git."

The girls just silently shook their heads, not sure if they could speak in their alien voices without breaking up. Instead they grinned at each other, in a way that they hoped didn't look too human.

'Party on the moon!' With the aid of a drone, all the new gear was secured inside. Courtney was given an alien EVA belt similar to the girls', with brief instructions on how it worked.

Colonel Hill stood at attention, nodding formally at his alien guests. "Ma Z, Aram At, it was a pleasure meeting you two. It was nice that our two species could come together like this in peace. I hope this is not the last time we meet." Then, relaxing his stance somewhat and smiling at them, he stepped closer. "I don't know how to thank you for fixing my old ticker," he patted his chest, in case they didn't understand the expression. "You probably added a few years to this old gray fox."

"We understand. The thanks are from us." They each took one of his hands and held it to their chests, bowing their heads and mimicking the gesture Ma Z had offered earlier.

After a long moment, hoping to break the solemnity of the moment, he whispered, "I was joking about throwing him out of your vessel. Don't do that."

Sam purposely gave him a blank stare, and then smiled back, reassuring him that his friend would be safe.

He offered his hand to his second command. "Be careful buddy, don't do anything stupid."

Court nodded. "Guess I'll see you in a week ... unless I can talk the gals into giving me a lift home."

Colonel Hill chose not to comment on this, and stepped back, resuming his formal posture, crossing his hands behind him. "Ma Z, you can take off right from here, directly exiting the atmosphere. Do not deviate more than a mile downrange or the air force will be all over you like burrs on a hound. Do you understand, young lady?"

"Yes, straight up. Not deviate. Thank you, Colonel Hill."

"Could I escort you?" asked Badger, making his continued presence known, and stepping forward. "I mean, as far as I can?"

Ma Z stared at him for a long moment, and then nodded, smiling mischievously. "Try to keep up."

The gathered crowd at Area 51 stood and watched as the sleek and shiny alien ship slowly rose from the ground, silently, without disturbing a single grain of sand. When it was about ten meters above the ground, it quickly accelerated, overtaking their escort, who was already at maximum speed and climbing vertically. Sam matched his speed, and then the ship decided she wanted to show off. She did a loop around the F22, and wiggled her wings before accelerating to her maximum speed of 540,000 kph, disappearing in the blink of an eye.

"Damn, that's impressive," Hill said to no one in particular, as the crowd looking up cheered for their new friends. "I'm glad they're friendly."

☙ CHAPTER 26 ❧

With Ma Z and Aram At on their way to Earth to pick up the parts they needed to salvage the mission and get back home, the remaining astronauts and aliens got back to business.

Worthy continued to be impressed with their technology, particularly with the drone's ability to transport the sergeant to the habitat in a protective air bubble. She found that walking on the moon with an EVA belt allowed her freedom from her bulky, damaged suit, and she enjoyed it tremendously. Comfortably set up in HAB1, she worked with Noi Ro to reverse the damage to Butcher's health. Using a drone, they had put him in a hyperbaric pressure bubble, to address his decompression issues. Using the alien scanning technology, and her knowledge of internal anatomy, they focused the healing power of the crystals.

Booker and Pierce were on *Endurance* examining Butcher's equipment, trying to determine what had gone wrong. There was no reason his suit's power supply should have been so seriously compromised, and Booker suspected that the issues with the suit, which had almost killed Butcher and had led to his continuing health problems, went beyond their original assessment of a power-supply issue. He just had a feeling.

They found his suit covered in black moon dust, which was expected. The air pack with the supplemental extended air tank and re-breather seemed to be functioning normally, but was almost out of oxygen. The CO2 filter was mounted on the front, easily accessible and designed to be swapped out by the astronaut, with a spare that was sealed in a pocket on the wearer's lower torso.

Booker turned to the young corporal. "Pierce, check the carbon dioxide filter to see if it was really a power issue or if it just malfunctioned, allowing too much CO2 to build up in his blood." As an afterthought, he added, "Check the spare as well."

"Yes sir."

With medical gloves, which Worthy had suggested they wear to avoid contaminating evidence, Booker carefully examined every inch of the suit, with the zoom ability of a hand-held digital camera.

He started with the helmet, because an excessive amount of sand at the back had caught his attention. Using the zoom camera as a magnifying glass, he discovered a small dent in the fiberglass, embedded with ice and sand. Lacking a measuring tool, he used a NASA ballpoint pen as a reference holder, and took a series of photos, rivaling any forensic crime investigator with limited equipment. After examining the inside, he concluded that the dent had not compromised the integrity of the head gear. The neck seals showed no signs of damage, nor did the shoulder joints. The gloves were heavily scratched, but that was expected, and they were designed to take the abuse. The left arm also passed inspection, but the right needed extra scrutiny, because of deep scratches on the elbow and forearm. He took extra pictures, using the pen as a measuring reference once again. The front pack, containing communication controls and CO_2 filter, had been removed by Pierce and was in the process of being examined by him on the other side of the suit-storage bay.

The front of the suit showed no sign of damage as he had assumed, although it was covered in the dark gray, almost black, dust. Flipping the heavy upper section over, he investigated any areas not covered by the massive backpack, containing air and power. He noticed that the small aerial used for communication had been broken off. It had been purposely engineered to be attached midway down the right side of the backpack, and relatively protected from being damaged. He hoped that pictures might eventually reveal some answers.

He was about to remove the upper torso and start his inspection of the lower half when something caught his eye. There was a streak of white on a now mostly gray surface. The streak started from under the large pack. This pack, like the one on the suit's front, was attached by heavy plastic zippers on three sides and internal straps that attached to the shoulders. The bottom was not attached, allowing for ease of movement. This was where the streak started, about two inches up from the lower edge of the pack; more pictures were taken before he separated it from the suit.

If not for the gray dust, and the spray of pressurized air escaping, which had blown the dust off, clearing the area, the tiny hole would not have been discovered. Realizing that such a puncture could have led to any number of problems, he checked inside the suit. At first it revealed nothing. Pushing a section of the insulation aside, he discovered a drop of red, on a surface that should have been pure NASA white.

"Shirl, do you copy?"

"Go ahead, Ty."

"I found a small puncture on the suit's back, on the right side, about four inches in and two inches up from the lower edge of the air pack. And there's blood, although only a drop." He hesitated, realizing the seriousness of what he was about to suggest. "Looks like it may have been caused by a needle. Too small to have been much else."

There was silence on the line for a long tense moment. "Thanks Ty, we didn't see any visible wounds on Butcher, but probably wouldn't have seen a small puncture."

"How is he now?"

"Still unconscious, but stable. We have him in a hyperbaric chamber."

"How did you manage to pull that off?"

"Don't ask, I'll explain later."

"Sir, I think I found something?" Pierce interrupted, as he crossed the bay caring some canisters.

"What do you have?"

"Sir, this is the CO2 filter in his pack. It looks fine and still has a few days of use left, as indicated by the test strip. Now look at the second one, which was in his pocket. It's also been used. See? The seal is broken. It has a few days of use left too. Notice how both have a little piece of suit repair tape on them? Well, I tested it on my suit, and after a few minutes, I could tell carbon dioxide was building up, even before the CO2 alarm went off."

"Are you okay?"

"Oh yes, sir, I didn't inhale much. Anyway, I checked the serial numbers and they don't show up in the equipment log. Actually, they're a different sequence completely."

"So you're saying his two filters both look perfect on the surface, right down to the test strips, but in reality they might have been tampered with?"

"I don't know about tampering, sir, just that this batch doesn't work."

"Check the rest of the filters in storage and in our suits."

"I already did and they are all good."

"Excellent job, Pierce. Jon, isn't it?"

"Yes sir. Thank you. I still have to look into why his CO_2 detector failed though."

"Copy that. I have some numbers I have to run down. I will be up on the flight deck if you need me."

***

Van der Hoose and Nom Iz were outside the damaged *Endurance*, crawling around the landing struts and paying particular attention to the wiring harness.

"I never would have imagined I would be outside on the moon wearing only yoga pants and a tee shirt."

"Yes," Nom Iz said. "The force shield protects you."

"I feel like I'm back on earth, with the same gravity. How is that possible?"

"I adjusted forces on you, to mimic the gravity on your world. These belts create a field around us providing necessary environment to survive."

"But why would you need to adjust gravity?"

"When on the planet with rings, we needed to adjust the gravity so the force was not as great, or we would not be able to move. Let me show you." Activating his arm bracelet, he touched an icon and they felt lighter.

"Bend your knees and push off with your feet."

As soon as she did so, she began to fly straight up. Thinking quickly, she bent at the waist and started to move horizontally, in the direction she was facing.

"I love it! I can fly!"

"Yes. When I was younger, I would … pretend to be a flying hero, saving my people."

"Just like Superman."

"Yes, like a super man."

"Hey, your use of the English language is getting better. A lot better than when we first met."

"Yes. We are fast learners. The more you talk, the faster I learn."

"Are your people telepathic?"

He paused to thinking of a response, knowing that this woman saw him as an alien, and not the male friend who had helped her back at MIT.

"Telepathic," Natalie explained. "It means being able to read minds … like listening to people's thoughts."

"It is not a trait that is common with my people."

"But you guys can do it, right?"

"As I said, it is not common. I know of only two people who possess such ability, and it is only between the two of them."

"Let me guess, you and that long-legged girl who left in your ship."

He paused, surprised. "Yes. How did you know this?"

"Just a lucky guess. You two look related; when you lowered your shield, and showed us your faces, I could see a family resemblance."

Even using the shield's masking abilities to project alien disguises, the modifications had apparently included similarities.

"Yes, she is my sister, and this telepathic ability is recent to us." He felt he could tell her a version of the truth. After all, he was never going to run into her again as Nom Iz.

"Can you read other people's thoughts? What about me?"

"No, only between Ma Z and myself."

"Would you tell me if you could?"

"Yes, I have no reason for subterfuge."

"Have you visited Earth before?"

"I have not."

"But you know about it and speak our language?"

"The ruling council has banned us from entering the sector around your planet and making contact. In our planetary studies, Earth is studied and discussed."

"Yes, but how did your people learn about us?"

"I'm not sure. Most likely from studying signals from your planet.

"So your people have visited us at some point in time?"

"There is no reference in the history journals." He was beginning to worry about the direction her rapid-fire questions were taking.

"Did your race abduct our people?"

"I do not believe so. There is no reference of that in the history journals."

"But it is possible?"

"There would be no need. As you have witnessed, our technology is more advanced than yours. Our people could launch a remote probe and scan a person from a distance without their knowledge. Our knowledge of your language and culture was likely gained from transmissions broadcast over many years. Ours is an old race. We have been exploring many worlds for a long time now, most likely before yours discovered fire." He was getting frustrated, and his conversation was becoming more animated.

"Oh ... I'm sorry, I did not mean to imply that your people were evil monsters. Are there other alien races out there, and could *they* have abducted my people?"

"You are asking questions that I should not answer. This is the reason why we were not to meet with your people."

"Why? Because humans are naturally curious? Please tell me a little more about your people and some of the other races you have encountered." She reached for his hand and held it tight, pleading for information any human would want to know.

"I no longer wish to talk on this subject. I will tell you that there are other races out there who may have visited your world. Most of the ones we have studied have been morally outstanding and would not have caused harm to humans. Life is sacred. Now let me inspect the power compartment that malfunctioned."

How could he continue this charade? He didn't know about other aliens, not really ... only what Orion had showed him on the first day they met. He remembered seeing a different colored icon on one of the outer planets, and it was explained that it most likely represented a crashed probe from another race. He also recalled seeing different color icons that represented interactions around unknown planets in a distant part of the Milky Way. Orion explained that one group was involved in a planetary war, while another was made up of trading partners. Most of what he told her was what he had learned from Hollywood and from his gut, which hoped advanced races would be benevolent. He understood why Mac and his mother told them not to talk too much.

"Fine!" She said, clearly frustrated. "You're just like a guy I knew back at school, pig-headed and stubborn! Can you give me more gravity, so I can walk around?" Van der Hoose pushed herself out from under the base assembly and electronics compartment they were inspecting. Nom Iz activated his bracelet controls and returned gravity to her. She watched as he pointed the scanning beam inside the compartment.

"Natalie, I have discovered something!" he exclaimed, a few minutes later as he popped his head out and showed her his findings on the 3D display. He pointed out the thing that had caught his interest. "That is the remains of a glass vial of acid. I do not believe this should be here."

"What the hell is that doing there? And how do you know it's acid?"

"The chemical analysis tells me it is a sulfur-base component that is extremely corrosive," he explained with an air of superiority, something he should have maintained from the beginning. "I can only speculate as to the reason for its presence. If the pressure in the vial was equal to your atmosphere, when your vessel encountered the zero atmosphere of space, the glass would break and the liquid would be released. This is an area containing critical wires. It may have been put there to damage those wires."

"Someone sabotaged us? We have to tell the commander!"

***

Looking around to ensure that he was alone, Booker accessed the list of personal journals from the account menu in the ship's database. Astronauts, like the rest of society, commonly documented their daily activities, to help keep their thoughts in order or even in the hopes of writing a book or a blog someday, for others to enjoy. Selecting Butcher's account from the crew menu, he was prompted to input a six-numbered access code. This is what he was waiting for. Closing his eyes, he brought up the image of those six numbers Butcher had scribbled into the dust, probably as he was struggling to stay conscious. Taking a deep breath, he opened his eyes and responded, keying them in.

A few seconds later, a document opened with a header in clear bold print: CIA: *Endurance* Mission. It was addressed to Sergeant Donny Butcher. It was a final briefing update regarding his secondary purpose for being on board. His mission was to uncover a mole on the crew roster, because he had a working knowledge of his military team-mates. The document went on to discuss espionage from China and a belief that vital information had been leaked. A second screen page indicated those on the team who had been vetted and could be trusted. He was pleased to see his name at the top of the list, followed by Shirley and then Pierce. A second list showed those who had not been confirmed, starting with Major Adam Carson. What shocked him was that the flight engineer, Natalie Van der Hoose, was not on either list.

The last page discussed a recent development, indicating that a person or persons with NASA had sabotaged equipment that could impact the safety of the crew. No detail had been given as to what had been tampered with, but Booker had a good idea.

He radioed his friend in the habitat. "Shirley, do you copy?"

"What's up, Ty?"

"Are you alone?"

"Except for the professor. Why?"

"Is Van der Hoose around?"

"No, she's out of communication when she's wearing the EVA belt. I believe she's with the student, Nom Iz. Why? What's going on, Ty?"

The commander briefed her on the numbers scratched in the dust and the documents they had led to.

"Can you think of a reason why she wouldn't be on either list?"

Without hesitation, Worthy replied. "No I can't … unless it's just a timing thing. Nat was brought in after Doctor Corinne Piech broke her leg skiing. With the accelerated time-table for the launch, Corinne couldn't pass her FIT EVAL. I have worked with Corinne, nice gal. I had heard of Van der Hoose. She was the flight engineer scheduled to be on the Mars mission next year. They pulled her out of training in Florida. She's given me no reason not to trust her."

"I agree, but who do we ask in Houston without showing our hand?"

"I don't know, but I'll keep an eye on her."

"Thanks Shirl."

"Hey Jon, is the commander around?" Van der Hoose asked as she and Nom Iz entered *Endurance*.

"Yeah, he said he was going to the flight deck."

"Thanks Jon." She left the suit bay with Nom Iz and headed into the elevator. "We have to tell the commander about the sabotage. He'll know what to do." As soon as they exited the elevator, she announced, "Sir, we found something!"

"Give me a moment," he said. "I'm on the radio with Worthy. Apparently Butcher is stable but still unconscious. Stay on the radio Shirl. What do you have, Van der Hoose?"

"The power regulator that the sensors connect to has been damaged, purposely. Nom Iz, please explain to the commander what you found."

He did, describing the location and the vial of acid, as well as his conclusions regarding sabotage.

"We found it using his scanning device," she added.

"Van der Hoose, could that area be accessed during flight?"

"No sir, that area is protected by an insulated outer cowling. The cowling is designed to come off when we separate from the service module."

"So the only time it could have been tampered with was during assembly or when we landed. That will be all, Van der Hoose. Dismissed. Worthy, I'll talk to Houston to see if we can get a replacement module. Do you think they left yet?"

Nom Iz and Natalie exited the ship without saying a word. Nom Iz, who was relatively new to deciphering the female emotional code, in either of his personas, had learned to remain silent until women decided to tell him their problems. He didn't have to wait long.

"He dismissed us! Dismissed *me!* How could he? *Why* would he?"

"Perhaps, as your commanding officer, he is privy to information that he cannot share."

"Bullshit! We have been open with each other, right from the start, when we were first introduced back in training. Something else is going on, and I don't like it!"

"I suggest we take a walk and relax. Enjoy the beauty of this moon."

CHAPTER 27

After seemingly countless hours traversing the crater's depths, Major Adam Carson, with Lieutenants Carlo Santos and Ben Nuzzi, stopped to rest in the specially pressurized 'Ricklar' tent. Ricklar was a new space material, like Mylar only stronger, and invented by a scientist, Richard Larstein. When a coded radio frequency was applied, it would turn rigid. Another frequency would return it back to its normal flexible state.

Satellite photos of the ledge they were on had showed that they would have a relatively easy march ahead of them, to the top of the "item", which was five kilometers from their elevator entry point. Unfortunately what had been presumed to be a shadow was in fact a collapsed section of the ledge. The seasoned military men needed to climb down two kilometers of the frozen rubble left by the ledge. The near vertical descent had been broken up by relatively flat horizontal surfaces. It was on one of these rest areas that the tent had been erected so the team could eat and sleep.

"I take it that rock or glacier climbing on the moon was not on anyone's bucket list?" Carson asked, while eating one of NASA's ready-to-eat meals (MREs)—this one hot Salisbury steak and potato—inside the warm shelter.

Santos shook his head. "Man, that last wall was a bitch."

"Yeah, "Nuzzi added, "I couldn't tell if I was attaching my carabineer into black ice or volcanic rock glass."

"This is like a climb into hell."

"But without the heat."

"I hope Butcher made it back okay," Carson said.

"Second that, but he shouldn't have come with us if he was feeling dizzy," Nuzzi commented.

"He told me he had a headache shortly after we exited the elevator," Santos said. "I think, after a little rest, he'd be good to go."

Carson nodded. "Yeah, copy that. Booker and the rest of the team would have started a search by now and found him, assuming he didn't make it back on his own. I'm really pissed that COM is still down; useless piece-of-crap gear," Carson grumbled.

"That broken ledge was sure a snafu. If we had known, we could have constructed a bridge of some sort in advance," Nuzzi said, as he ate the last of his meatloaf dinner.

Santos shook his head, still enjoying Sheppard's pie. "Yeah, the crew of the next mission will have *all* the luxuries."

"Well Santos, you're last to finish eating, so you take first watch," Carson ordered. "Monitor the generator and keep your eye on the pressure. If it drops suddenly, we may not get time to put our helmets back on."

Santos smiled at him, sipping on a power drink and enjoying the warmth. "You got to love these new generators, silent power with heat as a by-product."

"Yep." Carson said, settling down for his rest. "Nuzzi, you have second watch in two hours; I'll take the third. Let's get some shut eye. In six hours, we make the final trek to the item."

***

"Don't you want to ask me questions about humans?" Natalie prompted.

"I find observation a better method of learning," Nom Iz said. "We have already studied human evolution, cultures, and your obsession with taking what is not yours, leading to the numerous wars that have shaped your history."

"Ouch! Is that really what they teach about humans?"

"I condensed it."

"What about the good parts? As a race, we're not that bad. I'm sure you know of other planets that are worse?" She absentmindedly kicked a small moon rock that was in her path.

"Yes, but they wage wars against other races of people. Other planets. Not among themselves. That is why your planet has not been approached by other races. You cannot be trusted to act as one voice. You are an immature species."

"Nom Iz, tell me, as one sentient being to another, what would you recommend we do, so that there are no more wars?"

"Real peace starts with the children. Two, maybe three generations and war could be eliminated if you started by teaching the children."

"That simple?"

"No. Not simple. It is hard work. If the educated, wealthy nations, which I believe you call 'the West', helped educate and feed the poor, which I believe you call the 'Third World', that would be a good beginning."

"We have been doing just that for many generations, and it hasn't worked."

"I did not say it would be easy, but think of the resources being allocated to war, that could be redirected to education and peace."

"Have you studied other races that managed to move from war to peace?"

He had no clue if there were many other races that had practiced what he was preaching, but he had to believe there were. Orion told him about the Alnilam people's history, with nations who had fought among themselves until they united as one people and focused on education and technology. There was even evidence on Earth that peace was possible through education.

"Yes."

"Well I'll see what I can do when I get back to Earth, to eradicate hunger and create world peace," she mumbled sarcastically, getting tired of her alien friend's sanctimonious preaching. "Can you raise us up so we can look at the lunar base from the top of the crater wall?" she asked. Moments later they were standing three hundred meters above the landing site, on the crater's rampart wall.

"So do your people procreate like humans?"

"Yes, but not quite the same way as you do," he smiled, knowing that would peak her curiosity and change the topic.

"Oooh, that sounds like fun." Her smile disappeared as she noticed something out of place. "Hey, what's that?" she asked, pointing to two parallel lines in the lunar soil, leading towards the solar panels.

Lowering the two of them to the surface, Nom Iz directed his scanning beam at the lines and displayed the results in 3D, while Van der Hoose got down on her hands and knees to study them her way.

"They look like tire tracks from a vehicle, and not one of ours," she said. "At least not from this mission."

"I agree. One wheel is damaged and leaves a scrapping pattern," he said, referring to the image displayed.

He redirected the beam, following the tracks. Below the fine dust powder left by the landing of *Endurance*, a trail was revealed, which they followed through the center of their little compound toward the Cameron Cut. The trail continued over the edge and into the crater. He elevated them above the deep pit.

"Oh my gawd, this is freaky. Put me down on solid ground." Nom Iz complied with her request but continued scanning down into the abyss.

"There is something down there."

"Yes, that's why the GI Joes went into the crater." The second she said it, she realized that their alien friends were not aware of the item, or the presence of the military. "Oh crap!" she whispered to herself.

Nom Iz was studying his display. "I am detecting a small wheeled object moving slowly at the bottom, near the far wall; its tracks are the same width as the ones we were following. There are radio signals coming from it, being received by a metal device embedded in the wall. Come with me to the ledge, and I will show you."

"No, I think we should get the commander first."

"I am also detecting an anomaly in the scan: a large blank area ... a void. Yes, you must speak to the commander, and I must speak with the professor."

***

While his fellow army officers slept, the soldier on watch quietly retrieved his cell phone, plugged in the ear buds, and selected the music of his generation. The earphones and wire also doubled as a powerful UHF aerial. The cell phone looked like the latest Apple model, with a protective case, but was in fact the latest spy gear from China.

From his sitting position, he had an unobstructed view of the crater floor, although there was nothing to see but blackness. He typed in the coded alphanumeric entry and waited for a reply. The source of the sending relay was in the shadows, rolling over the frozen water at the bottom of the crater, and connected to an unknown face with a large bank account. He received the reply and began his report.

> *'Unexpected delay. Route collapsed.'*
>
> *'Understood. Opposition resolved?'*
>
> *'Yes 1 down, 1 to go. Have you confirmed object yet?'*
>
> *'Yes 10 minutes ago. Object is the same as child, but enormous. Will send homing signal in 1 hour. No further delays.'*

***

Nom Iz and Van der Hoose ran to HAB1 to talk to the professor.

"Professor, what do these scans mean?" he asked, showing him the results of the scan.

Orion pulled Simon to the far corner to talk quietly. "The void in the scan is due to a large quantity of crystals," he whispered. "*Our* crystals. My ship would register nothing as well. I think it may be the old ore ship that left Guatemala the same time I did."

"Natalie has informed me that three soldiers went into the crater, and they are heading toward it," Simon whispered back. "What if it's one of your father's ships?"

"We cannot let them discover it."

"It may be too late. What we need is a good cover story."

"Hey Shirley, how's the patient?"

"Hi Nat. Still unconscious but stable. The drone thing has created a hyperbaric-like chamber to filter out the carbon dioxide from his blood. The professor has been scanning him to make sure it's working."

Van der Hoose stared at the hovering stingray-like object that was holding Butcher cocooned in a bubble, and bathed in an eerie bluish glow.

"How was your walk-about?"

"We found rover tracks running right through our camp and to the ledge of the crater. Nom Iz also found radio signals coming from the rover. We think it rolled off. I have to tell the commander, but the last time I gave him bad news, he freaked out and dismissed me."

"I'm sure it's just your imagination; besides, he and Jon are on their way over, so don't sweat it, girl."

CHAPTER 28

Kai Yung took his private express elevator down to the subterranean labs. He entered a secure door, requiring a biometric scan and voice-authenticating password, and was greeted by two lab techs bowing reverently. He returned the greeting with a slight nod of his head, and casually walked over to the glass enclosure. The creature came over to him immediately, knowing who its master was.

Yung opened a small door and stuck his arm through. The egg creature, now with an eight-meter wing span, crawled over to him and rubbed its smooth jet-black skin against him. This was a ritual performed daily since it had hatched three years before. Young then took a bunch of wild mountain flowers and held them for the creature to eat. The flowers were just part of its diet, gleaned from the text written on the shell. The monks had documented the foods the mother had eaten while convalescing on the Tibetan plateau so many years ago. He was curious as to when this offspring would grow into the shape of its mother. From the drawings, the parent was angular, with beautiful swept-back wings, looking almost like a stingray. This poor juvenile beast was an odd ugly mixture of aquatic stingray, flying bat, and tree-crawling squirrel. What it lacked in looks, though, it made up for in intelligence.

Yung had trained it to respond to the various tones of a flute. One set of notes would cause the creature to perk up and go to the sound. This was first discovered accidentally, when a flute was played by an off-duty lab worker, at the far end of the building, while the creature slept in its pen. The creature had tunneled under the floor to a shocked and scared flutist. It just lay there, listening to the trill of the flute, and making what had been described as a purring sound. The sound of the flute was synthesized and the exact frequency isolated.

Further tests revealed that the sound could be heard by the creature, or perhaps felt, over great distances. The creature was moved to Yung's private and isolated island in the South China Sea. A special research vessel was dispatched to the South Pole, where the tone was played. Within minutes, the creature had perked up and flown out of its pen, landing on the research ship a short time later, twelve thousand kilometers away, and been greeted by its master.

The same test was repeated over and over, varying the volume and eventually being tested in a vacuum. The results were the same. Yung could now control it. The creature had incredible speed both in the air and under water. When the Cameron Cut was discovered, his scientist had examined the shape of the unnaturally formed crevice, and determined that it had been created by the creature's mother's wing, as it crashed into the crater wall. A plan was formulated then to investigate the bottom of the crater and determine if the great winged beast was in fact there. Confirmation from the Little Jade Rabbit and the symbols it transferred was enough to change his plan slightly.

Outfitted with a camera collar, the young creature was going to be released to rendezvous with its mother on the moon.

"Okay gentlemen, now is the time to activate the homing signal." He directed his command to two technicians in white coats, who were hovering over computer terminals nearby.

Keys were pressed and the signal was uploaded to a commercial satellite, and then transferred to a Chinese Military one. Then it was routed to the lunar satellite his government had in orbit to monitor and communicate with the little Jade Rabbit, the rover that was now sitting at the bottom of a frozen crater. Total time lapse was three long minutes. He watched the screen impatiently as the signal was handed off at each transfer point. Finally the destination point was reached.

"Thirty seconds, sir."

The tone was about to be re-broadcast to earth. They turned and watched the creature, passively lying on a mat of straw. Without warning, it became agitated and its ears perked up; then it ducked through the hole in its enclosure.

An array of cameras and monitors, including the one attached to its neck, were active, following its movements. It exited the tunnel directly into the South China Sea and swam under water, heading to their secluded island, a procedure it was trained to do each time it left its enclosure. Reaching the sandy beach, it sat still, staring up through the clouds.

"I think this exercise is a failure, sir. It is not moving."

"Wait, I have faith in my little egg creature."

They watched as a muscle twitched in its leg, then another. Slowly it hunched itself lower into the sand. Then whoosh, it rocketed up at a blinding speed. The motion-controlled cameras followed it as far as they could before losing it in the clouds. In the lab, they were already watching the radar and watched it climb, at two thousand kilometers an hour, on a direct course to Earth's only naturally orbiting satellite.

Yung had another team of technicians monitoring military radio chatter from China, Russia, and the US. The little creature, small in comparison to a jet or rocket, did not give off a heat signature from exhaust. The likelihood that it would be detected was remote but possible, just like the chance that he would be discovered as the perpetrator of this unorthodox launch. If it was spotted, how would they describe what they saw? There were no sightings reported.

Once the child reached the moon and attached itself to the mother, the two would be recalled ... and be his to control. That was the plan. It would be quite a sight: an enormous dragon beast descending from the heavens and landing on his island. China would take notice. The world would take notice.

༄ CHAPTER 29 ༅

Gregory, with Mac's stingray spaceship, was preparing to take it out for a swim among the whales that were migrating through the North Sea when it became agitated and broke the telepathic bond.

The big friendly gentleman spoke softly into his portable radio. "Mac, Gregory here, your space ship is acting strange. It keeps breaking the bond as soon as I establish it. Can you come here and have a talk with it?"

"Lin Una, Gregory is having a problem with the vessel creature again," Mac said. "Come with me please. It may be that the creature does not trust him. He only has a quarter of my blood."

"Well Orion's creature took to Sam and Simon, and they only have a quarter of your blood too."

"Yes that is true, but your children are different. They have half of you know whose blood, not to mention whatever the blasted Nazis did to him."

"Yes Father, let's not start that again. And damn it, stop calling me Lin Una," she snapped at the older man. "I prefer Lyn."

"You sound like your child, Sam. Now hurry lass, and don't fret about a name. You've had many and will have more still." The old 'Scotsman' activated his EVA belt and elevated himself off the patio, heading towards the cavernous pen of the flying creature. Glancing sideways, he noticed his daughter had caught up and was flying beside him.

They reached the cave and found the creature shaking, trying to fight an urge. Mac floated into the vessel, followed by Lyn and Gregory, and sat in the control chair.

"Come on my big beastie, what is troubling you old friend?" Although he spoke outwardly to his ship, Lyn and Gregory knew he was reaching out to it on a deeper level.

The creature settled noticeably and telepathically informed its master what was troubling it; then it activated the 3D display in front of the control console. An image of the outer islands of China came into view, where a small object had launched into orbit. Mac zoomed in on the object, which was now in space heading to the moon. He studied the odd-looking object and then turned to his puzzled daughter.

"What is it, Father?"

"You all best be sitting down. We're off to the moon. That object is what *this* creature was before it was engineered to look the way it does now. *That* is its primitive form," he said, looking at the image.

"Why is it heading to the moon?" Gregory asked.

"I don't know, but I have grandchildren up there," he said, as they felt the creature start to move.

The creature slipped into the water and swiftly swam to an empty part of the frigid North Atlantic, where it broke the water's surface and propelled itself skyward and out of the earth's atmosphere. On Mac's command, it slowed to follow the young creature at a distance, watching as it vectored in on the moon, unaware of their presence.

"We better create similar disguises to the ones the kids are wearing, so we can blend into their charade," Lyn said, as she adjusted her appearance.

"I don't feel like going back to school, as a student *or* a teacher," Mac grumbled.

"What are you two talking about?" Gregory asked. "Was Tamara here, with Simon?"

Lyn explained to him about the children wanting to help Tamara's fiancé, Tyrone, and the other astronauts. She went on to describe their cover story and character choices. "So Father," she laughed, "you know more about your planet's hierarchy than we do. What is a rank that would best suit your role?"

"Well, it *has* been a while since I did any acting. I think I will be the chancellor of the education council; Gregory will be my disciplinary marshal, and you, my dear, will fill the role of headmaster of the school."

"Sounds like a plan. Oh, and Father, you have been acting as long as I have known you," she smiled at him fondly. "How many characters have you played?"

"Far more then I can remember, my dear."

"Should we inform our children?" Gregory asked.

"No. This may just be a coincidence. Let's not concern them. Besides, it will be fun to surprise them." Mac smiled at him, enjoying the possibilities. "I do like a good adventure."

CHAPTER 30

Booker and Pierce entered HAB1's air lock, stripped out of their suits, plugging them into the chargers, and entered the common area, where they were greeted by a content pilot, a hesitant engineer, and two cautious alien men.

"Hi all," Booker said. "What's happening? How's everyone doing?" He reached for a MRE.

"Well, I'm fine," Worthy said calmly. "Couldn't be better. The arm is back to normal and the sarge is stable." She turned to Natalie with a smile and a nod.

Taking that as her cue, Natalie spoke up. "Sir, we have evidence that a rover cut through our base right around the time the solar panels were being setting up. It looks like it rolled off the edge and into the crater. My friend, Nom Iz, also discovered that it is still sending out a signal." She licked her lips nervously, and steadied herself for the bad news she was about to deliver. "He also knows about our GI Joes down there, and that there's something else as well. Please don't dismiss me like you did earlier." She said all this quickly, on a single breath.

Booker turned to Noi Ro and waited.

"I do not wish to be part of your human games. Why is your military in the crater? What are they looking for?"

"Ice."

The professor looked him squarely in the eye for a long moment. "You would send scientists down there, if that were true. In our experience, military personal support the interests of a nation, and are usually authorized to use deadly force to meet their objectives. I ask you again, why are they here and what are their intentions?"

Booker looked at the student, Nom Iz, who had his arms folded on across chest, posturing support for his teacher. The young alien man was glaring at him and waiting for an answer.

The commander turned to Pierce, who was chowing down on his own hot meal, watching events unfold before him as though they were in the middle of a play.

"What about you?" Booker asked. "You got anything to complain about, son?"

"No sir."

"Good." He gave the situation some thought. "Gentlemen, if you give me a moment, I will explain everything, but first let me clear up a concern I have with my flight engineer. What I have to say, and the answers she provides to the questions I will ask her, may resolve some of your questions."

The commander proceeded to explain about the attempt on Butcher's life, the CIA memo about a sabotage attempt, the list of suspects and coinciding list of those who had been cleared of suspicion, and the fact that Van der Hoose was not on the list.

"So," Booker crossed his arms in front of himself, "you have anything to say for yourself, Natalie?"

"No sir. This is the first I heard about an attempt on Butcher's life or the CIA's involvement."

"Are you working for any other agency or government?"

"No! I only work with NASA," she replied, red-faced and upset. "The only country I have ever visited was Mexico, and that was a vacation with some girlfriends."

"Do you believe her, Shirley?" Booker turned to ask his close friend.

"Yeah Ty, I do. I think Butcher has it wrong."

"You are partially right," Sergeant Butcher interjected suddenly from behind them, as he sat up in his protective bubble, much to the surprise of everyone in the room. "I hadn't updated my information. Sorry Commander. My apologies Van der Hoose. Now could someone please tell me what the hell is around me?"

Worthy did her best to explain the alien presence, and her strong belief that they were friendly, but before she could finish, Orion walked up to the tough sergeant and scanned his vitals.

"Sir, your vitals are back to normal, but I suggest you avoid any strenuous activities for the next twenty-four of your hours. My name is Noi Ro, and we are here to offer aid."

"Holy Crap! You're aliens! Well, I'll be damn! I never thought you were real. Does the rest of the world know? Are you guys here to solve our global warming problems? Or to stop nuclear proliferation? Would you tell us if you were an advance team preparing for an invasion?" The sergeant asked one question after another, bewildered and in shock.

"Answers later," the tall alien replied with a smile, "but for now, just know that we come in peace." He turned to the commander. "Our questions about the military presence have still not been answered?"

"Professor, before launch, we were informed that a Major Carson and his two lieutenants were on board to assist in the retrieval of ice from the crater, and to set up the oxygen generator. As for the item at the bottom of the crater, the news of its presence was given to us by Major Carson just prior to landing. That seems to be the real reason the military is here."

Butcher interjected quickly, "With all due respect, Pierce and my mission was not of a military nature per say, not in the traditional sense that you are thinking. We were ordered to Vanderburgh Air Force Base to train on the set up of the habitats, solar panels, and the OX-GEN, like you said, as well as the normal astronaut stuff you guys underwent. In fact, we thought we were flying up on *Endurance* with you. We were shocked when they secretly put us aboard an unmanned supply ship. As for what the hell is in the crater or why they are here? No clue." He paused to catch his breath, acknowledging the rest of the people in the room before continuing.

"In the interest of preventing a galactic war with your people, I *will* say that I was approached by the CIA with information that an attempt would be made on us, or the ship, to prevent our return. This attack was to be orchestrated by a person or persons from another country, who hired Americans to carry it out. My job was to identify who up here couldn't be trusted. They selected me because I have passed information to the CIA before, when I was in the Middle East. My brother in-law also works at NASA, and they trust me."

Worthy took advantage of a brief lull to ask the obvious question: "Why the hell would one of us sabotage our own ship and prevent a safe return?"

"Yeah, I don't understand that either," Butcher said. "The information they gave me did not suggest a suicide-type terrorist attack, so maybe they had another way to get home. The lists I received identified people that the CIA had vetted and those they didn't. I'm sorry again, Natalie. You were a last-minute replacement and not on the list. I did hear from my contact, just before *Endurance* landed, that you were now on the good side of the list."

Relieved, Van der Hoose smiled. "I feel like I have just been taken off Santa's naughty list."

"Sergeant Butcher, has your confidence in everyone in this room now returned?" Noi Ro asked.

"Yes, I trust the humans anyway, and I guess I have to believe that you don't want to kill us or you probably would have done that already. Now what's with this weird bubble thing you have me in?"

"It provided you with a safely pressurized environment in which to recover. My scans indicate that your vitals are now within normal parameters for a male your age, but perhaps you should consult with a human medical person." He indicated Worthy.

"The big lug's okay," she said. "Let him out."

"I have a question for our new alien friends," Booker said. "Do you know what's in the crater?"

"I cannot speculate until I have visual confirmation," the professor said to the roomful of curious on lookers, "because there are many alien objects in your solar system of which you are not aware."

Booker took charge. "I say we take a field trip to that thing that's got everybody all riled up."

"My suit arm is damaged," Worthy noted.

"And my gloves are saturated with oil," added Van der Hoose.

"And Butcher's air system in his suit isn't functional," Booker said, nodding. "Can you help us out Professor?"

"We do not have protective field belts for everyone," said the professor. "Beyond our own, we have only the one that your engineer has been wearing and one other. You will have to decide who wears it. We have two drones that can transport those in space suits more quickly."

"Sarge, I fixed your suit," Pierce jumped in. "You shouldn't have a problem. I checked all of our CO_2 filters and topped up the air supply. Commander, our packs should be about three-quarter charged."

"I can improve on that using my crystal, and give you full charges," Nom Iz suggested, heading to the suit bay with Pierce.

It was decided that Worthy would get the spare belt and team up with Noi Ro. Van der Hoose, who was already wearing one of the belts, would continue her relationship and fly with Nom Iz, while Butcher and Pierce, wearing full NASA suits, would share a drone transport, leaving Booker alone in the remaining drone.

☙ CHAPTER 31 ❧

Carson and his team made their approach using a rock-ice outcrop as a defense against the unknown. Night-vision goggles, specially adapted for their helmets, allowed them to trek across the relatively flat ice surface and view their world in shades of green. Hot objects would theoretically show up as reds and yellows, but in this subzero barren environment, the only red images were the three of them. They paused to check weapons before advancing.

Their M4 assault rifles, which were specially outfitted to fit their oversized gloves, were capable of firing 700 rounds per minute; they each carried spare clips strapped to their thighs.

"Last check, Santos, you checkout Nuzzi, and I'll check you," the major ordered. "Santos, when we are done, climb up there and take a sniper position. Nuzzi, you're with me."

"Wait major, let me double-check *your* gear." Santos motioned for his commanding officer to turn around. With the pretense of an inspection, he retrieved a marker from his pocket and marked the back of the major's suit and helmet with an 'X' in infrared ink.

"You're good to go, sir," the lieutenant confirmed, tapping the major on the head.

The ground had gradually sloped up to the wall, where it formed the ridge they were now on. Santos watched from his position as the two men crept along the wall towards the building-sized object. Even at this distance, he could tell it was smooth and made of an unbroken seamless material that was not from earth. It was a little warmer than the surrounding rock-ice, emphasizing the fact that it might be biological, which scared him, He trusted his new employer, though, or rather the money that had been transferred into his account. With his goggles, he could see that the two red humanoid-shaped objects were just steps away from the monster-sized 'building'. The one with the 'X' was trailing as the other reached out and touched the steep smooth wall of the thing. Nothing. No movement. No reaction. The butt of a gun was used as a stronger contact, and still nothing. Not surprising.

They did not expect the organic item to move, or even notice their presence. The body of the item continued out into the crater floor, in a sweeping angle, as far as their limited scopes could see. They were at the edge of it, the part that was leaning up against the crater wall with its top partially embedded in the rock, almost a kilometer above them.

"This sucker is huge!" Carson broke the silence over the command frequency. "I bet it would take a platoon of men weeks to explore it, and even then we would have barely scratched the surface."

"Sir, we can get between it and the wall, over here." Nuzzi pointed to the boundary where rock-ice met organic material.

"Santos, you copy that?"

"Yes sir. What do you want me to do if we lose COM?"

"Let's hope we don't. Haul your butt down here and watch this opening."

"Copy that."

They slipped between the smooth biological wall and the rough ice, with more than enough shoulder and head room. With the absence of even the minimal starlight, the green ghostly images vanished as was expected. In unison, they broke mini glow sticks and shook them. Carson dropped his just inside the darkness, while Nuzzi tossed his ahead. Now with the chemical radiance of the sticks, there was more than enough illumination to continue.

"Santos, you still out there?"

"Yup, no little green men following you. I'm almost at your location."

"The walls are clean," Carson said. "No sign of an entry point yet."

"Understood."

Eight glow sticks later, they detected an interruption in the symmetry of the smoothness: a ragged breach to the interior that extended up as far as he could see.

"Santos, we have an entry point. The outer wall is about a meter thick. I'm entering the rupture now. Do you still copy?"

"Negative. You cut out, I'm guessing when you made it through the wall."

Nuzzi reached in and tapped the major on the shoulder. The major was already aware of the COM drop, but wanted to get a quick peek inside. Retrieving three glow sticks, he tossed them inside, in different directions, as far as he could, and stared in awe at the marvel of alien bio-engineering before him—a sight no human had ever seen before. He started to turn and exit the vessel, to regroup with his men, when he felt something touch the back of his helmet.

The image of the organic interior of an ancient alien ship was the last thing Major Adam Carson saw. He never heard the bullet in the silent vacuum of the moon, as he dropped to the frozen floor of the vessel.

CHAPTER 32

Professor Noi Ro led the group into the crater's depth, following the presumed route the earlier crew had taken. They glided down past the elevator, descending into the pitch-black nothingness. He activated the drones scanning beams, the images from which were displayed inside each drone's protective bubble, and to the 3D displays above his and Nom Iz wrists. The images that were displayed were similar to the military-issue night-vision goggles they were all familiar with, but a hundred generations more advanced.

Worthy and Noi Ro were flying together, while his student, Nom Iz, was with Van der Hoose, sharing the display image. Van der Hoose was slightly relieved to be able to see where they were going, but still terrified of the height. She gained some comfort by holding the muscular alien's arm.

"There is the spot we found you, Butcher," Booker announced, pointing. It was agreed that, while in the protective alien shields, they would use the drone's technology to communicate.

They drifted down to the ledge, and along the path that the major had taken, while Noi Ro and Nom Iz directed their scanning beams to the ledge and the wall, looking for any anomalies. They came to the broken ledge and discovered aluminum spikes in the wall, complete with repelling lines. They proceeded onward, quickly reaching the base, where evidence of humanity was found in the form of a discarded power-bar wrapper and numerous boot prints in the dusty frozen surface.

They effortlessly glided over the icy terrain, following the footsteps of their predecessors.

"It's good to see they made it past that broken ledge. At least no other crew member was left behind," Booker casually stated, breaking the stillness as they watched the wonders of this foreign ice world float by.

"You know Professor, traveling like this sure beats bouncing around with our suits. It would be nice if you could leave us a few," Worthy casually commented, knowing what the answer would be.

Butcher and Pierce's drone was flying higher and farther out from the wall, creating a larger field of view on the displays. They spotted the large item first, as it loomed out of the darkness like an apparition from a ship graveyard.

Noi Ro instantly recognized the shape as the item lay, resting on its side. It would be what his own ship—his home—would look like, except this was the ore ship, and ten times larger. Activating a floating icon, he retrieved confirmation and vital information about the big ship. He halted the fleet and floated in front to address the crew.

"The object before us is one of ours. It was an ore-processing ship lost over a thousand of your years ago, in this sector. The ship is a living creature, similar to the drones and the vessel in which we arrived. This creature is not registering any life signs however."

"Did you know about it?" Booker asked.

He lied. "I speculated that it might have been one of ours, but in our field studies, we have discovered many derelict ships and probes from other races."

"What was it doing here, so long ago?" Worthy asked.

"Mining, I presume."

"What and where was it mining?"

"I do not know." He lied again, uncomfortable doing so.

"Does that thing of yours say anything about the crew?" Butcher prompted.

"It departed our planet with a crew of three." He told the partial truth, but knew that this ship, and another big ore processor, were remotely controlled by his own ship, now resting in the ocean. He knew the whereabouts of two of the crew members. His father was buried in Guatemala, near the mining site, and the other he'd just met in Scotland, quite alive. He guessed that the third would be found frozen inside this ship. He remembered the man—his father's assistant. His face surfaced from the deep recesses of memory, and he felt a wave of sadness wash over him.

"So where are they?" Butcher asked, getting agitated.

"The answer will be revealed once we enter the ship," Noi Ro snapped, uncharacteristically.

"Is it dangerous?" Van der Hoose hesitantly asked Nom Iz, whom she was gripping tightly.

He reassured her with a smile. "No, it will be safe."

Booker was studying the screen before him, and detected a small purple object to the left of them beside the big ship. He accidentally touched the object in the display and a zoomed-in version materialized. The same display was shared with everyone.

"What is that?" Worthy inquired, as the object was partially obscured by the large ship.

"I will go closer to get a better scan," Nom Iz suggested.

"No don't leave me!" Van der Hoose begged, holding tighter. "I'm freaked out as it is."

"Then come with me. Professor, we will stay in communication and catch up later."

Their two glowing white bodies became dimmer as they sped off from the group towards the mysterious object, which was registering a trace of heat. The professor and the remainder of the group moved forward toward the dead vessel creature, uncertain of what they would find.

***

The little creature was tiring, yet it pushed on through space towards the big shinny orb, driven by some unexplained desire. It cautiously approached the crater, momentarily fearing for its life, and then realizing that its master would never harm it, as the tone beckoned it onward. With this renewed feeling of confidence and energy, it dove into the blackness.

Its sensors picked up the source of the sound it had felt, which had led it to this place, but other sensors revealed something more. All creatures, even the most primitive, recognize their own mothers. Such was the case for this strange little being. The draw toward the sound was imposing, but the need to be with the big creature was greater.

Without hesitation, it attached itself to the slick smooth skin and crawled toward the head. It tried to make sounds, attempting to communicate, but in this airless environment, nothing could be heard. Instinctively, it attempted to form a mental bond—something it had tried to do with the master, but failed. A flood of emotions consumed the little creature, as it realized it was truly alone.

***

Nom Iz and Van der Hoose floated down to the crater ice base, like two bright fireflies in the night. The combined glow of their protective shields illuminated the ground all around them, and revealed the small four-wheeled machine, tucked beside the big creature. Using his scanner, they determined that it had battery power and was actively transmitting.

The Little Jade Rabbit's infrared camera was switched to normal mode, as the bright object approached. The observer studied the glow as it hovered in front of the twin cameras. A signal was sent and the range of focus was adjusted, dialing in the digital iris of the lenses. Two humanoids were part of the glowing apparition. The observer confirmed that this vision was being recorded. He watched as one of the humanoids pointed a beam at it, and the collected data was projected on a display in the glowing sphere. Another signal was sent, this time directing the machine to move toward the light and deploy its secondary ground probe.

This backup probe was a last-minute addition to the rover's instrumentation, unwittingly approved by the administration. The probes were designed to penetrate the soil and analyze total water composition, particularly around Shackleton Crater. The second probe was the same on paper, with major changes left undocumented. A fragment of a crystal, embedded in the little creature's egg shell, was incorporated into the hypodermic-like needle apparatus. Tests on the little creature confirmed that the radiation from the crystal was the only way the needle could penetrate its tough hide, allowing for a sample of its DNA. The rover had just completed the same process on the large creature.

Reloading again, it was ready to withdraw a second sample. The presence of floating, glowing extraterrestrials was an opportunity. The two samples would easily be retrieved by his agents on site and returned to earth for a detailed study.

Taking an action from nature, the little rover crept passively toward the glowing lights, its probe un-extended. Dialing down the light input on the cameras iris, it rolled until it touched the protective glow of the taller humanoid.

"Awe, isn't that cute," Van der Hoose mused. "It likes you." Van der Hoose mused.

"It is more likely attracted to the light, in order to charge its power system," Nom Iz commented, preoccupied with his scanning results and unaware of the danger until it was too late.

"Ow! What the—" Looking down, he could see the rover retracting a needle from his leg. He elevated himself and rubbed the sore spot before he realized that his crystal would quickly heal him. He also realized that Van der Hoose was scrutinizing his very human reaction and verbalization.

"You certainly have learned to embrace human language."

Nom Iz ignored her comment, and went to retrieve his blood sample, but the little four-wheeled menace ducked under the big creature's wing, making it almost impossible to catch.

The rover backed up into the tight space until it could go no farther, spinning its wheels into the rock-ice. It continued, like a burrowing animal, depositing the excavated debris in front, and blocking the presumed attack from the alien being.

When the last of the open space was sealed, the transmission of the tone and the signal to Earth were lost. Like a badger confronted with a solid underground wall, it followed the path of least resistance and dug around the smooth edges. The big creature-vessel, being part biology and part technology, had hatches engineered into it, with access panels, keyed to the biometrics of DNA and crystal radiation. The rover had trace amounts of both, enough that the technological part opened and the rover rolled in. On board, autonomous default programming of 'explore and record' was activated.

***

Kai Yung watched with keen interest as his little Jade Rabbit approached the glowing shapes. The light the objects gave off was enough to confirm that they were humanoids. There was no technology that could do what he was seeing; otherwise he would be involved with its manufacturing. These beings were definitely not from Earth.

The blood sample from the alien would add nicely to his wealth, when it was returned with the big creature.

His excitement faded when the view screen showed the rover retreating, and its transmission halted. That was understandable, if the rover was shielded by the big creature or if it managed to get inside it. He would wait patiently, because the remote antenna at the crater's rim would signal when the creature was leaving. Success and good fortune was close at hand.

***

Van der Hoose floated over to Nom Iz, who was struggling to get under the wing, and tapped him on the shoulder.

"Forget it; it's long gone. Let's get back to the others."

They glided over to the group, now down by the icy-rock wall that the creature rested against. Boot prints and a discarded glow stick indicated that this was the route the astronauts had taken.

"Carson, this is Booker. What's your status?" the commander repeated over the command frequency, when he exited the drone.

Santos, hearing the radio, handed his co-conspirator his rifle while he slowly exited the crevice, leaving his fellow lieutenant hidden.

"Commander, Santos here; are we glad to see you." He stopped short, surprised to see two glowing beings standing with Booker. Still in shock, he noticed two overgrown stingrays floating next to them. The stingrays were the same shape as the behemoth ship he was standing alongside. His night vision goggles also detected two astronauts behind one of the floating things.

"What the hell is going on? Who or what are they?" the confused lieutenant asked, pointing to the glowing beings in fear.

"I was going to ask you the same question. Where's the major?" Booker asked authoritatively.

Santos lied. "We don't know. He told us to stay out here while he went to the ship to investigate."

"Where's Nuzzi?"

"He is by the gouge in the hull that the major went through. We were about to go in and look for him."

"When was the last time you heard from Carson?"

"Maybe an hour or so."

Taking Worthy's hand, Booker became engulfed in the protective field. "Worthy, do you smell bullshit?"

"Yeah and a lot of it."

Booker exited the protective force shield, and gestured to Santos. "Come out here, I will get Nuzzi."

"No sir. We have orders to hold this position. Besides, you didn't explain what those things are," Santos insisted, stalling for time as he motioned to the alien objects.

Unaware of the events unfolding below, Nom Iz and Van der Hoose unexpectedly ascended, landing in front of Booker.

Military reflexes took over. Santos retrieved his gun from Nuzzi and the two opened fire on the glowing beings. Van der Hoose and Worthy, in fear for their lives, backed up to Booker, expecting protection. Unbeknownst to them, their shields were the protection, absorbing the kinetic energy of the bullets. Booker realized this and moved with them to safety behind a drone. The other drone took up a forward defensive position. Noi Ro and Nom Iz, who had already witnessed the stopping power of the shields in the Guatemala jungles earlier that year, stood their ground and waited for the military men to run out of ammunition.

"Stand down, Lieutenants!" Booker ordered, attempting to diffuse the situation. "That's an order!"

Noi Ro activated his arm bracelet and instructed the lead drone to move forward to better protect those without shields. This action was interpreted as a threat, forcing Santos and Nuzzi deeper into the crevice. Seeing them retreat, Butcher and Pierce advanced to the entrance, but were stopped by Booker.

"I'm not looking for a gun fight. Any suggestions, Professor?"

'Sam, how far out are you?' Simon called. *'We have a problem in the crater and could use your help, ASAP.'*

CHAPTER 33

Working in Area 51, Courtney Williamson was no stranger to the weird and unexplained, but stepping into the sleek alien ship through the glowing blue portal, into the alien women's ship, was a heart-pounding moment, and a definite first—redefining weird.

"Mysteries always have a solution in science." This was his favorite saying, picked up from one of his many professors, at either MIT or Cal Tech. Having an IQ score in the 300-plus range was probably a major contributing factor for his successes. Once he completed a degree in Bio-Molecular Engineering, NASA brought him in to head up a team to develop the next generation of launch vehicles for future missions. It was this work on bio-engineered space crafts that had attracted the attention of the NSA, leading to a job at Groom Lake Operations.

One of the first projects he had worked on was analyzing debris found in the 1947 Roswell New Mexico crash. It wasn't the light-weight pieces of metal, with the peculiar glyphs on them, that were so prevalent in modern Roswell mythology. It was what else they had found that he dealt with. As extraordinary as the unidentified crashed object was, and the prospect that it was not of this world, the item found near it was even more alien. It was a biological entity. It was hurt, and by duplicating its living environment to that of an aquatic creature, combined with some dumb luck, he managed to bring it back to health. It only communicated with him once, and that was through a computer screen. He wished he could have talked to the controller of that drone, and learned where it had come from, not to mention a million other questions he had. But he had never gotten the chance before it escaped.

That was earlier in the year, and he hadn't seen it since. When the NSA invited him to comment on a grainy photograph taken with night-vision equipment, and magnified a hundred fold, he recognized the shape as the extreme version of his probe friend. He later learned that the photograph was of something on the moon, and that a team was going up there, under the guise of confirming water presence.

The NSA also saw the similarities, which was the reason for soliciting his opinion. As second in command of Area 51, and in charge of all extra-terrestrial sciences, as well as being the only human who had legitimately communicated with a non-Earth entity, he was given the project. Major Adam Carson, already scheduled for the mission, was to be his eyes up there, with the intent of determining if that object was remotely controlling the little probe and if there were others like it.

When the alien rescue ship made an appearance on the scene, he was almost certain that it was connected. All doubt was removed when the ship sent out its own probe, identical to the one he had helped.

This was the break that he was looking for. And anyway, he couldn't pass up a chance to fly in an alien space ship to the moon.

"So what do you ladies do for fun at school?" he asked, after ten breathtaking minutes of mind-blowing excitement, as he felt the freedom of gravity being lifted from him. Ma Z had asked the ship to make the ceiling transparent again, providing the 'VIP ride' sensation.

They didn't answer, so he tried again. "You know, when you don't have to study or fly around in this wondrous vessel." Courtney relaxed his grip on the chair, as he tried to start a conversation.

After getting no response, he decided to try another tactic to get them engaged. "How about a piece of pizza?"

At the mention of food, Aram At turned to face their passenger.

"Is that edible?" she asked, gesturing to the boxes on the deck, and getting ready to have a bit of fun.

"Damn straight it is. It's pizza. It's the most popular food on Earth!"

"Do not leave it there," she said, "or the ship will consume it." She smiled, getting a look of fright in return.

"This ship is alive? Wow, what does it eat?"

"Anything *she* wants," Ma Z replied, turning her pilot chair towards him, laughing, and accepting the offered slice. Aram At joined them as the three ate slices of pepperoni and cheese pizza, realizing they were famished.

"I hope the food agrees with you, because I don't know how to fly this thing," Courtney suggested with a chuckle in his voice.

Realizing her error, Ma Z quickly made the motions of scanning the food, knowing that their charade had almost been blown.

"It is safe. I believe our physiology is not that different. Aram At, this food has animal product on it, and you said you would not eat any flesh." She smiled, knowing that her friend had just started a vegetarian diet to fit into her wedding dress.

'Crap, you know I love pepperoni. It doesn't count as real meat, does it?' Tamara silently sent her, upset for being called out. She then turned to the big Jamaican. 'This tastes good, and I am enjoying the flavor." She did her best to pout alien style.

"We're just saying, girl, it's pork meat, with all kinds of good tasting nitrates added," Courtney joked with them, enjoying their company and poking fun at the vegetarian.

"□ʕאך" Aram At cussed, and dropped two large slices of the meat to the deck floor, watching as the ship absorbed them.

"Did you see that!? Wow, remind me not to walk around in bare feet!" He broke out laughing, pointing at Aram At, who was blushing.

"Do not swear when we have guest!" Ma Z mused, laughing with Court at her friend's expense.

"This ship is like the perfect bachelor pad; any food you drop, it eats. Better than a pet dog."

Ma Z nodded. "It eats anything."

"So," he said, "this has to be exciting for you too, being students and getting to meet another alien race. That is, unless you do this all the time?"

"No, not all the time. It is exciting as you say," Aram At replied nervously, not wanting to get into a geopolitical discussion.

Sam picked up on her friend's discomfort and decided to change the subject. Then it donned on her that Court had no way of confirming anything they said. Who knows? Maybe alien women their age partied.

"You asked what we do for fun, at school. We do this." Ma Z stood up, pulling the big man with her, and proceeded to slowly move her hips in a sensual fashion, directing the rolling action towards him.

"Damn girl, that's hot even on Earth. Hey, let me add some tunes." He fumbled with his phone and accessed his collection of R&B. Then, as an afterthought, he switched over to his favorite Reggae artist. Within seconds, the island lilt of Bob Marley, singing "Could You be Loved" resonated from the small speakers, as he matched the slow hip slide of his dance partner.

Ma Z mentally asked the ship to boost up the volume and base, and all were rewarded with rich reverberation of tones and a beat rivaling any night club in LA or Paris. Both girls were familiar with the artist, and enjoyed the way it made them feel and move.

When the song ended, Aram At moved into his arms, ready for her turn. Not wanting to stop dancing, Courtney instructed his phone to play "Jammin" from the same artist.

Ma Z swayed with them, and the three got their groove together, with slow hip-moving motions directed at various partners. It had been a while since she had danced, or for that matter, had a good time holding a man this close. She had been under cover in Afghanistan for the last twelve weeks, and dancing was definitely a mission breaker. Aram At loved to get out and party too, but the last good bash had been on the trawler, earlier that year. Her fiancé just wasn't around much to give her that pleasure.

Courtney watched these two sensual alien beings, brazenly gyrating their hips, knowing that their attention was directed at him. Whatever might have been going on in their heads, he thought he saw sadness on their faces. As the song concluded, he played another: "No Women, No Cry". He loved this song, and the way Bob Marley's voice could melt a women's heart. More than one women had left with him for the evening as they stirred to its beat.

If the world only knew of the galactic powers of Bob, he thought, as he held Ma Z close, realizing that these alien girls, with their body hugging onesies, were responding just like humans.

***

'Sam, how far out are you? We have a problem in the crater and could use your help, ASAP.'

"They need our presence in the crater. We must hurry," Ma Z informed her bewildered shipmates, as the vessel accelerated to maximum speed.

'Simon, what's going on?'

Five minutes later, after a detailed explanation that included visuals, she was caught up and filtered the information back to the others on board, just as the South Pole lunar base came into view.

❧ CHAPTER 34 ☙

Mac, Lyn, and Gregory were in the second ship, monitoring everything from the shadows as Sam brought her ship down to the group in the crater.

"What the bloody hell is going on. They are reckless! Sharing our technology. Look, Sammy brought another one up from earth. What the bloody hell are we now? A taxi service? Do you have any suggestions Lyn? Because I don't?" Mac was angry and agitated as he watched the events unfold.

"First thing is to calm down and direct some of that anger into your acting," Lyn suggested. "We have a cover story; let's use it. Let's make a bold entrance, and I will exit and talk to them as the headmaster of the school."

Mac instructed the ship to project a larger, grander image of itself, using many lights, Hollywood style, as they came in for a landing.

True to form, they presented a dazzling display that any FX director would have been proud to put their name to. Lights shimmered like an aurora borealis, gradually changing to various shades of green, blue, and purple, pulsing with life. Their presence instilled shock and fear in both the humans and the fake aliens, and got their full attention.

Continuing the Hollywood style, a burst of steam billowed out from under the craft, increasing the drama and mystery.

A door slowly formed in the side of the vessel, and Lyn hovered out onto the icy surface, wearing the same one-piece white material but with a regal purple sash that covered most of her body. She masked her hair to show small braids woven into her long green mane, a hairstyle that any queen would be envious of.

"I am Lyn Una, the headmaster of the school. Professor, students, you will come with me. The chancellor of the education council is inside and demands your presence." She said this loudly and in English, on the alien frequency, but with a strong alien accent.

Those not in a shield, and the communication network, looked stunned and confused and went to the nearest person with a shield for answers.

"What's happening Professor? Who are they? Do you know them?" Booker was the first to connect with Noi Ro.

Butcher and Pierce moved to Nom Iz, who was connected with Van der Hoose and Worthy. Courtney, Aram At, and Ma Z had already exited their ship and were almost with the team when they saw and heard Lyn Una.

'She certainly has a flare for the dramatic, doesn't she, bro?' Sam whispered to Simon silently.

'Yuup, she missed her Broadway calling.'

After the message was relayed to Booker, he stepped out from the glow, but kept his hand in contact with Noi Ro, to communicate with the new person in authority.

"Headmaster, ma'am, I am Major Tyrone Booker; I am in charge of the humans here on this moon. Your professor was only offering aid and—" he was cut off with a wave of her hand.

"Professor Noi Ro, NOW!" This was her last command, as she turned and headed into her ship.

"Are you in trouble?" This was asked by more than one human.

"Yes most likely; we must go." Noi Ro did his best to look upset, knowing that it was not real, but something had prompted his friends' mother and grandfather to show up and pretend to be their superiors. He was curious and would act the part accordingly.

"You can't leave us down here like this; we will be stranded," Worthy said, as she grabbed the professor's arm.

"Does the headmaster know of your telepathic abilities?" Van der Hoose whispered to Nom Iz.

"No he does not. None of them do."

"Sorry, but I think you should stay and ask your sister to communicate what's going on."

'Sam, what do you think is going on?'

'Not sure but she wants us inside.'

'Our friends are worried. They think the headmaster will detain us and discontinue our aid. They fear they won't get out of the crater. I'll stay and comfort them while you go and tell me what's happening.'

'You should go; she's your mother.'

'She's OUR Mother, and she won't bite. I thought you guys had buried that hatchet back in Scotland.'

'Fine I'll go, but they don't know about our ability.' Frustrated, she floated off towards the impressive ship, catching up with her friends, Noi Ro and Aram At.

Out of the corner of her eye she saw Courtney running towards the human assembly, stumbling, unaccustomed to the low gravity.

"Bravo Mother! Bravo!" Sam criticized, applauding slowly as she slipped through the opaque shimmering door. "I wonder how much of that arrogance was real."

"Thank you, Sam, I'll take that as a compliment of my acting skills. I was listening to you and your interactions at Area 51, and I must say you have become quite the thespian yourself. Well done!" Lyn quickly replied, defusing the situation as she applauded back.

"Well, if we are finished complimenting each other," Mac said, looking around, "we have something important to share with you." He looked around. "Where is Simon?"

"He decided to stay outside with the humans."

"Why would he do that?" Lyn asked her daughter.

"They were afraid you would force us to return to school and face disciplinary action, leaving them stranded."

"I suppose I did come across as a pretty stern headmaster." Lyn smiled and winked at Mac.

"How the bloody hell is he going to know what we have to say? Our communications aren't transmitting from this ship, what with most of the damn humans now connected to our external network."

"I'll keep him in the loop. Don't worry," Sam responded guardedly.

"And how the bloody hell are you going to that, lassie?"

"Duh, by using their telepathy," Tamara answered.

"What?!" Mac and Lyn responded in unison.

"We believe it has something to do with the DNA of their parental lineage," Orion stated casually.

"NOT from my side it didn't!" Lyn loudly announced.

"Who else knows about this ability?" Mac asked the group.

"Just the four of us and now you three," Tamara confirmed.

Lyn moved to the other side of the ship and embraced her daughter for the second time in her adult life.

'You have his gift,' Lyn said silently to her daughter. *'Be careful. It will lead to danger.'*

'You have it too?'

'Yes, with Simon, although he never realized. It only worked when I touched him. It would seem by touching you, I get the same results.'

'Si, thinks it's a twin thing.'

'Tell him that the three of us need to talk about this further.'

'Okay Mother, we understand and will talk more about this later, won't we Sam?' Simon added, listening to his mother's internal comments to his sister, through his bond with Sam, and causing her to break the embrace, startled and confused. Sam just smiled back, smugly.

"Lyn, deal with your family issues later," Mac said. "We have more pressing concerns. Less than an hour ago this happened." He brought up the display showing the little egg creature, launching itself from an island in the China Sea.

"That creature is the primitive form of the stingray vessels, and if not controlled properly, could become extremely dangerous."

"How is that possible?" Orion asked.

"I don't know, and that worries me. Is your father's ship still gathering data?"

"Yes, it has since it landed on Earth. Scanning the skies with microprobes, and now with the internet and wireless communications, it has amassed all forms of information. I should have data on its origin."

"Good, connect to it and find out everything that has ever been recorded about it. Start with the launch, and go backwards to when and where it was found. I think you will discover an egg, measuring about a meter high, at the end of your search. We need to find out if someone is controlling it. Orion, do it quickly and keep us updated on our secure frequency."

"I will do it now," Orion remarked, glad to have real abilities to share that the others did not have.

"You will have to make it quick," Mac said, "because the creature is here right now, on the ore ship, trying to bond with it. I will board and attempt to talk to it."

"Three soldiers have also boarded. They entered through a rip in the lower belly, probably near the light-speed drives," Orion added.

"Bloody hell, I've spent a millennium trying to keep our existence and this technology hidden, and now we're on the brink of being discovered. We've gotten shoddy!" He shook his head in frustration and anger, then turned to Sam. "Any military strategies you can suggest?"

"Simon informed me that they are armed and dangerous. They shot at him and the humans. We should split up, with one group going after the creature and the other tracking down the soldiers. Uncle Mac, can you get into the ship from the top?" Sam asked.

"Yes, I will take Lyn and Gregory with me. You and the others follow the rogue soldiers where they entered. Be careful and try not to harm them."

"Simon wants to know what he should do with the others outside. They will want to be part of the capture."

"Tell him they will not be safe. They stay outside," Mac instructed firmly.

"If we are ever to befriend them and gain their trust in the future, as an alien race, we have to allow them to help and witness the capture of their fellow shipmates. We have purposely presented ourselves as superior in intellect and in ethics; we must once more prove that we are honorable. The soldiers will ultimately be dealt with by the human authorities," Orion suggested strongly, gaining approval from Tamara and Sam, who relayed the statement to Simon, who was in full agreement.

"It is *because* of our superiority and intelligence that we *cannot* allow the humans to enter the ship!" Gregory objected excitedly, standing firmly with his mentor. Yes, they could get hurt, but more importantly, we will be exposing ourselves! Mac is correct. We should *not* allow them to enter the ship."

"Buddy, we know them!" Tamara said, jumping into the discussion. "They are good people and can help. They will *want* to help."

"No, you do *not* know them," Gregory lashed back. "They will turn on you in a heartbeat, and no one but the group here can help you, because we are family, and I am not your 'buddy'. I am your father; show some respect."

"What?" Tamara gasped, in shock.

"Well, if you hadn't all been so impatient to leave and rescue your fiancé, you might have learned something from your elders," he scolded. "But no, you are just as pigheaded as Sam."

"Silence!" Mac shouted, frustrated with all the drama and distraction. "As the last of the three original travelers, and the patriarch of this dysfunctional family, the burden of judgment is on me. I am proud that everyone has debated in true Alnilamtian fashion, heatedly and passionately. And good points were made on both sides but in our planetary council tradition, I defer the decision to my seconds in the family tree." He turned to his nephew and daughter. "What are your opinions, Orion and Lyn?"

Lyn spoke up first. "Orion made a good point about the future, if we decide to greet them as an alien race. The groundwork, whether we like it or not, is being set right now. It is our responsibility to show the world that we are an honorable group. I can't speak for all of Alnilam, just our little family and my oldest cousin, Orion, if he will allow me." Orion nodded and she continued. "I say we allow our new friends to help in any way they can, working side by side, aliens and humans." Lyn made eye contact with Sam, who was wiping a tear away. She then went to her daughter and held her hands. "Tell your brother we will let them help."

"We will still need to protect the three astronauts not in the environment shields," Orion quietly added,

"Bloody hell," Mac huffed. "We have more than enough belts for them, but I need fully charged crystals."

"I can help you with that; I brought extras," Orion said. "Oh and Mac, I also have an idea as to why the ore ship's nervous system burnt out."

Mac gave him a quizzical look. "What, you scanned the ship? You think it was the blue-ring crystals?"

"Yes, they are more powerful then the red-ring ones that came from your planet. Some of the blue ones have defects, which Simon and Sam found a way to correct last year."

"Really, how?"

"It was an accident on board the *Dragon Spirit*. The defective crystal came into contact with a spilled glass of wine. It would seem that the chemical elements in Merlot correct the defects."

"Well bloody hell! Smart young bugger. But it seems like a waste of a good bottle. I'm changing the teams around. I want you with me. Lyn will take Orion's place out there."

"I would be honored," Orion replied, "but my knowledge of the crystals is vastly surpassed by Simon's. Besides I have to find out where the little creature came from."

"Okay then, Simon is with Gregory and me. I think I should greet our human guests first."

As the group broke up, collecting the necessary supplies of crystals and EVA belts, Orion pulled Sam aside. "Sam, can you help me with the ship? It won't talk to me, and I need it to link with my home ship on Earth."

"Sure buddy," Sam laughed, punching Orion on the arm. "I guess I spoiled her."

CHAPTER 35

"Greetings, I am the chancellor of the education council, and this is my disciplinary marshal. You have already meet Lyn Una, the headmaster of the school. I speak to you with grave concerns about the actions of Professor Noi Ro and his students. It is our planet's philosophy to observe and monitor new space-faring races, like humans. Our intent is to never interfere with such development; such is the course of your evolution, your destiny." Mac paused and looked at each earthling, acknowledging each in turn before continuing.

"We are an ancient race of people with an old, and some would say wise, council at the top, but still with antiquated ideals. There has been a growing movement over the last thousand of your years that would suggest that our people get out of our comfort zone, and teach and share our technology with races we feel have potential to use this knowledge wisely. The professor and the students, it would seem, feel the same way and there is little I can do to stop him or his students, short of imprisoning them. The time has come to listen to the next generation."

The astronauts murmured their gratitude, as they applauded.

Holding his hand up, the chancellor halted the acclaim. "Do not thank me yet. I believe you have an expression, 'Be careful what you wish for.' What I have to offer may put hardship on your society and your way of life, and may actually threaten your existence. Your people have enjoyed innocence, unaware of other races, and for the most part these races have ignored you, primarily since you had little to offer. If, and I do say *if*, we part with our knowledge and technology, other races may attempt to take it from you—races with horrific morals, which would then use our own technologies against us and you."

The human team grumbled their concern.

"Chancellor, sir," Commander Booker said, "as appealing and freighting as your proposal is, it is not our decision to make. You should be having this conversation with the president of the United States and the UN."

"Son, how old are you?"

"I am 31. Why? What does my age have to do with this?"

"Everything and yet nothing. I have been alive more than 8,000 of your years, and the professor and the headmaster are both around 1000. The students average 126 years." He felt this small exaggeration would only help their credibility. "You are but a child in comparison. Do not think for a moment that I am going to simply give you the keys to the family car. Not right away. First we talk, learn from each other. Then we see if you are ready for the keys."

"How long will that take?" Courtney asked, stepping forward and speaking for the first time.

"You Americans, as I believe you call yourselves, have this need to 'fast track' proposals. When it comes to dealing with our race and other space-capable peoples, patience, you will find, is the wiser course of action. I believe you have another expression that is fitting: 'Stop and smell the roses'."

Commander Booker nodded. "Wise words indeed, sir, which I suggest we table for our own wise leaders to ponder. For now we have a pressing matter: Three of our men are in that ship down there. At least two of them are armed and dangerous, with the other unaccounted for. We cannot allow them to be killed by your people or that ship. We are willing to assist in their capture, however."

"I would propose nothing less," agreed the chancellor. "In fact, it is we who offer our assistance while *you* retrieve your men. But hear me, no being on *any* of our ships will be harmed. Are we clear?"

Everyone was in agreement.

The chancellor continued. "In our earlier briefing, Ma Z proposed a strategy. Ma Z, if you please...?"

"Yes thank you, Chancellor. My suggestion is that we approach the capture from three directions. The professor and I, with the rest of your crew, will follow the men inside using the same breach they used. The chancellor, marshal, headmaster, and Nom Iz will enter the ship at the command station farther up the ship."

"You said three directions," Booker said. "That was only two."

"The chancellor and Nom Iz will attempt to wake the creature itself, while the other two create a moving force shield, moving towards us and hopefully trapping the men between." She purposely left out how the little creature fit into the picture.

"Why would you want to wake the creature?" Courtney asked.

"It could contain the men without confrontation, and protect them from this inhospitable environment," the chancellor replied.

Booker cleared his throat. "I don't want to seem ungrateful, but the three of us in these bulky monkey suits could move a lot easier without them."

Butcher agreed. "I for one would not like to be mistaken for one of the bad guys and get caught in the cross hairs of an alien stun gun, or whatever you have."

The marshal handed the NASA-suited members their equipment. "Here are additional force shield belts. Once you have changed out of your ... 'bulky monkey suits', we can get started."

Mac and his group, along with two drones, floated up to the top of the big ship, where an entrance was revealed. They slipped through the large door, leaving it open behind them, and finding themselves in a large utility chamber. The ceiling was domed and curved down to the floor. The most prominent objects in the room, running the length of the chamber on the ceiling, were three large grayish-black conduits about two meters in circumference. Looking down the length of the room, Simon could see smaller conduits, branching off at regular intervals, and still smaller ones leading off of those, each about the size of an arm.

"Impressive, isn't it, my boy?"

"What are those things?" Simon asked.

"They're the creature's nerves and lead to its brain. Lyn, you and Gregory set up the drones and create the shields at the far end, to block the other hatch. Simon, you follow me." The big man, who had intimate knowledge of the inner-workings of the enormous creature, directed his grandson to a large black wall, where the nerve channels terminated.

"Behind this barrier membrane is the brain."

Using his arm bracelet, he aimed a narrow beam of light at the thick rubbery wall, sliced through it, and between the two of them, they pulled the incision apart and entered through it. The brain was a lattice-work of conduits, most of them ranging from the thicknesses of an arm to the thicknesses of a finger, with the smallest as thin as coarse hair, all covered in a chalky white fine dust. Simon spotted where the three main tubes intersected the cerebrum, with one on each side and the third disappearing into the darkness at the back.

"How big is it?" Simon asked in awe.

"It is slightly larger than two full-grown blue whales."

"Impressive. Should it be dry and dusty?"

"No, but it's not unexpected. That's one of the reasons I opened it up. I needed to confirm the extent of the damage."

"It looks dead."

"Yes it is. Electrocuted. See the rupture in that nerve conduit?" He pointed to the large pipe to the left of them.

Simon floated up and hovered over the deteriorated rubbery brain matter, inspecting the damage. The thick tube was brittle and pieces crumbled when he touched the jagged edge of the rupture. It looked to him like a pipe that had frozen and cracked—a very large pipe, which he confirmed by floating inside. The light of his suit showed scorch marks around the circumference, made by extremely high voltage.

"I'd say that nerve is fried," he said to Mac as he exited the organic tube.

"The others seem to be intact, so there *is* hope for this big beastie."

"I thought I would find little nerve filaments inside the conduit, like fiber optics."

"That *is* a filament. Electrical impulses travel inside it, and all the various other nerves throughout the ship, just like your own nervous system, but supersized." Mac chuckled, as he continued to stare at his scanner display. "I'm detecting a low-voltage reading in the third lobe at the very back. You need to head down that way; it should show up as a light pink color."

Simon pushed off the spongy wall and glided through the gap between the brain and the upper wall, in the direction Mac had indicated. He flew over a continuous pattern of nerves, crisscrossing over the dead white flesh, for almost twenty-five meters before detecting a change in the pattern. A fissure appeared, separating the two lobes.

He ran his fingers lightly over the delicate pink membrane, and saw tiny sparks of electricity leave his hand and dance on the surface of the living matter, before being absorbed. He communicated this information back to Mac.

"Keep doing what you're doing, but use both hands. When you think you've stimulated that area enough, place both hands on it and hold them there. Concentrate and try to create a bond."

He did as instructed, but failed to reach a telepathic bond. For his efforts, he did receive strange images flashing from the blackness however—images so bizarre they could only be created in the mind of an alien creature.

He decided to try what the strange old man at his mother's place had showed him and placed his forehead directly onto the creature's brain, while spreading his hands out to the sides. He felt electrons crackle around him and became immersed in their lightning bolts. He located a specific part of the brain: a bright flicker he was told to embrace. He followed it as it grew, and in his mind's eye, he could see a connection—a band of blue light joining him to the creature. The connection expanded, engulfing his whole body and drawing him tightly to the surface. The white glow of his suit was now blue, from the electricity flowing from the creature.

Simon lost all sense of his body, only his consciousness existed as he merged with the creature. Slowly he became aware of his surroundings—the giant creature's surroundings. He sensed everyone on board. He could feel their heartbeats, their heat, and the micro bursts of electricity they gave off. He could see all this coming through the strange color bands radiating off them—bands beyond the known color spectrum. As he adjusted to this form of existence, he found himself diving deeper into the creature's sub-consciousness, as strange alien shapes flew past him. Images were sharper now, and he could distinguish individual faces. He found Sam with Worthy, Van der Hoose, and Courtney on a lower utility deck. Booker was with Butcher and Pierce on the ore-processing deck. Orion was in his own ship, sitting at the controls with the 3D display active. Simon watched all of them for a while, before realizing that they were not moving. They were all frozen where they stood or floated. He sought out the presence of Mac, and found that he too was frozen, studying his scanner. With everyone motionless, it was easy to find two of the soldiers they were all searching for. There was no sign of Major Carson anywhere.

Lieutenants Santos and Nuzzi were hiding in a chamber between two decks, probably this ship's equivalent of an elevator.

'Sam, they are in an elevator room just ahead of you on your right,' he whispered to her internally. He couldn't feel her presence as he normally would. The strange phenomenon he had experienced back in Scotland was happening here. They were all frozen in time. He panicked for a moment, before gaining control. Breathing deeply, he relaxed and attempted to seal the elevator room, preventing their escape. With his mind, he willed his body—his host's body—to form a force shield around the door. He watched as the instructions were sent through the large conduit and then forwarded on to smaller ones, eventually terminating at a junction node near the elevator. A ripple of blue energy started to form around the door, yet he felt he could move through it. He wondered if his instructions were actually being carried out.

Suddenly another consciousness made itself known. It was weak and immature, yet inquisitive, seeking answers. Simon searched the big vessel with his mind, but found no evidence of the entity, so he decided to invite it closer in his virtual world. Slowly, from the shadows, a small creature sheepishly crawled to him. He picked up the jet-black creature, who nestled easily in the palm of his hand. It was the little egg creature Mac had shown them earlier. Why was it so small? It had to have been at least his height when he first saw it. Then it dawned on him: This was the egg creature's interpretation of itself, in relation to Simon, who it saw as the gigantic ore ship, with a massive intellect. It was Simon who was further interpreting himself as a human in this imaginary, or rather subconscious, construct.

He didn't know how to proceed. He wanted to talk to Mac, but he couldn't unless he broke the bond and returned movement to the timeline. He might even lose the connection with the little creature, which he didn't want to do.

Wait, the little creature isn't frozen in time, and neither is the one I'm connected to. Why?"

He knew nothing about the ability to stop time, other than a compilation of science fiction movies and what he had learned in physics. There was no evidence to support the existence time stopping, and yet he had witnessed it himself, twice. Then it came to him, in the form of a booming voice—the voice of the ore ship.

"OUR RACE OF BEINGS ARE NOT AFFECTED BY THE EFFECTS OF TIME. LIKE YOU, WE CAN PAUSE TIME AS IT PERTAINS TO THE SPACE–TIME RELATIONSHIP."

His rational mind realized that there was no actual voice, no sound. It was simply his way of interpreting the input. This massive brain, even damaged, was more intelligent than anyone or anything he knew, and that scared the crap out of him. He was at its mercy, and it was now awake.

"Am I doing this or are you?"

"IT IS OF YOUR CONSTRUCT."

"How am I able to pause time?"

"YOU, AND ANOTHER BEING WITHIN ME, ARE UNIQUE AND NOT OF MY HOST RACE, NOR OF THE RACE CALLED HUMAN."

"Where am I from then?"

"NOT WHERE. WHEN. YOU ARE FROM AN OLD, EXTINCT RACE, WHO COULD MANIPULATE TIME."

"But my mother is part human and Alnilam."

"THERE IS ANOTHER PART OF YOUR BLOOD THAT IS STILL DORMANT, BUT SOON WILL DOMINATE."

"What else can I do?"

"THIS FRAGMENT OF KNOWLEDGE I HAVE SHARED I RETRIEVED FROM THE DAMAGED AREA OF MY MEMORY. I DO NOT KNOW IF THERE IS MORE OR IF IT EVER EXISTED."

"That's too bad; I was hoping you could tell me more about this dormant ability and these time manipulators. How do I find out?"

"SEEK OUT THE ONES WHO CREATED YOU. THEY WILL HAVE THE ANSWERS. I DO NOT."

"I will. Thank you for the information. Are you hurt?"

"HURT, PAIN, NO. DAMAGED, YES, BUT WILL HEAL."

"There is a large portion of your brain that is injured. Will you be able to repair it?"

"NO, I WILL NEED WHAT YOU CALL THE EGG CREATURE, TO REPAIR IT AND SURVIVE."

"Yes, I will help, but what is that creature to you? Why is it so important?"

"IT IS ME, A PART OF ME, BEFORE WHAT I HAVE BECOME NOW."

Simon was unsure what that means. "What can I do?"

"STAY LINKED WITH ME AND GO TO THE CREATURE OUTSIDE. TAKE THE ALNILAM MALE WITH YOU. HE HAS KNOWLEDGE OF THE ACTION NEEDED TO COMMUNICATE WITH IT."

"How do I get him to come with me? He's frozen?"

"YOU ARE A CHILD, EXHAUSTING ME WITH YOUR INQUIRIES. GO, QUICKLY AND BRING HIM INTO YOUR MOMENT OF TIME. I CANNOT MAINTAIN THIS LINK MUCH LONGER."

❧ CHAPTER 36 ☙

Simon, severed his contact with the brain, yet could still feel the big creature's presence as a part of him. He retraced his route as he floated over the lifeless portion of the cerebrum to his old friend Mac.

He carefully touched the elderly man, but nothing happened. He remained frozen in the moment. *How do I bring him into my time?* He studied his friend. *Maybe I have to make a telepathic bond with him, like I did with the creature's brain.*

Using his newly awakened talents, he placed his hands on Mac's head and concentrated on that bright spot in his own frontal lobe. Deeper and deeper he dove into his being, seeking a connection. No response. His attempt was a failure.

He tried to remember what the creature had told him, about bringing him into his own moment of time. *What am I doing wrong?* He pondered the situation. *Could it be as simple as embracing him and pulling him with me?*

Simon gripped his friend by the arm and pulled the older man to him, like he was pulling him into a hug. He held him like that for a moment before he detected breathing.

"Okay son, I appreciate your affection and friendship, but Simon, this is a little more than I feel comfortable with."

"It worked! You're in my time?!"

"What the bloody hell are you talking about? Where else would I bloody well be?"

"Let me explain, we are frozen in time, or everything else is, and you have to talk to the egg creature, because the big brain told me."

"Do you hear yourself? You sound insane."

"No, come with me, and I'll show you."

Simon continued to hold Mac's hand, pulling him toward the far end of the chamber where his mother and Gregory were locked in their moment of time.

"Let go of me," Mac said, trying unsuccessfully to break the grip of the young man. "I'm not feeble."

"No! You'll slip out of my time. Just humor me and keep holding my hand!"

"Did something happen to you when you went to the back of its brain?"

"Yes, let me explain." Simon spent the next few minutes explaining the situation to an unconvinced Mac, but it wasn't until they came to the motionless forms of Lyn and Gregory that he truly believed.

"Bloody hell, you *have* stopped time. Okay, what do I have to do with the egg creature?"

"Technically I don't think I stopped time, just slipped between two slices of it."

"Whatever you want to call it, it's marvelous and bloody frightening. Now let's get that little egg beastie."

While still in frozen time, and connected to the ship, Simon led Mac to the portal through which they had first entered. The little creature was easy to spot. It was sending out erratic pulses of orange and yellow light waves.

"Why is it doing that?" Simon asked.

"The little guy is scared."

"Talk to it. Convince it we're friends."

"I'm not sure I know how," Mac said, frowning. "It's very young, and does not take well to a mental bond."

"The big brain said you would know how to communicate with it."

"Maybe if I touch it, we could create a link?" Mac suggested.

As he approached, the creature suddenly started pulsing in bands of red and infrared. It was also visibly shaking.

"Be careful, Mac!" Simon shouted, as the creature lunged at the older man.

Losing his grip on Mac's shoulder, the time slice they were in was broken and they both returned to normal time. Simon could no longer feel the comforting presence of the big brain in the background. The internal communications broke the silence as Lyn Una, the headmaster, gave instructions to the others, as they continued the manhunt.

Orion, who was tasked with searching for information on the egg creature suddenly broke into the conversation.

"Mac, I have detected something about the creature. A high-frequency sound wave was directed at it as it left Earth, originating from the China Sea. The signal is still being transmitted, from the antenna on the rover that was left on the crater's rim." He explained all this over the secure communication link.

"Block the signal and disable that antenna. Do it now, before this beastie strikes again," Mac commanded, then turned to Simon. "Can you do that time-stopping thing? I think I know what to do."

Simon knelt down and put his forehead on the big creature's body, extending his arms as he touched the skin. He felt Mac put a hand on his back, encouraging him. Quickly and easily, the young man established a mental connection, and as he was starting to dive deeper, to create the time-stopping feeling, the ship spoke to him.

"STAY IN THIS MOMENT. WHAT NEEDS TO BE DONE CAN BE DONE NOW. STAND BEHIND THE ALNILAM MALE AND HOLD HIS SKULL." The big brain spoke with renewed strength in its voice.

Simon did as instructed. Mac, who had been aware of the brain's presence, although only as an observer looking through a thick pane of glass, suddenly remembered what needed to be done. It was an old memory, and he wasn't sure if it was his. There were words in his native tongue, with a strange tone and cadence, utilizing the full spectrum of the language frequency.

Slowly he held his arms out in a gesture of friendship and peace to the little egg creature. Thoughts came to him that he processed into words. To him it sounded like a child's nursery rhyme. Some of the words he spoke had no meaning, only sound. Then he realized that he was unconsciously emphasizing the first, third, fifth, and seventh words in each line of the rhyme. He was sending the little creature code—base-programming code.

As he started the second stanza of the 'poem', he could see rings of purple light from the big creature radiating around them, converging on the small one. It had stopped shaking and its pulses of light were now slow and gradually changing to a light blue. By the time Mac reached the third stanza, the blue pulses began to mimic the big creature's and had turned purple.

Simon watched, listening to the sounds. It sounded almost like music to him. It was then that he realized that the frequencies of the alien language, that had hurt his ears when Orion first uttered them a year before, no longer caused him discomfort. The language was beautiful, and although he didn't understand all the words, he was able to grasp the gist of its meaning, like watching an opera in Italian.

Mac was just finishing the fifth and final verse when the big brain broke into their thoughts.

"COME MY CHILD! COME TO ME!"

The little creature, no longer pulsing, scurried passed Mac and Simon and entered the blue portal.

Following quickly behind, they watched as the child slipped through the brain membrane and crawl over the dead brain matter. Minutes later, the membrane sealed and the damaged nerve conduit started to build new tissue around the break, healing itself.

Mac and Simon both felt the sensation at the same time. The ship had forced a mental bond with them, powerful and primal. Mac had never experienced anything like it before. The ship revealed itself to them, showing the repairs being carried out. He watched as large nerve-conduit walls grew around the damaged areas. The ship was healing itself at an alarming rate.

"LEAVE. ALL OF YOU. IT IS NOT SAFE. THE CHILD HAS TAKEN OVER."

They felt deep rumbles, as the ship shook, trying to free itself from the crater's wall.

'Sam, get everyone out of here! he sent to his sister. *The ship is awake and dangerous."* He could already hear the voices of the human astronauts, asking for answers. As the ship began to shake violently, he heard a female scream over the COM

"Give them time to leave, damn it!" Mac yelled to the ship through his mental link with it.

He could see and feel the big ship breaking away from the ice wall that had entombed it for so many years. Then he heard a distinct sound reverberating through the ship: the sound of the light drives building pressure. There was also a hissing sound, evidence that an atmosphere was forming.

"Everyone get out now!" Mac shouted, and then pointed at his grandson. "That includes you, Simon!"

"ALNILAM MALE, YOU STAY AND CONTROL THE LITTLE CREATURE." The big ship's bond was now only with Mac. Its connection with Simon had been severed.

Out of the corner of his eye, Mac detected movement. It was Gregory.

"Mac, we must hurry!" he exclaimed.

"I cannot go. The ship needs me and I need you. Stay, please."

Gregory stared at him for a long moment, and then nodded. "I have never felt a part of this era. Even my daughter does not want me. Yes Grandfather, I will accompany you. Do you know where we will go?"

"Out there," Mac pointed to the stars with a youthful twinkle in his eyes—the same look he'd had in his eyes years ago, when he first left home. "On a wild adventure."

The ship had opened its elevator doors and forced the two lieutenants out of hiding. Pierce and Butcher held them as the headmaster, Lyn Una, caught up. They were about to exit through a nearby portal when Santos pulled a revolver and opened fire on his fellow soldiers and countrymen.

Even with the protection of the EVA shield, the instinct to duck and hide overpowered both Pierce and Butcher. The untested and unproven alien technology was not enough to make them hold their ground and re-apprehend the traitorous astronauts. When the last of the shots were fired, Butcher gave chase with Pierce and Booker close behind. Professor Noi Ro and Van der Hoose exited through the hatch.

Courtney Williamson and Aram At, who had exited earlier, helped those still trying to get out of the large shaking beast.

Simon had barely escaped the upper hatch when the big ship started to rise out of the crater. He floated, watching as the ship cleared the outer rim and slowly vanished into the blackness of space.

He was submersed in silence again. It the same sensation he felt when underwater. The presence of the big brain had taken a toll on him. His head hurt, and he was exhausted and breathing hard. Then a voice from the depths of space penetrated his thoughts. It was Mac.

'Simon, my old friend, look after your sister and mother. They will need your strength. Tell them why I had to leave. Explain to Tamara that her father did not belong in this time, but that deep in his core, he loved her. Lyn can explain what I am trying to say. Tell Orion to look under my favorite bottle of scotch on your boat. There he will find a code I left him; it will unlock answers on his ship. Convince Sam to love her mother and to trust her. Simon ... take care, grandson."

Then there was silence—the background noise of the cosmos.

***

Deep underground in his office building, Kai Yung stared at the computer monitor. Something had happened. The sound frequency he had been sending to control the little egg creature was no longer being received. The remote antenna picked up the movement of the big ship as it left the crater, but it was not heading to Earth.

He held his head in the palms of his hands, squeezing his eyes closed and trying to will the impending migraine to recede. His skin was flushed; starting at the top of his head, the red tint slowly traveled down, covering most of his upper body. The pounding in his head would not ease up, nor would the hammering of his heart. All that money, all that time, gone. Years of research, plus his ancestral legacy, vanished. How could this happen? He was ruined. He felt a sudden pain in his left arm.

He reached into his shirt pocket and pulled out a pill case, from which he extracted a small capsule. Tucking the nitroglycerin pill under his tongue, he waited for the pain to stop.

CHAPTER 37

Simon floated down to the ice at the bottom of the now empty crater, to join up with the group who were resting by the ships. A quick count revealed that six people were missing. Where was Sam?

He rushed to the group and his mother, just barely remembering to maintain their alien pretense in his panic, "Have you seen Ma Z?"

"I saw her heading down the corridor with the NASA pilot, past the drive engines in the big ship. Did you see the chancellor and the marshal?" Lyn Una asked, with fear in her voice.

He took his mother's hand and pulled her into his protective shield, touching her cheek gently.

'What is it, son? Where's Mac?' She was in tears.

'They stayed behind to control the egg creature that had bonded with the ore ship's mind. The ship asked them to stay. Mac and Gregory.'

Aram At interrupted as she broke their embrace and the connection with her hand. "Simon, Butcher just told the professor and me that they saw the ship absorb the two lieutenants, as they tried to escape through the damaged hull. I guess they weren't fast enough. Did you find Sam?"

"Mom told me she was with Worthy, back behind the drive engines. We're not sure if she made it out. Mac and your father stayed behind. I'm so sorry," he told her, as his mother wept, hiding behind the protective shield.

The professor was connected to the rest of the team, trying to ascertain what had happened during the commotion. He watched as Courtney's eyes widened, as the newest member of their group overheard the conversation between Simon and Tamara on the open alien frequency.

'Hey Si, can you send a drone to get us?' Sam asked, finally getting in touch with her brother. *'We got out on the other side of the ship, and in the process, Worthy's belt got snagged as the hatch started to close. She's in my protective shield, but I think the battery is running low because the field is pulsing. Please hurry Simon; part of the ice wall fell on us and we're trapped.'*

"I've got them!" Simon shouted as he hugged Tamara and his mother. "They're okay, but need our help!" He quickly activated his arm bracelet and sent a drone to find them, almost a kilometer away. Tamara followed, as he raced to find his sister—his soul mate.

Butcher, seeing the group float off in the direction of the collapsed wall, took off after them. Had he known how to operate his belt, he would have floated; instead he did what he was comfortable with, running and hopping.

With the aid of the drone and its powerful lifting beam, they easily freed Sam and Worthy just as Booker caught up and hugged his old friend. "Shirley, we were all worried about you! What happened?"

"I was following Ma Z and heard gunshots. I dropped to the deck, and that's where I found Major Carson's spare filter cartridge. I showed it to Ma Z, and she discovered a trail of blood. So we followed it until she heard someone urgently telling us to get out. Ma Z found a hatch and managed to get it open. We barely made it out."

"Do you wish you'd stayed in the *Endurance* as instructed?" Booker asked grinning.

"Hell no," she laughed, feeling more relaxed. "I wouldn't have missed this for the world." It was only then that she realized that all her rescuers had formed a circle around them, fortifying the protective shield. "Now can someone tell me how we get out of here without decompressing my body?" she turned, asking the aliens of the group.

"Yes," Nom Iz said, "the drone will carry you back in a bubble."

"Just a second," Booker said, looking at the professor, "is it possible for Shirley to float with us, if we're all holding hands? Will the protective shield be strong enough?"

"I believe that is another option, although the drone would be more comfortable and efficient."

"Well if Worthy doesn't mind holding my hand, we could task the drone with carrying those big chunks of rock and ice back with us. No point making this trip without completing our mission." He grinned at his friends, who were in total agreement.

Nom Iz led the group back to the ships, holding hands with Ma Z, who held on to Worthy, who held tightly to her friend Booker, who completed the connection with Aram At. The drone followed behind them, with a hundred kilograms of ice and rock in its lifting beam.

When they got close enough to the ship, they found Pierce pacing in the fine dust outside Orion's space craft.

"Where is everyone?" Booker asked.

"They're all inside," Pierce said, eating pizza and drinking beer. Courtney, the guy from Area 51, brought them up."

"Holy crap! Really? You know Shirley, I have a craving for some good old American pizza. Care to join me?" She did, and the big man escorted her through the force shield and into the ship.

"Excuse me, Nom Iz?" Pierce said softly, pulling the tall student aside and connecting to his shield. "The headmaster was quite upset about the chancellor and went to her ship alone. I think she was crying. I thought you should know, because you two seemed to be close."

"Thank you."

'Sam, where are you? Mum's upset about Mac; I'm going to her ship.'

'I'm in here, eating. I'm famished and this pizza is delicious! You should try a slice. Wait—what happened to Uncle Mac?'

Instead of explaining, he sent her images of the two men staying on board and their reasons for doing so.

"Wait. I'm on my way."

Shirley could smell the distinctive aromas of pizza, as she passed through the blue shield protecting the doorway.

"I'll take a slice of that, dear," she said, gesturing to Courtney, who had taken it upon himself to once more be the bartender and host of this impromptu party.

Worthy looked around and saw all the familiar human faces, laughing and enjoying the hot eats and cold beer. She smiled when she saw Van der Hoose, and went up to her and gave her a hug.

"Hey Nat, you okay? Any cuts or scrapes getting out of the ship?"

"No, the professor tended to all our minor injuries with his crystal thingy. I only had a small bruise on my elbow, when I fell on the deck. I'm fine now. What about you? I heard you were buried under a ton of rocks?"

"Oh it was nothing. Didn't feel a thing. Those protective shields really work." She said this with all the confidence she could muster. Then as an afterthought, she continued in a whisper. "I was bloody scared, yet excited too." Taking a deep breath and looking around, she smiled at Nat. "So what do you think of all this?" She gestured at the now-crowded ship.

"This was more exciting than the trip coming up here."

"Copy that girl. I hear you."

Tamara, can you come here? Mum has a problem and needs your help. Sam internalized this to her friend, hoping her friend still had the link with the ship and that they could take advantage of it.

Aram At heard her, and leaned close to the professor. "Hold down the fort, pal. Lyn Una wants me over on the other ship."

With extra beers and pizza slices in hand, she entered the headmaster's ship. Sam and Simon were both quick to help themselves to the treats, but Lyn had more pressing matters to deal with.

"Oh thank you, Tamara, but you didn't have to. I'm sorry for summoning you like this, and taking you away from your party."

"What can I help you with?"

"Well, we have a problem with this ship. I don't know how to fly it."

"What? After all these years, you can't fly?" Tamara laughed, lightening the mood.

"No dear, I never tried." She laughed as well. "Mac and your father did all the flying. I was just chauffeured around. There was no need to learn."

"No probs, Mum, I can fly it for you," Sam mumbled, through a mouthful of pizza.

"Sweet!" Tamara shouted. "I get to fly Orion's ship!"

"Wait a minute, T," Sam said, interrupting her friend's excitement. "She's a pretty powerful creature. She may not like you taking control. Now this old tug is more your speed."

"Tamara, why don't you try to bond with this ship first?" Simon asked.

"This ship *has* got more kilometers on it," Lyn said, trying to mediate, "and has had many operators. It may take to you, dear."

"Fine, I'll try!"

✿ CHAPTER 38 ✿

"Hey it worked. It's talking to me!" Tamara exclaimed after a few minutes of intense concentration. "*He,* I mean. *He* said he would teach me to fly with him, and you too, Lyn."

"I knew you could do it, T." Sam hugged her friend, excited that she was the new pilot of this ship.

"Okay, now that we have that settled," Simon said, "let's get back up to the surface and help the astronauts fix their space craft."

The humans were given the opportunity to choose which ship they wanted to fly on up to their habitat and the return craft. Natalie and Pierce decided they would fly with the headmaster and Aram At, while Butcher and Booker preferred the professor's more familiar ship. The pilot in Worthy insisted that she would take the co-pilot seat next to Ma Z.

'Hey Si, you want to come with me back up top?' Sam asked, in their special twin voice.

'No, I think I'll walk back. The big ship told me some things when I was connected to it and I need to think them through.'

When Courtney found out that one of the aliens was walking back, he opted to join him. After all, this was the first time—and most likely his last—that he would ever get this 'once in a life time' experience.

"Hey friend, do you need company?"

"No."

"It's probably not safe to walk around alone without a buddy," he said, hoping this would give him the opportunity to get some answers. "Besides, I could use the exercise."

Nom Iz knew that this proposal was logical and smart, in light of the mishap with Worth's EVA belt, and Ma Z's nearly drained battery.

"You can come with me, but I will not be good company. After being in the big ship, I need to think about some things I saw."

ORION - Escape Velocity

The groups lifted off the crater bottom, anxious to get into sunlight. Even with the EVA's force shield protecting them from the environment and extreme cold, the lack of light and closeness to the ice gave them the impression of being chilled to the bone.

The two glowing beings watched the ships head out, and then started a silent and leisurely walk, with just enough gravity effect to mimic Earth.

Simon's thoughts were filled with visions of his long-time friend Mac. He'd always thought of him as a fatherly figure and a mentor, but the revelation that the old Scotsman was his grandfather, spying on him and using a phony accent, was disturbing. Why didn't Mac, or his mother for that matter, ever tell him about his alien heritage? Why leave it to chance? He might never have known at all if he hadn't accidentally discovered Orion and his secrets. He might never have learned about his twin sister either.

The big brain had said, "There is another part of your blood that is still dormant, but soon will dominate." What had it meant by that?

It figured it had to be connected to his father, his biological one. *"Seek out the ones who created you. They will have the answers."*

He found himself getting angrier and angrier the more he thought about it. *This is critically important information that you would think a mother would tell her child!* He kicked a chuck of ice and watched it soar off into the distance. It was only then that he remembered that he wasn't on Earth but on the moon. Stopping, he looked around, noticing the drone following behind him with the ice samples. He turned and stared at his walking companion.

"Are you okay, friend?" Courtney asked. "You look like you have the weight of the world on your shoulders. Do you want to talk about it?"

Simon thought about it. How could he possibly explain? Court was completely human. He would never understand. Verbalizing his emotions was uncomfortable for him, but he knew that this guy was a scientist, trained in the same logical thinking processes as he was. Maybe he could help.

He sighed. "I don't know how to explain it. I am confused. I've recently learned that I have been lied to my whole life. Things I believed in as truths are in fact false."

"What, like that big ship mining ore on Earth, and your council keeping it from you?" Courtney guessed.

"No. Well yes. Possibly."

"Maybe Sam or your mother will have answers," Courtney speculated, reaching for answers.

"Yes they might know more, but I can't trust my mother. She lied to me about everything. She didn't even tell me about my own sister. My twin!" He kicked another small rock, unaware that Courtney was smiling, or why.

When they had raised themselves to the crater's edge, Courtney figured he would ask another question.

"So when this is all over, are you going to your home or your mother's?" He had pieced together bits of information, and listening to his intuition, he took the gamble. Would the student answer truthfully, without the alien façade?

"Tamara will most likely take Mum back, while Orion and I—" He stopped suddenly, shocked at what he was saying ... at what he had *said*. He turned away from his companion, for fear that he would see the look of humiliation and betrayal written all over his face. Simon increased the speed on their belts, wanting to get to his friends as quickly as possible. He wanted to get off this moon and get home.

"I am still learning to speak human. I think I used wrong words to explain my thoughts!" Nom Iz exclaimed, struggling to undo the predicament he had put himself into. Now the whole team was in jeopardy!

"Sure I understand," Courtney smiled inwardly, knowing he was onto something much bigger. "The English language is tricky, with multiple meanings for most words."

Van der Hoose, Pierce, and Aram At were finishing up the last of the repairs, while Worthy confirmed their effectiveness with the sensors from the cockpit, it would seem that the scientist they brought up from Earth was not needed for the repairs after all. Booker and Butcher were in deep conversation with the headmaster and the professor, discussing Alnilam customs and the political fallout of this 'first contact' meeting. Ma Z hovered near the top of the crater rampart, waiting for the return of her brother.

'Hey Si, how's it going? You almost here?'

'Just about. We can see the cut in the distance. Sam, I think I told him too much about us.'

'Oh crap, really? How could you!'

"It just happened. Sorry. Don't tell Mum or Orion; I'll explain it to them."

With the aid of the drone, the samples were loaded into the cargo hold of *Endurance*. They would be departing within the hour.

"We will miss you. It was our honor to make friends with your people." Professor Noi Ro offered his hand to Commander Booker.

"It was our honor to meet you and your crew. We are forever in your debt." Commander Booker accepted the handshake. The backdrop was the same as for their first encounter, with the stars and stripes and the red maple leaf both boldly unfurled in the low sun.

All crew members were on board their respective ships. Tamara and Lyn were the first to leave, followed by the big Odin ship, *Endurance*. Sam, in Orion's space ship, waited on the surface in case there were last-minute complications.

With everyone's fingers crossed, the NASA ship lifted off the desolate lunar surface, kicking up a wave of dust.

The two alien crafts watched as the *Endurance* successfully rendezvoused with the large departure-rocket engines.

Worthy watched as her new alien friend, Ma Z, maneuvered her sleek craft in front of the *Endurance's* main view port and gave a very human wave.

Worthy responded with a thumbs up and waved as the large rockets ignited. As the G-forces started to build on the humans, Worthy could see the alien ships accelerate, in the opposite direction, presumably returning to their studies around Saturn.

Endurance completed their final moon orbit with an Earth-insurgence trajectory. The moon would once again be without a population, until the humans returned.

❦ EPILOGUE ❦

The old trawler lay at anchor over a coral outcrop, some miles from the shores of the Exuma Islands, Bahamas. The moon was full and cast its reflection over the still waters. The light danced on the transom highlighting the ship's name: *Dragon Spirit*.

The sounds of Bob Marley's Reggae music wafted through the air, as did the smokey odor of apple wood and barbecued chicken.

"Is it ever going to be ready? I'm starving," Tamara whined to Simon, monitoring the stainless-steel industrial barbecue on the stern deck.

"Honey, you can't be that hungry," Lyn said from the lounge under the canopy, as the young brunette paced back and forth. "We had a big lunch. Where are you putting it all?"

Sam chuckled. "That low gravity must have really burned up the calories."

"When does Tyrone get out of isolation?" Lyn asked.

"The NASA doctors say two more weeks."

Simon frowned, squinting over at them from his spot at the grill. "That's cutting it close, for the wedding."

"Why is he in quarantine a week longer than the others anyway?" Lyn asked.

Sam couldn't resist teasing her friend. "Because he was 'sucking face' with an alien babe on the moon. Isn't that right, girl?"

"Yep," Tamara laughed along with the others, "and he has a lot of explaining to do when he gets out."

As the laughter died down, Lyn broached a more sensitive subject. "Tamara, did they tell you anything about Lieutenant Nuzzi or Santos? Nothing has been said in the media." Lyn shuddered just thinking about the big ship absorbing them before they could escape.

"No one said anything to me, and they didn't acknowledge Major Carson's disappearance either. Don't forget, they returned with three extra crew members, who covered for the missing guys. Do you think Carson's still alive on the ship?"

"Well Worthy and I did see a blood trail, but no body," Sam said.

"Who knows," Simon added, "maybe he found one of the crystals and healed himself."

Tamara nodded. "Yeah, it's not like there wasn't a shipload of them on board."

Sam wandered to the rail and looked out at the ocean. "There was no mention of alien's helping them out either. Government cover-up if you ask me." She smiled ruefully, thinking of her uncle Mac. He had always loved a good conspiracy theory. "Bloody Hell."

"I miss the old coot," Lyn added, sounding somber.

"Me too. I hope he's safe; Gregory too," Sam said, hugging Tamara, whose hungry pacing had brought her within reach.

She returned the hug, sighing. "I didn't even know my dad, and now he's gone."

Lyn got up from the lounge and joined the girls at the rail, wrapping her arms around them both. "One day, I will tell you all about him."

The squeal of a dolphin lightened the mood as the big mammal broke the surface.

"Sheera!" Sam shrieked in excitement, as she ran down to the swim platform. "How's my big girl?"

The big dolphin responded with clicks and squeaks, repeating the vocalization while a bluish light appeared, rising from the depths. It grew in size and brightness until it reached the surface.

"Orion's here," Simon stated unnecessarily as their tall friend floated above the water and onto the boat. "I hope you're hungry, buddy."

"Yes I am. Do you have enough for Sheera? I promised her a piece of whatever you were cooking."

"You bet. I have three large chickens ready, and Sam has spent most of the afternoon making salads."

Everyone took a seat at the table, as Simon set down platters of chicken.

Orion, looked around at the group. "I have discovered some interesting facts about where the egg creature came from."

"Really? Let's hear it, buddy."

"Mac was correct with his hypotheses. I have learned that it was launched, by a reclusive billionaire, from a private island in the South China Sea. The man acquired it from his grandfather, who stole it from a monastery in Tibet."

"Was this billionaire dude controlling it?" Tamara asked.

"Yes, with a special modulated frequency, but he will not be troubling us anymore. His staff found him slumped over a control station. He had a brain aneurysm and is in a coma."

Tamara looked shocked. "Oh wow, did we do that?"

"I do not believe so."

"Sounds to me like he lost it when he lost the little egg creature." Sam chuckled as she snagged a piece of chicken.

***

The sound of an approaching airplane cut into the dinner conversation as it circled above the vessel. The group watched as the small float plane landed, gliding over to the stern of the trawler. With the illumination from the deck, it was easy to see that there was only one occupant. Simon jumped up to assist the pilot in securing his craft.

"Permission to come aboard, captain?" a tall Jamaican man asked, and without waiting for a reply, he stepped onto the swim platform and came aboard.

"Hi, everyone, I'm sorry to interrupt your dinner. I'm Courtney Williamson, but you already knew that, didn't you?" he said casually, walking over to the table of bewildered faces.

"It took some doing, but I finally tracked you down, Samantha. It is Lieutenant Samantha Harding, isn't it? Assuming that's the name you're going by now?"

"I prefer to be called Sam, if you don't mind."

Courtney nodded. "All right Sam, explain to me why your fingerprints showed up on a glass I witnessed being drunk from by an alien female?" Seeing their expressions change in reaction to his question, he quickly went on. "Before you do anything stupid, know that I have told no one, but *have* left a very detail report of this for my supervisor, who will get it if I don't come back."

Sam shook her head. "I don't know what you're talking about."

"I see the whole moon gang is here," he acknowledged, looking at the various people gathered. "Good job by the way, but I would like to know how you managed to pull off that little subterfuge." He paused and tried to decide how to proceed. "You all look scared, but you don't need to be. I just want to work with you as your inside guy at Area 51." He picked up a chunk of chicken from one of the platters, and took a large bite, letting the suggestion sink in for a few moments before continuing.

"That trip we took in your space ship, and walking around on the moon, well … it doesn't get any better than that, does it?" Pointing at Simon, he asked a question he'd been wondering about for weeks: "You resolve your mother issues yet?"

'What do we do now?' Sam silently asked her brother.

Simon shrugged. *'I think we should listen to what he has to say.'*

***

No one noticed the glowing orb that appeared at the bow of the boat. It happened in a blink of an eye, although no one was looking. In that frozen moment between blinks, it grew in size and brightness. Two humanoid shapes exited the orb and walked to the stern, where everyone was gathered. The female walked up to Simon while the male walked up to Sam. Simultaneously they embraced their objectives and brought the twins into their moment of time.

"What the hell!? Who are you?" Sam asked, ready to fight.

"Sam, it's me, Simon. Well not the Simon you're with now, but it's me from the future."

Trying to wrap her head around what he was suggesting, she looked at her Simon and then at the man who was holding her. Then she looked at the women who was holding her Simon. She realized that she was staring at herself … only a little older.

"So we have learned to move *through* time then," her Simon said to the older pair. "I have not shown Sam any of this yet."

If anything this confused Sam even more. "We can do this?" Sam asked anyone who would answer.

"Yes," Sam from the future replied. "This and more."

"You guys should listen to Court," Simon from the future told their younger counterparts, "but be careful, because he has another agenda. Oh, and above all, don't work with the president, like he's going to suggest. We did and ... well, let's just say it didn't go as planned."

"Can you tell us anything else about the future that may help us?" Sam asked.

"Well yes, don't discount Senator Debra Stevens. She is a very influential friend, just don't tell her about Ma Z." With that, future Sam laughed and hugged her junior self.

"Can we tell the others?" Simon asked.

"Absolutely," future Simon replied. "You will need Orion and his ship's database."

As the pair from the future disappeared back into the glowing orb, and it vanished, the twins looked at each other and smiled.

Future Sam punched future Simon on the shoulder when they were safely on board the time bubble.

"Why didn't you let me warn them about the alien white cylinder in the trench?"

"Because we figured it out so will they."

The End?

More Orion adventures to come in *Orion - History Walkers*.
Read how it all started in Orion Surfacing.

CPSIA information can be obtained
at www.ICGtesting.com
Printed in the USA
LVOW11s2033241017
553642LV00001B/1/P